White Bird

by Ruta Sevo

First Printing: August 2014
ISBN 978-0-9905862-0-3 paperback

Momox Publishing
Contact: ruta@momox.org
www.momox.org/whitebird
www.goodreads.com/sevo

Available for order online as a paperback, Kindle, or iBook

Cover design: Ruta Sevo
Cover photo of stupa: Copyright © Erwin Voogt www.erwinvoogt.com

This is a work of fiction entirely and does not portray any real people.

Thanks to Steven Bauer (www.hollowtreeliterary.com) for a full review and
guidance. Thanks to Bette Hileman (bettehilemanblog.wordpress.com) for
editing. Their advice led to countless improvements, large and small.

Dedication: To Pat McNees, a catcher in the rye

White crane, lend me your wings,

I will not fly far away.

From Litang

I will return.

-song of Tsang Yang Gyatso, Sixth Dalai Lama,
predicting his next birth

TABLE OF CONTENTS

THOMAS HAD FLOWN BEFORE but never exited a ramp to face signs he couldn't read. The signs were written in Chinese, with a few clues in English about where he should go next. Landing in Hong Kong felt like landing on another planet. On every side were swarming travelers, including Asians saying things he couldn't understand. He'd been warned about pickpockets and felt leery when people bumped into him. He was used to being on his feet nearly every waking hour, so the thirty-six-hour trip from Seattle to Kathmandu would be excruciating.

Because he was jet-lagged, sore and cramped and would have to spend eleven hours in Hong Kong, he rented a space in an Asian-style, sleeping-pod hotel. The hotel was primarily a strange but airy room with shelves holding prone guests filling every wall. He eagerly squeezed his long body into a cocoon.

Before falling asleep, he put his backpack safely at the foot of the sleeping pod. In the bottom of the pack was precious cargo: a box wrapped in brown paper. It was nothing he needed to declare through customs—not snacks, not chocolates, not a traveler's treasure—but ashes. Human ashes. His brother Paul.

The box resembled a cigar box, but it was heavy, heavier than the cigar boxes Thomas and Paul had used when they were kids to mount butterflies on needles and build a collection. The two of them had been budding lepidopterists. Inside this box, Paul, a pound of dust in a plastic bag, had joined Thomas' memory of dead butterflies. The undertaker in Flagstaff had told Thomas he'd run out of plain cremation boxes and would he like a vintage box instead?

Paul had had shaggy blond hair, a wide burly chest, and an amused smirk that women found charming. Now, he would never have to fade into old age. It was yet another way he would be excused. No one would see an elderly Paul. No one would know how Paul would deal with the free time or the physical indignities of old age.

After eight hours of sleep, Thomas felt the walls of the pod closing in on him. It was time to get up and catch the next plane. He had to take care of business, no matter how awful. *Think of scattering the ashes as a job*, he thought, *like tearing down an old barn. Scattering the ashes would clear some of the garbage from his past, clear it for something new and fresh, even if it was just a nice field of clover.*

***

After arriving in Kathmandu, Thomas, along with about two hundred other travelers, had to navigate customs. They scattered across a room, grabbing forms to fill out and pushing their way to stand in lines. He imitated what the others were doing. Many tourists were told to get out of the screening line and go to a photo booth for a required visa photo. Thomas found it reassuring to see a mix of people: Young and old, Americans, Indians, Germans and Russians. A young man in tattered clothes and dreadlocks who was returning for a repeat six-month stay. Tall, muscular, German-speaking men, dressed in the finest outdoor, lightweight, breathable jackets, holding giant bags of mountaineering gear for Everest adventures. Clusters of tourists from a church in Kansas, with lumpy bodies stuffed into sweat pants, who stuck close together every step of the way, determined to be patient. Clearly, they were not headed to Everest. Strangely, they showed no fear although Thomas knew this was their first trip to Kathmandu.

He'd exchanged some dollars for Nepalese rupees in Hong Kong and resented the difficulty of figuring out exactly how many rupees he needed for transport to the hotel. Jetlag made it hard to concentrate. He was wary of being tricked out of his money. Though he had fastened his cloth money belt tight against his midriff to foil pickpockets, he still worried about getting conned for Nepalese money.

As soon as he exited the airport, he was stormed by short, dark cab drivers trying to grab his bag so they could own him before other drivers got to him. He didn't know how to pick one. He waved them off, trying to be polite. He'd never been around people who were so pushy, touching him and grabbing the handle of his bag, ignoring his protests. Were any of them going to murder him? It was the last thing a tired traveler needed: a mob shakedown. He started to show the drivers an angry face and found a tourist desk where he was warned to hold onto his bags and insist on a metered scooter-cab. He went with a cab driver who spoke crude English and wore a cleaner shirt than most. Thomas gave him the name of the hotel he'd booked.

It was still daylight in Kathmandu. The three-wheel scooter-cab took off fast into dusty streets as if it needed to escape something terrible. The cab skimmed around dirty, large cows chewing their cuds in the middle of the unpaved streets. Cars and buses competed, intimidating each other to give way. Crowds were walking on both sides of the roads, jostling like the cars. Some pedestrians wore dust masks.

Finally, the scooter pulled into a narrow alley that led to a dark, dead-end lane with a hotel sign. A lethargic, Labrador-sized dog, splayed on the concrete steps in front of the hotel, barely looked up. Smoke, thick with the scents of Indian spices, wafted over a fence. Thomas practically jumped into the nearly empty hotel lobby. Two men who spoke English welcomed him.

Bewildered and drained by the street scenes he'd witnessed, he went to his room as fast as possible. The hotel was highly rated, but reasonable. He'd been warned that the electricity would go out for hours every evening and generators would keep a few lights on. In the bathroom, the shower directed water toward a drain in the middle of the floor. There was nothing to keep water off the toilet or the sink. There were no hooks on the door to keep clothes or a towel away from the water. There was no space on the sink to put toiletries. He'd read a pamphlet, "Kathmandu Warnings and Dangers," but it hadn't explained everything.

He escaped into sleep.

***

Seven months before, in a gray reception area in Flagstaff, Thomas had put an arm around his mother, Livia, who was sitting on a cold plastic seat, and handed her the box of ashes. She looked as if she wanted to wail into a flimsy Kleenex.

"Not a spectacular resting place, but we've got him," he said.

His own vigor embarrassed him. He was lanky and thin from spending most of his time on his feet in the woods. His skin was both rough and smooth, like river rock, scrubbed by rain, wind and dry air. A short, groomed beard softened the angles of his face. Women who appreciated gardening and manual labor, such as painting and building, liked his hands. He remembered Caroline holding his hands as if to soften them and soothe their roughness, treating them like a pair of versatile tools. She said they were sexy—rough and soft at the same time. He rarely wore a hat to fend off the Northwest drizzle because he thought his hair and beard were shelter enough. When it was sunny, he exposed as much skin as possible. That was the Northwest way.

He was not at all like the guy reduced to coffee grounds, his brother.

In the waiting room, Thomas felt Livia's frail hand on his arm and wished she'd put up more of a fight against weakness and weight in her old age. She had the extra flesh of a woman in her eighties but her eyes were kind, her face soft and wrinkle-free. She normally wore a long full skirt, an ample shirt, and a bright silk scarf draped around her neck and sometimes her head. Today, the scarf was uncharacteristically dark-blue.

On this trip to Flagstaff to claim the body and arrange for cremation, Livia's frailty had been a challenge. As she and Thomas walked off the plane into the airport, she'd barely lifted her feet. Thomas was handling their carry-on luggage and couldn't propel her forward physically. He dashed to an airline counter and asked for a wheelchair.

The Flagstaff airport was small and relaxed. Thomas and Livia finally made it to a rental car. As he held onto her, she swung heavily into the passenger seat. They drove to the hospital through the flat, dry town, a geo-space far from Seattle's wet greenery. *What if the stress of the trip kills her*, Thomas thought. *Thanks, Paul.*

"I never imagined coming to a hospital to see somebody already dead," she said.

"Can't be helped. We'll make it short."

"After all of Paul's adventures, he ends up in a fridge in a basement."

"We all might, you know. At least, we know where he is."

They slowly walked through several empty, antiseptic corridors, took an elevator to a chilly lower basement and found a door marked "Morgue." A technician led them to a wall of large drawers that looked like those for frozen specimens in a museum. He pulled out a drawer.

Livia started crying. "He's all swollen."

"He's not really here, Mom." Thomas had never seen a dead body. It was a blowfish version, or a bad caricature, of Paul. A Paul-looking dummy made of gray-white blubber. Thomas was repelled by the distortion. *So this is what happens*, he thought. *Really ugly*

Thomas nodded at the technician. They walked back into an office area. Thomas and Livia decided not to transport the body back to Seattle. It was going to be cremated anyway, and they would have the ashes. They knew Paul wouldn't have objected. He hadn't liked fancy rituals, such as memorial services. None of the family did. Because Paul had almost no relatives in the U.S. and few friends after his long absence, Thomas couldn't imagine who in Seattle would come to a memorial service.

Thomas helped Livia back into the rental car and drove her to a nearby motel.

5

She put on her robe and settled on the bed. She watched him putz through his things.

"We have so little family," she said.

"We have some. You have Clara and me." His aunt Clara had stayed back in Seattle.

"I've lived too long."

"How can you say that?"

"I outlived Paul."

"Then, stick around for me."

"Why did he have to go do something dangerous?"

"A raft trip isn't that dangerous."

***

He set out to find the Peace Corps office in Kathmandu.

He saw hundreds of little shops open to the street, fronted by stands and tables precariously set on brick, concrete and mud. The shops displayed pots and pans, saris, scooter parts, electronics and groceries, all of which seemed to be pouring into the street. Going through Kathmandu was like walking through a carnival that allowed vehicles to drive through the center. There were car horns, bells, shouting and loudspeakers, pedestrians all over the streets, vehicles coaxing them to step aside. There was cow dung in the middle of narrow dirt roads. The odors of diesel fuel, spices, mounds of loose tea, food cooking on open coals and cow dung blended in a mix that changed every few feet.

Nepal felt unreal, like a fast movie. Thomas couldn't turn his head quickly enough to take it all in and make sense of it. He looked up and saw a utility pole with a scramble of lines extending ten feet from the pole like a globe of black spaghetti dangling in the air. The handyman in him was horrified. Clearly, the authorities weren't keeping people from tapping lines. Nobody was fixing the dangerous, dangling live cables. *Who debugged this tangle of wires when it failed?* he wondered.

The instructions for finding the Peace Corps office worked well enough. It was a modest place with simple furniture. A fan pulled street air into the office through an open, barred window.

6

An amiable Nepali woman looked up Paul's Peace Corps record from the early eighties, more than twenty years earlier, wrote down where he was assigned and pointed it out on a map. It was 2009 now and the Peace Corps had survived in Nepal in spite of a suspension of a few years, with records intact.

"Did you know one of the other volunteers in his cohort is still in Nepal, a woman named Helen Simons?" she asked.

"Really?"

"Her parents are well-known here." Thomas hadn't thought he would find anyone who'd been acquainted with Paul. His next step was going to be to find a guide to take him into the lowlands to look around Paul's old territory. Paul hadn't specified where he wanted his ashes to be scattered. Finding someone who knew Paul was vastly more interesting.

The Nepali woman wrote down an address: that of Jeri and Donald Simons, Helen's parents. Since the phone call was local, she dialed the Simons' number and handed the phone to Thomas.

"Hello?" a woman answered.

"Hello. Um. I'm from the States. Thomas Rusak. Can you help me find Helen Simons?"

"Well, yes. Why do you ask?" Her voice was warm. American English.

"My brother Paul was in the Peace Corps with her. She might have known him."

"Why don't you come by and see us?"

He could hardly believe the invitation. The opportunity to visit Americans was a shower of sunshine. "Sure! This afternoon okay? I'm at the Peace Corps office."

"Yes, yes. Come on over. I'm home, and Donald will be back in an hour. Do you think you can find us?"

"I'll ask people here to help me. Thanks. See you in a bit." Thomas hung up slowly, savoring the security of knowing his next step. The trip was looking up.

The Nepali woman found him a scooter-cab outside, negotiated a fee, and told the driver where to take him. The novelty of the vehicle distracted Thomas from the danger of darting past larger vehicles on muddy, pockmarked roads full of pedestrians, dogs, goats and cows. The scooter-cab stopped at a large iron gate in a white concrete wall. Thomas gave the driver the agreed-upon fee, thankful he didn't have to negotiate. A young Nepali man came to the gate, nodding like a servant or assistant. They entered a small garden of trees and flowers with a path to a carved wooden door.

An elderly, slight white woman met them. "I'm Jeri. How are you?" She had a healthy glow and strong energy. She was a bit younger than Livia and Clara, slim and quick. She was wearing light sandals and a blue Indian kaftan that covered her knees. *Ah, Mother Kathmandu*, thought Thomas. He was relieved to be talking to someone in American English.

"I just got here. Nice of you to invite me."

"Are you touring?" She waved him through the door.

"Not really. Family business."

"How so?"

"I've brought my brother's ashes. I'm trying to figure out where to scatter them. Your daughter might help me."

Jeri led him through the house to a large sitting room with one wall fully open to a veranda and garden. To Thomas, the room looked like an Asian art shop or museum filled with Indian and Tibetan artifacts and artwork. The fabrics were glorious, and the wood furniture had carved frames. Books and papers were stacked neatly everywhere. Judging from the density of favorite belongings, he decided the room had been settled for a long time. Another Nepali servant brought in a tray of tea with milk in a brass tea set with English cups and saucers. On the tray, there were also cookies and small pieces of mango and oranges.

"During her Peace Corps days, Helen taught in a school up in the hills," Jeri said. "She talked about her volunteer friends, but she worked hard to keep her independence because we were right next door. It was like having your kid go to college in her hometown, which happened to be Kathmandu." She laughed.

"Helen and Paul were here in 1986. You were here then?"

"Yes. Donald and I were with an NGO that works with Tibetan refugees. Donald used to run it, and I ran the schools. The work is still going strong. Many Tibetans are still in this area. We help out informally now."

"I don't know much about Tibetans. Or Nepalis. Or much about anything else here." Thomas struggled to translate NGO and remembered it was code for non-governmental organization, or non-profits that work abroad.

"Donald can find you a guide, if you like, to take you around. Nepal is beautiful. You're going to be amazed."

They heard the front door open and a large, burly man came in. He had unruly gray hair, a mustache and ruddy skin. He wore a loose white shirt over khaki pants.

"Oh my. We have a visitor. Hello. I'm Donald." He reached out a hand. "What brings you here?"

"I'm Thomas."

"Visiting from the States?" Thomas was wearing his Northwest rain jacket, jeans and boots. His cotton shirt might have implied "not seriously hiking."

"Yes. I was looking for Helen."

Donald hugged Jeri. "Jeri, let's have some tea." He went to wash his hands. Jeri left to order more tea.

Thomas took a closer look at the artwork. There was a large, brass, standing Buddha. There were small soapstone carvings of Indian gods. One wall had a large canvas—a mountain scene with a simple, large, white Buddhist *stupa*, or dome-shaped shrine. He'd seen pictures of *stupas* in the guidebook.

He heard a sound in the courtyard and looked in time to see a young, white woman with long, blond dreadlocks rushing by. He thought she might be Helen, but she was much too young. Jeri came back.

9

"Tell me about yourself." Jeri sat down, moving aside colorful pillows.

"I'm really a handyman. Washington State. Haven't travelled much."

"What do you know about Nepal?" She asked.

"Almost nothing. Read a bit in Paul's letters."

"I can lend you a few books if you like. It'll give you some context. Of course, we've been here so long, it's hard to imagine seeing it with totally new eyes."

"Sorry to be so naïve."

Donald came back, sat down and poured himself some tea. "How do you know Helen?"

"I don't. She might have known my brother Paul."

"And where is he?"

"He died," Jeri said. "Thomas is here to spread his ashes. Do you think Dorje is free to guide him around?"

"That might work just fine. I'll check."

Thomas was relaxing, listening to their chatter and drinking the warm milky tea. "What does Helen do here?"

"Helen went back into the hills," said Jeri.

Thomas sat up as if he'd won a free drink in the bar. "Is it possible to visit her?"

"Certainly. She's a lay Buddhist nun."

"What does that mean? Is she cloistered or something?" He leaned toward Jeri with interest.

"No, no. She runs a hostel associated with a monastery. She caters to trekkers and travelers. And meditates."

"Can you check if it's all right to visit?"

"Sure. We'll phone someone in her village."

He wrote down his hotel's number for Jeri and Donald.

"What are you hoping for?" Jeri asked, reaching for a piece of mango.

"I don't know. She might tell me about places for the ashes. Isn't being a nun unusual for a Western woman?"

"It happens. Lots of nuns here. And dozens of goddesses, of course. People here think goddesses are real." Jeri laughed. "*Dakinis* don't sit at home tending yaks. There are stories of wild women who become yoginis and mystics and who don't belong to anyone. They're free spirits. That might have been part of the appeal for Helen."

"So she earns a living running the hostel?" Thomas was starting to be embarrassed by his interrogation but not so much that he stopped.

"Most monks, male and female, depend on the community," Jeri said. "They beg, perform rituals, and so on. Much like female nuns and saints in the West. Maybe you've heard of Hildegard von Bingen, the medieval German saint? She ran a large convent, among other things. The hostel generates a good income for the monastery, which is unusual in Nepal. Just the way things turned out."

"Sounds unusual. I mean to have a nun in the family."

"We like having her near, of course."

Donald laughed. "There are plenty of families proud to have spawned a priest or two. Holy people. It enhances your own karma, as they say."

"Is it common here? I know Italian Catholics push their sons into religion." Thomas thought of his own parents, who, disgusted with the godless horrors of the Second World War, left religion behind.

"We didn't do that, for sure," Donald said. "I think we left her to her own fate. It takes a lot of guts to break from the norm, even in Kathmandu. The temptations of love and family life were not strong enough for Helen."

Jeri added, "She had a calling. Earned more merit in prior lives, as Buddhists might say. Of course, we think she had a reasonable example of a good family life." She laughed. Thomas heard a little strain in her laugh.

"I would think so." Thomas smiled.

"That may be more than you wanted to know," Jeri said, as she took his teacup.

Courier

A FEW MONTHS AFTER PAUL's ACCIDENT, Thomas took the boxes containing Paul's belongings sent from Washington, D.C., into Livia's well-lit kitchen. He hadn't been involved in the logistics of closing out the minutiae of Paul's life. Livia had taken care of that. In one box Thomas found a copy of the will, lists of accounts, and notes about companies to notify in the event of Paul's death. The will had been made using a simple template and signed properly. It gave everything of value to Livia. Apparently, the biggest asset was a retirement fund of $300,000, which Livia transferred to her own retirement, as direct withdrawals from Paul's fund would incur taxes. With this inheritance, Livia would have enough to reside in assisted living for several years, if she needed it. Thomas appreciated that the will benefitted him indirectly. Livia's house would never need to be sold.

A second box contained things people keep in their desks or storage boxes— the emotional trivia of private lives. Livia had already unpacked and repacked the box several times. There was a red, Swiss army knife. Several colorful carabineers. Computer disks. An old Instamatic camera. Headphones. Photographs, in small batches. Postcards. Foreign coins. Hikers' patches from the Peace Corps, the Swiss Alps, Mount Rainier, and Rocky Mountain Park. Matches from Picholene and Victor's Café in New York, 1291 Bed and Breakfast in New York, Nepenthe at Big Sur in California, Dianthe in Vancouver, and exotic places like Tokyo. There were sticky notes galore, with obscure phrases like "Control Shift += Control Shift _", "stay as sharp as a knife," "bookmooch.com," "A Dead Hand Paul Theroux," "dead lamas," "Heidegger hermeneutical studies," "expect heavy traffic," "cull the herd."

Deep in the mix was a two-inch, obsidian arrowhead, black, shiny and sharp as a diamond. The shape was unmistakable. It was hacked into a flat point that could go right through a sizable deer or a human. Thomas felt a pang of sweet recognition, then immediate anger. The arrowhead threw him back to a hike in Utah with his father Nicholas. Nicholas had a Geiger counter and hoped to strike it rich finding a uranium mine. They had walked and walked with their minds in a fantasy as thick as the Gold Rush. Long distances into the dry wilderness of southern Utah, with the choking smell of sagebrush and with dust, lizards, and beautiful orange rocks everywhere. Thomas was ten years old and close to the ground. While Nicholas scanned the earth, Thomas and Paul were glued to the dirt path, picking up neat rocks.

Thomas found the arrowhead. Obsidian was rare in that area. The glossy black stood out against the background of rusty dirt. Indians had had to procure this black gold from the obsidian fields in Oregon and traded it all the way across the country as far as the East Coast. Thomas had shouted with glee and held the arrowhead up before calling Paul and Nicholas. The three of them shrieked at scoring such a find. Thomas was the hero. He'd bested Paul. When they arrived home, Thomas put the obsidian with other treasures in the back of his desk drawer. Now and then, he would take the obsidian out and hold it, dreaming of Indians, horses, hunting in cedars. It was his piece of heaven.

Long ago, when Paul was still living at home, the obsidian had disappeared. Now, it was back in Thomas's hand, cold and sharp. It was evidence that Paul had stolen it from him, that he could not resist the wonder of it, that when he packing up for college, he'd gone to Thomas's secret stash and helped himself. The boy in Thomas wished Paul dead, right now. *Die. You took my arrowhead, you swine. You always put yourself first.*

There were a few photos from Paul's Peace Corps stint. One was of a young woman sitting on the stoop of a doorway painted bright red, dressed in a maroon, kimono-style, rustic top over a brown skirt. She was holding a small, yellow potted plant. On the back was written "Helen, 1986." There was a shot looking up the side of a large *stupa* in Nepal. There was a shot of the corner of a rustic stone house. There were several photos of mountains looming over valleys, some lush green, others barren gray stone.

Thomas tried to picture Paul touching these things. Thomas wondered what his own box would hold. He wouldn't have a picture of a woman in his drawer. He hadn't gotten close enough to a woman to regret parting so much that he treasured a photo of her.

For a stranger, all the precious things Paul stashed in desk drawers and boxes would be like an array of useless novelties on a flea-market tray. The precious things would seem like junk. Silly objects and notes with inscrutable messages.

Hello, Paul, Thomas thought to himself. *I guess this is it.* It was easier to think about Paul now that he was dead. Now, about happenings in his own life, Thomas wouldn't have to think, "What would Paul say?" Paul was silenced, forever. His life was framed by birth and death, and everything in between was locked in. It was a story with a beginning and an end.

To Thomas, Paul had always seemed intense and daring. When Paul ventured away from home into the world, Thomas was too young to be interesting to a brother five years older. And they'd never caught up much as adults. They'd shared a spotty childhood of struggle, but as adults, they did not help each other through crises or depend on each other to make sense of their early years. As adults, they'd always met at Livia's house, with its old family dynamics and conversations directed by her presence. The brothers shared much familiarity, mutual tolerance, and acceptance, but no burning interest in brotherly bonding or chasing adventures together. They remained far enough apart to avoid the friction and competition of antagonistic brothers and seemed to like it that way. In the course of Paul's intermittent and usually short visits to Seattle, they never had fun, built any great rapport or had any gripping personal conversations.

On reading the handful of letters that Paul had left, Thomas discovered snippets of interest and an enduring sense of his brother's affection for Nepal, but he found no revelations. He picked up the arrowhead, hesitated, then grabbed Paul's cap and sunglasses and headed to the guestroom to sleep.

***

In the morning, Livia waited until he'd had his coffee. "Thomas, I found one thing that's important." She was preparing an omelet for him and was staring at the toaster oven, waiting for a croissant to brown. "Paul wanted his ashes scattered in Nepal."

"What?"

"I can't do a trip like that. Clara can't either. Will you do it?"

Thomas felt as if a ceiling fan had fallen on his head. He'd listened to the reminiscences the night before, the fondness for Paul, his distant brother, the one who was never home, never taking care of things in Seattle, too far to be much fun or comfort. Paul had not shared in the maintenance of the family home. Now, Thomas knew that he himself would inherit it. But Livia was asking him to stop his own life and finish Paul's. To do something that seemed wild.

"After all the hardship we went through leaving Lithuania, the family split up forever," Livia said. "You and Paul didn't suffer so much. Maybe you can suffer a little to give Paul what he wants. We don't have control over the past. We do have control over this: the luxury of a graceful death. At least his ashes, I mean." She took the croissant out of the oven.

Thomas was used to reminders of the family's emigration after the War. It was their family culture to "never forget" the devastating trauma of separation from family and country in Livia's lifetime. He himself, in great contrast, never went anywhere exotic.

"Mom, I've barely been to Vancouver or San Francisco. How do you think I'll do in a foreign country?" He found Seattle too busy and too big, so how about Kathmandu? Did they even speak English there? Would Paul have done something like that for him? He wasn't sure.

"You can do what any other tourist can do. I'm sure there are lots of Americans there and people who help Americans. Your biggest problem will be very long flights."

"Why don't you get one of the travel groups to do it for you? That makes more sense."

"That's so impersonal. You're between jobs, aren't you?"

"I am."

"For Paul?"

Thomas felt his neck tighten. His mother had asked him to do a lot of things, but asking him to favor Paul was going too far. "Paul was the one who liked to travel. You're confusing us. I'm the one who stayed close to home—stuck in my pickup truck. Why did Paul choose a place that has nothing for us? Why so far?" Thomas dug into his meager omelet. A few leaves of basil spiced it up. Nothing fancy.

"Clara and I will book it for you. Think of it as a long ride to an interesting place. Don't do it for Paul. Do it for me."

Thomas shrugged his shoulders. He remembered Paul's saying goodbye at the airport when he went off to college. That was when Thomas finally realized that he was irrelevant in Paul's life. Thomas was the dutiful son left behind, the designated forever child. No exotic cities, girls, world's greatest places to visit. Now that Paul had died, Thomas was competing with a myth, a myth locked in time: the man of the world, the man with fun stories, jokes and crazy souvenirs. Although Thomas didn't want the life that Paul had made for himself, he was sure he didn't want the life he had created for himself—a life that primarily consisted of obligations to take care of his mother and stay close to home. He was the one who'd had to compensate for what she'd lost when she was torn from her native country, her family, her youth.

Thomas left his mother's house, noncommittal.

In a bar in Winthrop, Washington, Thomas was having a drink with one of his clients. He was often invited to hang out after working on a property. Only a few restaurants had a small bar, and they'd become happy settings for familiar faces, his surrogate family.

"The fencing should get delivered tomorrow," the rancher said. "Now that we've got posts up, the work should go fast." His face was flush with comfortable fat, and he had kind, satisfied eyes.

"I bet the horses will be glad to get back in that field." Thomas said. He felt good fixing things, especially when it kept money flowing into his bank account.

"By the way, my wife's driving into Seattle for the weekend. Can you bring me a package tomorrow? She'd rather I smoke when she can't see it." The rancher lifted his glass to Thomas, a co-conspirator.

"Sure. Glad to. Is it helping your headaches?" Customers with medical needs were Thomas' clients for his secret supply of marijuana. They weren't wasted or slothful social outcasts. They had earned their money honestly. They wanted to relieve pains and discomforts using pot instead of strong, expensive drugs with damaging side effects.

"Oh yeah. Sweet relief." The rancher cupped his glass.

Thomas liked taking care of his community. Dealing marijuana was like running an invisible pharmacy in a small town. In Winthrop, he was getting to know a new set of people, slowly, through encounters in local shops and invitations to stop by homes, often with spacious fields around them. People did not move to Winthrop for an intense social life, but they appreciated camaraderie. Many had already made a nest egg while working in the city and were retreating to fresh air and sunsets. They had money for luxuries. Feeling connected to locals was part of their rural adventure. With his clients, Thomas could talk about current affairs and deeper issues like whether the country was going to hell, water rights and man's relation to wildlife. He equally appreciated gourmet cheeses, fine wines, and an omelet and a beer. He was an ideal dealer: congenial, safe, accommodating, available. Nice.

Six months earlier, he'd moved to Winthrop after a stint in a national park in Oregon. He'd lost his secure federal job, when it was discovered that he'd succumbed to the temptation to grow marijuana in deep recesses of the forest. Although his marijuana plot was not on land within the national park, it was an infraction that threw him off a secure financial base and forced him to relocate to the Winthrop area to start over. He had a degree in forestry and loved maintaining remote areas in the Pacific Northwest. Now, he'd ruined that line of work. Still, he enjoyed smoking pot and considered it a staple in his daily life. He firmly believed that it was harmless and should not be controlled, especially for medicinal uses. This made him popular wherever he lived.

The loss of his federal job did not weigh heavily. He felt it was a misunderstanding. He also believed that what he'd done was not wrong. In his mind, the Forest Service was unreasonable and bureaucratic. If he could support himself in Winthrop, the job change would not be so bad. He would be around more people. More women, too. His mother had harped on the lack of a social life in the forest for a single man entering his fifties, and now he could "circulate."

Like Paul, he'd never felt the need to settle down and had a wide variety of friends. He'd had no conventional home with a family, mortgage, pets, and a yard. But finally, when he moved to Winthrop, he did get a dog—a Weimaraner mix called Sally, who slept with him and satisfied his need for daily conversation. He rented the top floor of a finished barn, primarily for sleeping, as he spent most of his waking hours outside.

Thomas wasn't thrilled that Livia was pressuring him to travel to Nepal. She tended to forget that her children had their own lives and that now there was only one child. Her small social circle in the U.S. hadn't distracted her much from her family, in which she had enjoyed the role of queen mother.

"I have to go into Seattle myself soon," he said to the rancher, who was his neighbor. "My brother died, and my mother wants his ashes taken to Nepal."

"Nepal? Wow. You? Were you close to him?"

"Not really. He was five years older and always away. Far away. We didn't see each other except at my mother's. We led separate lives. Just didn't click, you know?"

"Well, I have at least one brother like that." The rancher set his empty glass down at arm's length, as if moving the thought far away.

"Not even phone calls. I hardly knew him."

"You're sure nice to do this for him."

"More for the family. Not many of us to choose from. I'm the only one fit to travel that far." Thomas took a sip of beer.

"Is Caroline going with you?"

"Oh no. No. She and I broke up. Just friends. You know." Thomas, too, set his glass down, but very near him, wishing there were more beer in it.

Women did not stay with him long. He was a magnet for those who wanted to get away from crude, blue-collar bar hounds. One of his old girlfriends said he seemed honest, like his fellow rangers and handymen, direct and in touch with the earth, tools, machines and animals. He tended to be quiet, not boisterous. He was thoughtful. He would remember to listen to a woman and patiently hold her through a rough spot. He didn't pressure for rough sex, or drunken sex, or inconsiderate "drive-by" sex. He seemed to appreciate attention and softness.

However, his women tended to pack up and walk out, regrettably, because he didn't seem to want more than simple affection and shallow friendship. He never talked with anyone about a future with a house, garden, farm or children. He didn't express any great passions or particular pleasure in intimacy. He knew he didn't strive for another reality. More money, more things, more property, more power, even more sex—these were matters of indifference.

Unlike Paul, Thomas didn't set himself up for some destiny, some grand adventure and a bigger world. Sometimes, he suspected that his long-term use of marijuana had tempered any deep urges and left him feeling that his current life was a pleasant and high-enough state.

His last girlfriend Caroline was a buxom, extroverted woman in her forties who worked as a hostess in a Winthrop restaurant. She had a good job that made it possible to live in a simple but pretty cottage beside a river and to ride other people's horses during off-hours. Of course, she attracted all the single males passing through, but she'd learned how to keep them away. Her protective force-field was her announcement, soon after meeting, that she had an invisible, degenerative disease that would soon require the services of a very generous care-taker. If she got to know someone and liked him, then she would tell him it was a lie. The lie worked for the most part. Transient men had a horror of being tied down to a sick woman. Her luscious body tempted them to pursue a friendly short dalliance. But she soon tapped into their sense of independence and managed to chill their shallow lust.

In retrospect, these insights came to Thomas. He'd never heard about a deadly disease. Caroline didn't put him off, nor do anything to dampen his lust, for that matter. Neither was she overly clingy. They were both matter-of-fact and liked that about each other.

She let her emotions go with Thomas only to discover his own invisible disease of apathy. "You're wonderful company, but you're starting to feel like a loyal cat that comes back only when he wants something," she said. "Most of your rhythms are apart from mine. I want to own a horse farm someday. I want to build a future." He knew that she closely tracked the ownership of properties around Winthrop, talking with restaurant customers about who'd moved, who planned to move, who was selling, who was buying, what price people were asking and what the buyers paid. She'd saved and invested her own money.

Thomas found his small apartment inside the old barn perfectly satisfactory. During her visits to his place, Caroline discovered how he was using the extra space in the top of the barn. She saw the seed pots, growing lights and drying bins. But Thomas wasn't ambitious, even about raising marijuana. He didn't experiment with varieties or try to grow original strains. The foodies among the marijuana crowd would have dismissed him as a hack and an amateur.

While pot fans gathered in places like Amsterdam every year to talk about the quality of plants and propagation, Thomas was painting somebody's barn. Marijuana growers met at private parties and talked about raising pot on a large scale, building greenhouses, supplying medical marijuana dispensaries. Thomas didn't feel competitive. He'd read some basic botanical texts and learned fundamental growing methods to minimize failed plants. His product was regular, adequate and in high demand.

As a handyman he worked small jobs all over Winthrop and stopped by for a cup of coffee and a discreet sale at dozens of homes. Many of his regular customers booked him for work on their houses and farms, in gratitude for the convenience and safety of his delivery method and to make sure they would see him again.

Hike

ON THOMAS' THIRD DAY in Nepal, Donald sent Dorje to meet him at his hotel. Dorje was young, slight and dark, and was dressed in khakis and a starched, plaid Madras shirt. Like most locals, he wore plastic sandals. He was a Tibetan refugee who'd grown up in Kathmandu and spoke good English.

Thomas and Dorje spent the day walking around Kathmandu. It was not unusual to see a short, dark, nearly barefoot native, towing a tall, white Westerner dressed in jeans and hiking boots through the streets.

Thomas tried to picture Paul in Nepal. He knew Paul had spent two years walking the muddy streets and living a fairly rustic life. Thomas didn't expect to get to know him by visiting Kathmandu, but he wanted to learn more about Paul's fascination for travel. Decades ago, the Kathmandu Paul had seen was even more primitive.

Even though Thomas had arrived in Kathmandu with great reluctance, he was suddenly jealous of the adventures he imagined Paul had experienced. Safely following Dorje, Thomas could watch people who were completely strange to him, dressed in ways he'd never imagined. Rickshaw drivers, shopkeepers measuring out tea on scales next to the street, vendors walking the roads with bags or hats or beads draped over their arms.

Thomas and Dorje stopped to look at a courtyard where dozens of people gathered around a goat tethered to a post. A man grabbed the head of the goat to hold it firm and sliced through its neck with a large machete. The goat's body fell bleeding as a child took the head, held it aloft by the horns, and danced around. Although Thomas had worked on ranches and farms, he felt queasy. He thought about his dog Sally, who was about the same size as the goat, and left behind in Winthrop. Dorje pulled Thomas back into the street, away from the scene.

***

Thomas and Dorje caught a bus to Pokhara. From there, they planned to hike up to Paul's old village. Thomas didn't know what to expect, except that he was following Paul's footsteps.

When the bus left for the six-hour journey, it was not full. About an hour out, a crowd of Nepalis and goats boarded. Passengers squeezed into every possible space, some sitting in the aisle, while goats huddled under the seats. For Thomas, the bus ride was a sensory onslaught. He thought of the pristine, air-conditioned cocoon provided by an American bus. Here in Nepal, strong-smelling people were squeezed against each other, wearing all sorts of caftans and vests and shawls. The odors of humans and goats and spices blended in a noxious vapor, which most of the time was sucked out the window by cold air.

Thomas and Dorje stayed overnight in a simple guesthouse in Pokhara, eating an ordinary meal of rice, lentils and vegetable curry, called *dal bhat*. Thomas hadn't come down with serious diarrhea yet, but he knew he would eventually. He took a separate small room, while Dorje slept in a shared bunkroom. The guesthouse was one step up from camping. The blanket smelled bad and was inadequate for the cold.

They embarked on the hike in good weather. The long, winding, stone path was surrounded by lush vegetation, including hundreds of blooming rhododendron. Because it was the main route into the higher valleys, it was four or five feet wide. Processions of Nepalis with animals passed by, some moving very quickly, like people in rush hour who walk the path every day. As Thomas and Dorje climbed higher, beaver-like marmots on alpine slopes on both sides looked at them in panic and lumbered for cover. Several times Thomas saw hundreds of butterflies flocking in flashes of color that, like fireworks,

24

dissipated as fast as they formed. The colors of the vegetation changed constantly.

The path was a popular tourist-trekking route. Thomas and Dorje passed other foreigners, including a party of Japanese men and women. They were dressed in the latest gear as if they'd just walked out of an outdoor-adventure equipment store and were on their way to pose for commercials with the mountains as backdrop.

The first river Thomas and Dorje crossed used a short zip line for transport. Thomas could see what he had to do: Sit in a plank seat that was like a swing suspended from a pulley on the main rope, hold onto his belongings, and grab onto the ropes on each side of the seat. He was sent zipping down the line to a dip in the rope over the center of the river 100 feet below with trees crushing on both sides. Bouncing high over raging rapids, he felt excited by the danger. At that point, the ferryman pulled a towrope to haul him to the other shore. Thomas tried not to pay much attention to the condition of the ropes, knowing very well they could have weak spots.

Thomas and Dorje passed vigorous, cheerful trekking groups who were paying for the fun of this hike. Thomas wondered if there were so many hikers in Paul's time. Dorje told him the stone steps were less than a decade old, built by hand on steep hills. The steps seemed to have been constructed on a scale similar to that of the Egyptian pyramids, using similar technology, except that the base of the Nepali steps consisted of muddy, steep slopes instead of flat, sandy plains. Thomas' hike was a journey back in time.

A short, three-rope bridge appeared. Thomas had to walk on one rope while holding onto two higher ropes on each side. There were a few interim ropes holding the three in a "V" shape. If he slipped off the foot rope, he would have to catch himself by holding onto the support ropes. The trekkers queued up to transit one at a time. Even though these bridges had probably been used for centuries, Thomas wondered if anyone kept records of fatalities. Looking below, he wondered how many centuries of tragedy had been flushed down the river.

A number of smaller bridges consisted of ropes with boards lashed together to form a walkway, with additional ropes as handrails. On each side of the river, the bridges were secured with board, rope and rock constructions. Multiple hikers walked across at the same time, moving carefully to prevent too much swing in the walkway. Thomas saw fully loaded donkeys waiting to cross behind the hikers. He looked toward the wide river below him and suddenly pictured Paul floating by.

***

After Paul's death, Thomas had a long phone conversation with the tour guide in Arizona. The accident happened in June in the Grand Canyon, when the dams on the Colorado River release the maximum amount of water and the river is high and fast. The fleet included several large rafts. The tour group camped on the side of the river and ate gourmet dinners the guides cooked.

Thomas' family knew Paul loved active vacations. He was single and had a high-pressure job at the Peace Corps headquarters in Washington, D.C. He'd said that he wanted to photograph the Grand Canyon and that his friends told him the trip would be a spiritual experience.

The guide explained to Thomas that all the guests on the trip were equipped with life preservers and were expected to paddle. Paul's age of fifty-four was average among them, and he was fit. Thomas knew Paul ran about twenty-five miles a week, biked and hiked for fun, and watched his diet. The guide said women on the trip liked flirting with Paul, who told endless travel stories and had a knack for charming every member of the tour group, male and female, in a way that left them loving him.

On the fateful day of the accident, the rafters navigated mostly Class IV rapids with boulder gardens, large waves and small waterfalls. Those rapids require quick maneuvering but don't usually pose life-threatening dangers. At Bedrock Rapid, though, the twisting and spinning water splits around a large rock outcropping, and rafts must steer to the right. Paul's raft did not make the turn and, instead, veered left. It smashed against the steep rocks on the side of the river and turned over, dumping everyone on the raft. The raft ahead of it waited below the rapid and picked up three of the six occupants, including the guide. They grabbed hold of the upside-down raft with the supplies strapped inside. Paul and two other guests were swept down the river. They had been instructed that if they fell in the water, they should float feet-first with arms tight against the body, holding onto their life jackets.

When Paul passed the guides, they saw that he did not look their way and appeared disoriented. They thought he might have hit his head. They couldn't go after him. They watched where the two other rafters were drifting and had to wait for another boat to make it through to provide help. The Dubendorf Rapid, rated up to VIII, was just a mile downriver. Dubendorf had multiple large, rough holes, big boulders and high volumes of cascading water. Paul was swept into that turbulent water, which worked like a blender on anything passing through. The guides found his body another mile downriver. The other rafters, who'd made it to rocks on the shore, were found alive.

The guides radioed for a helicopter rescue. The accident was rare for the company. Paul's body was carried to a hospital in Flagstaff, where he was pronounced dead.

***

On the other side of the river, Dorje called Thomas out of his reverie.

They passed a high plateau used as a site for the disposal of the dead. It was surrounded by beautiful fields of alpine flowers in purple, pink, yellow and white, and a fierce river raged in the valley below. On the site was a circle of small boulders that looked like a mini Stonehenge, with a small building on one side and a *stupa* on the other.

"That's where dead bodies are cut up for vultures," Dorje explained. "Some think the vultures are *dakinis*, or goddesses.

Shamans like cremation grounds because of all the spirits. People do blood sacrifices here, too." Dogs and birds prowled the area looking for remains. It was both a cemetery and a feral feeding ground and made Thomas curious and fearful. *It's a good thing Paul didn't ask for this,* he thought. *I couldn't do it.*

He stepped off the path to urinate, going into bushes for privacy. When he stood up, he saw an army of small leeches climbing up his boots onto his legs. They were fast. He quickly finished his business, stepped back, and swung his pack to dig inside for a pocketknife to flick the leeches off. There were many. They were on his pack, too. He ran back to the trail.

"Dorje, Dorje! Leeches!"

"Thomas, no knife. It'll leave part of the leech there. Wait, I'll get water."

Dorje got his water bottle and dug in his pack for a small jar of salt. Some of the leeches were swelling fast. "Don't worry. They inject anesthetic that kills your pain. You won't feel them. But what they inject also makes blood flow to them. Water and salt make them let go. Take your boots and socks off."

Thomas reluctantly exposed his feet and stepped over to a patch of dry dirt, clear of any grasses that could hide more bloodsuckers. Dorje poured a little water down his leg and salted each leech. They went into spasms and fell off, one by one. Some were as large as Northwestern slugs and reddish-brown from drinking blood. Thomas' legs were covered with little holes, dripping red.

"That sure trumps mosquito bites. How many does it take to kill you?" He used his knife to flick those that still held to his backpack. He thought, *Paul should see me now, looking like Saint Sebastian with dripping, bloody holes all over. Of course, nobody is persecuting me, unless it's some leech-demon. For you, Paul,* he thought. *Bleeding for you.*

"I suggest you look for a dry place next time, my friend," said Dorje.

They finally went up a stone stairway onto a terrace that was part of the village where Paul had lived and worked. The village consisted of concrete and stone buildings scattered over a hillside, with worn paths between. Thomas expected he would feel some rush of recognition, but there was nothing. Paul had not described the village in detail. It could have been anywhere in Nepal. The novelty of the structures was interesting, but not fascinating, to Thomas as a builder.

Dorje asked around and found a school building. A sleepy dog lay in the dirt in front. It was dusty-tan, skinny, but affectionate. Dogs were in the class of animals considered sacred in Nepal, Dorje explained. Monkeys, pigeons, and dogs could wander and be taken care of, especially in temples. They could attach themselves to a family, but could be assured of treats and scolding anywhere they went. This dog stood up, as if he had just been assigned tour duty, and followed Thomas and Dorje around.

"You're a good fella," said Thomas, leaning down with an outstretched hand. Because he'd left Sally behind in Winthrop, he missed canine conversation. The dog licked his hand. When he stood up, the dog jumped up against him, smiling.

Suddenly, Thomas was stricken with recognition. The face was familiar. When he was eleven, his parents had given him a dog like this because they'd thought he was too shy. He'd doted on Charlie, spending hours at play, sleeping with him. His parents were right. A puppy changed his life for eight months, at least. Long enough to feel as if he and the dog were extensions of one another.

At the time, Paul was in high school. He'd joined track and field and started jogging in the early morning. Because the young dog needed to be let out at daybreak to avoid accidents indoors, Paul took care of that. Then, he'd go running.

Thomas later learned that when Paul saw other people running with dogs, he decided to take Charlie with him, thinking since he was the only one up in the morning, the rest of the family wouldn't notice. Paul thought running would be good for the dog. Thomas suspected, too, that Paul wanted a piece of Charlie without getting in Thomas's way.

A few days into this plan, Paul let the dog run off-leash. He didn't realize a young, untrained dog would run after anything exciting like a squirrel or another dog. It finally happened. The dog ran off into the street and was hit by a car. The driver stopped, and Paul caught up with the dog, hundreds of feet from the running path. Charlie was clearly dead. Paul picked up the bleeding, mangled carcass and carried it nearly four miles.

When Paul arrived at the house, Thomas was waiting for him, missing his dog. He saw Paul walking with a bundle of fur in his arms and screamed. Paul handed him Charlie and said, "I'm really sorry. Sorry. Sorry." But Thomas thought Paul had acted like he'd just done him a favor by bringing the dog back. He burst into tears on the back steps of the house. Nicholas and Livia finally realized what was happening and tried to console him. Paul was punished, but no punishment could make up for taking away the love of Thomas's young life. His parents offered Thomas another dog, but he wouldn't accept the offer.

The dog in Nepal brought back the whole incident. *Did Paul send you?* Thomas thought. *Not really good enough. You're nice, but you're not Charlie. Paul owes me big.* Still, Thomas gave this dog special attention as they walked. His child's broken heart still hurt.

Thomas and Dorje found the government guesthouse where Paul had lived. Very few residents in the village remembered Paul from his picture, and they had almost no stories to tell about him. He was a curious historical fact: the American who was here for a bit. However, they did point to a concrete latrine that came of Paul's efforts. It was a proud feature, part of Nepali change toward a more sanitary environment. Thanks to Paul, the funds had been found, and the village surpassed others in term of development. A villager took Thomas and Dorje behind the concrete structure. Near the base was an inscription in the concrete: "Peace Corps, Paul Rusak, 1987."

The village tour was disappointing. Except for the latrine, no spot proclaimed itself as "the spirit of Paul." *Yes, Paul made his mark all right,* thought Thomas. *The only physical marker of his very existence on earth is not a tombstone.* Someday, Thomas would have to resist telling this story in a bar.

No spectacular point along the hike stood out as a perfect site for scattering ashes. Thomas and Dorje could have been walking through a forest in the Cascades of Washington State. The hills were beautiful, surrounded by mountains, full of glades and valleys and streams that could be precious for some personal reason. Thomas was frustrated and hoped Helen would give him a clue. What was plan B if he couldn't find a good spot? Maybe, instead of a natural setting, one of the little temples on a hillside would be appropriate. He didn't know if Paul was a Buddhist, but the mini-*stupa*s covered with prayer flags and candles were unique in Nepal. They were like little guard stations for hikers on alarmingly steep hillsides.

***

Thomas and Dorje planned to visit Helen's monastery near Pokhara, too. Her current location was not directly on the path they'd used to get to Paul's village, but was close to where she was assigned during her Peace Corps stint. The traveler's hostel her monastery maintained was near a popular trekking path in the foothills below Annapurna. Thomas and Dorje spent another night in the crude Pokhara hotel.

They set out on a three-hour hike toward the monastery. Thomas's stomach had quieted from the day before, when his distress was compounded by leeches up his legs, and he could enjoy the scenery.

Thomas and Dorje arrived at the monastery in mid-afternoon. Dorje knew the place and took them directly to a whitewashed guesthouse. There, Thomas had his first view of prayer flags on lines extending from the tops of buildings to stakes in the ground like flags on the rigging of a sailboat. Some flags were multicolored while others were white. The lines with flags looked like strings of handkerchiefs hung out to dry, so beaten by the wind that their edges frayed. In the wind, they sounded like flocks of birds. Inside the guesthouse, directly off the entry, was a tearoom with low benches and low, rough wooden tables. The guesthouse had areas for leaving backpacks, sticks and hiking shoes. Directions to an outhouse were prominent. Dorje asked for Helen. She was away but would return that day, so Thomas and Dorje sat for a meal and waited.

After about two hours, a thin, middle-aged, white woman with short, reddish hair walked in from the kitchen area. Her face was lean from living at a high elevation and rosier than most of the natives' faces. Thomas knew from his climbing friends that living at a high altitude gives you more red blood cells, which, along with light skin, makes for a healthy glow. The red of Helen's hair and cheeks was echoed in the maroon of her vest, which she wore over a thick, cotton blouse and long, plain Nepali skirt.

Dorje stood up to greet her with his palms together.

"Dorje! How nice to see you," she said in Nepali.

"Helen. How are you?" he replied in English, signaling that Thomas was with him.

"Did you eat? Did they give you a room?"

"Yes. Helen, this is Thomas Rusak from America." Thomas felt self-conscious as she looked at him. He was holding a brand name Western daypack that was ragged and nearly empty. He was about her age.

"Oh!" She held her hands to her breast, then looked to Dorje. "Trekking?"

"No, Helen. He's here to see you." Thomas got up and reached out his hand. Instead, Helen put her palms together in the Hindu greeting. Thomas pulled his hand back and awkwardly imitated her. They sat down at a table in the dining area.

"I'm Paul's brother. Did you know him in the Peace Corps?"

"Ah. A long time ago."

"Yes. Paul died in an accident last summer."

"Oh! I'm so sorry to hear that. What kind of accident?" She folded her arms as if putting up a shield.

"Rafting trip. Drowned."

"How awful. What a shame!" She was silent for a minute, looking down. Then, she leaned toward the kitchen and signaled someone for tea. Her hands returned to her lap, tightly clasped.

"Were you friends?" Thomas asked.

"Yes. Only then. We didn't stay in touch."

"He worked for the Peace Corps in Washington, D.C.," Thomas said. "Training manager. Travelled a lot. Your parents said they hadn't met him."

"Ah. You met my parents?"

"Yes. The Peace Corps Office sent me to them. They set me up with Dorje here."

"Are you looking to follow Paul's travels?"

"Not really. I have his ashes. He wanted them scattered here. That's why I'm here. I'm looking for a place he might have liked. He didn't name any particular place. We were in his village yesterday. I thought maybe you could suggest something."

"Yes. A few places come to mind." She paused, without expression. "I'd have to think. Where are the ashes?"

"In Kathmandu." Now, Thomas felt foolish. If he'd brought them, he could have gone to a place she suggested and been done with it. Maybe he was afraid he would drop them in a river or something. *Why did he leave them behind? He'd not been sure what these hills were going to be like. How rough. It's not as if he were climbing to the Everest Base Camp. People lived here. Still, if the spot for ashes turned out to be close by, he would have to do this all over again. He could have asked Dorje whether to bring them. But then, someplace in Kathmandu could end up being the final site.*

Helen was silent again. Thomas and Dorje looked around the room. There were some *tonkas* on cheap poster paper plastered to the wall. Travel posters for Annapurna and the Himalayas. Some prayer flags. The décor looked like token accommodation to Western travelers, who probably ate, went directly to bed and spent only one night. Helen's crossed her arms and looked tense.

"Did you know him very well?" Thomas asked.

"Yes, actually."

"Oh?"

"Fairly close. We were a day's hike apart."

Thomas looked at her now, seeing a woman. *His brother's close friend? What were they like in 1986?* He tried to remember Paul's appearance as a young man. "I'd like to hear more."

"He was handsome. Cosmopolitan. He'd spent years in France. He could sing French songs."

"French?" Dorje laughed.

"We pretended to be family when we visited each other. It's common here to have far-flung family come and visit."

"Ah." Thomas could see that she was wringing her hands now.

She clasped her hands to calm them. "He was headed to Japan. He planned to wander on his way back to the States." She got up awkwardly. "Excuse me while I check on things. Why don't we talk after you settle into a room and wash up?"

Thomas and Dorje stood with her. She directed them to rustic guestrooms in back, explaining access to the outhouse and to water for washing. Other visitors had arrived and were looking for food and rooms.

Thomas was suddenly very tired. A steep three-hour hike was unusual for him. His guestroom was dark, lit mostly by one bulb. It was rustic like hikers' shelters just about anywhere. A mattress, pillow and a cheap cotton comforter. He fought the urge to sleep.

When Helen returned, Thomas and Dorje were back in the dining room sipping hot tea. The hostel did not serve meat or alcohol, which kept some trekkers away. It was a popular stop, nevertheless, because the novelty of a Western innkeeper implied Western standards for cleanliness. This meant that boiled water was probably available for drinking and used for cooking. Some trekkers carried their own meat and alcohol, anyway. Thomas saw that the hostel made an effort to provide Western food like spaghetti, pancakes, and omelets. In most hostels, austerity was the norm.

Helen gave Thomas a friendly look. She seemed much more relaxed than she was earlier. "Tell me more about Paul," she said.

"He spent more than two years in Japan teaching English. He learned Japanese well enough to work as a translator in that language as well as in French. A strange mix, but it got him some work. Then, he went to Tahiti and stayed about six months. It's French-speaking, so he was comfortable there, but Tahiti didn't offer the kinds of jobs he could do. The Tahitians didn't need French-English translators. Mostly he did a Paul Gauguin thing, I think."

"You mean the sex?" She seemed to swallow the question.

"No, no. I mean he enjoyed the tropical weather, the relaxed culture. Lush greenery, beaches. The fantasy of the South Seas."

"It doesn't sound very purposeful to me."

"That's true."

"He seemed more an idealistic doer when he left here."

"Maybe he was taking a break in Tahiti," Thomas said. "He came back to Seattle briefly and soon took a job in D.C. with the Peace Corps. That's how he spent about twenty years. Making good money and taking trips."

"He never married?"

"No. Don't know why. I think he had a girlfriend in Japan."

"What about you?" Helen asked. "How did you spend all those years?"

"Me?" Thomas suddenly realized that he and Helen were close to the same age and that Paul was older than both of them. She might not have realized it. It was hard to judge the ages of people in their fifties. There were too many variables. Now, he looked at her as a woman, instead of as Paul's long-ago lover. "I'm a handyman. I live in the middle of Washington State with my dog Sally. I didn't have Paul's ambitions. I've had a quiet life. My mother is in Seattle. Paul really believed in the Peace Corps. That was his mission. I don't have a mission." Thomas felt defensive now, thinking of his mother's life-long comparisons between Paul and him. He suddenly missed being in Winthrop, ignorant of Paul's business.

"Sometimes just living your life is mission enough," Helen said.

"What about your mission? Why did you stay here? It's an extreme commitment." Thomas realized he'd been seeking to know Paul's life and not hers.

"I found my beliefs here. They make me happy. The simple life makes me happy. The most exciting thing in my life is spiritual progress. It's not a totally monastic life. The hostel keeps me in touch with Westerners, news and values. Just enough. Enough so I don't miss the West. I can go to Kathmandu and catch up with the West."

"Sounds like you don't find the West as seductive as most of the rest of the world does."

"I don't find it at all seductive. I have the usual complaints about it: rampant obsession with material life and consumption, competition to get rich, struggle to build a good life, which is very much defined materially. Very busy. People working long hours, commuting long hours. There is too little contemplation or serenity or savoring the present. Savoring nature. The setting here is spectacular, every minute of it. I don't just visit it on weekends."

"Did you go to college in the States? Have a good time? Get inspired?"

"Actually I got uninspired. Women were treated badly. You were discouraged from complex jobs. Imagine if you pressured to be an elementary teacher, a secretary, a nurse or a helper of some kind. It wasn't a good deal. You could get fired if you got married. You could get fired if you had a child. America was very backward in respect to women. While I was there, a man broke into a dormitory for women studying engineering and killed fifteen of them just because he thought it was wrong for them to be studying engineering. That's crazy. A deep misogyny. Also a culturally embedded belief that women are inferior. I got away from that overwhelming feeling that I couldn't breathe and couldn't think as a whole, independent person." Thomas could see the American in her rising.

"Isn't some of that sort of universal, though? Is Nepal much better?"

"Buddhism is one of the most egalitarian religions in the world. There's a hierarchy of holy men running the show but nothing like the Vatican. It's mostly an individual pursuit within a community. God isn't a father figure. You don't get 'saved.'"

"Aren't most lamas men?"

"Yes. But Tibetan society is different. They practice polyandry and polygamy. Women can keep their family names, inherit property, marry two or more brothers."

"Still, isn't there a lower status?" He knew he was pushing negatives at this point and smiled to soften the question.

"There's spiritual equality. A woman can reach the same enlightenment as a man. We're not treated like inherently deficient humans. There are powerful nuns."

"Could you have been a Buddhist nun in America?"

"Not really. You need to align with a lama if you're a Tibetan Buddhist. Finding your lama is like falling in love: You're fated to find each other and form a strong, life-long bond."

"Did that happen to you?"

"That's personal."

"At least, you aren't a hermit. Or, you don't seem to be. Maybe that's my stereotype."

"I've done a retreat to a cave. But no, I'm not that far away from regular people."

"Like Christian saints? Many of them ran convents and monasteries."

"Maybe. I don't have to rationalize it to myself. I do what comes to me. Don't you?"

"Ah yes. I do what I do, whether there's a system behind it or not. You're right." Thomas laughed, thinking about his marijuana business. Did he think pot was spiritually sanctioned on any grounds? Would marijuana prove to be "a good thing" scientifically, eventually? Maybe selling it was just a fine thing for him to do, providing a lifestyle without complexity. That made sense to him if he didn't think about it too long.

Thomas realized he hadn't smoked pot in a week. He'd been warned to have nothing on him when he entered the country, but once inside, there were possibilities. "You know, I grow marijuana in a place where it's illegal." He was suddenly proud of his courage. Maybe that was his mission.

"So? Is it an addiction? Do you make money?" Helen said.

Thomas thought she was taking on a nun's concern for his spiritual welfare. It was off-putting. Maybe she knew it. "Not addicted. I make money other ways." He leaned back, withdrawing from the sudden attention she was focusing on him.

"You like the risk, maybe? The secrecy?"

Thomas wasn't used to women digging deep so quickly. They usually tried to flatter him. *Helen had probably talked to a lot of Westerners passing through. This wasn't bar talk. She was getting to the meat of things pretty fast.*

"Ah. Maybe."

"Maybe, we both like to be a little on the outside, Thomas."

He sensed she'd had enough mutual probing for now. He started to get up. "Let me know any ideas for the ashes," he said, lifting his legs over the bench.

"Call in a day or two," she said, also standing.

***

In the morning, Thomas and Dorje set off early. Other hikers were already heading in both directions, up and down steep steps off the main courtyard. Thomas and his companion hiked several hours and then rode a bus to reach Kathmandu.

They left the wilderness and quiet of endless hills surrounded by mountains for the dust, diesel fuel, noise and crush of the city. Thomas' nerves were rattled, but he was beginning to enjoy the carnival atmosphere of the city.

Tibetan Buddhists

WITHIN DAYS, Thomas was glad to get an invitation to visit Jeri and Donald again. They now served as familiar territory. They'd heard about his hikes from Dorje, who'd been a calming presence through several days of culture shock and had also been invited to Jeri and Donald's place.

Maybe, Thomas thought, he'd learn more about Helen. Her religious deportment was a puzzle: Was there a normal woman in there? At least, one he could recognize? He realized he hadn't interacted with priests in his own country much, and maybe it was not Buddhism that got in the way of understanding her, but the choice of a religious life. He didn't understand why she was attracted to isolating herself in a foreign country and being extremely devoted to religion.

It was late afternoon when Thomas arrived at Jeri and Donald's house. The sun was streaming into the dining area with an entire wall open to a patio and the garden. Like most expatriates, the Simons had a cook and servants, so the gathering was leisurely. In the U.S., their lifestyle would have been upper class.

Jeri said their cook had made some steamed dumplings called *momos* as an appetizer so Thomas could try them. They contained ground beef flavored with sesame oil, soy sauce, green onions and cumin. The cook also made an Indian meal with chicken curry, red lentils, rice, *raita* eggplant, *puris*, and slices of fresh mango. All the dishes were new to Thomas. He'd been eating in restaurants and felt lucky to get a taste of good, Indian home cooking.

"I bet they don't eat like this in monasteries," Thomas said, savoring the many dishes.

"Did you have a meal at Helen's hostel?" asked Jeri.

"Yes. It was all right. Didn't include any meat. Maybe they use fewer spices. I guess you're not vegetarians."

"We're not," Jeri said. "Practicing Buddhists, on the other hand, don't eat meat. Most likely they use less butter. Many natives really prize an occasional meal of chicken, pork, goat or lamb. You've probably seen that *momos* are the fast food of Nepal."

"I'm getting a taste for Indian spices. Of course, you can't get away from them here."

"How was your visit with Helen?" Donald asked.

"A big adventure for me."

"What's your biggest surprise?"

"Well, her choice to be a lay nun. I don't think she's the same person who was in love with my brother. I've heard about Westerners who go after Buddhism. I don't quite understand people who stay and assimilate as much as she has."

"Well, she grew up here," Donald said. "She still has a lot of contact with trekkers and tourists, so she's not as isolated as she would be in a remote monastery."

"Did you try to stop her?"

Donald laughed. "There's an old Chinese story about a father who tried to stop his daughter from becoming a nun. He wanted to marry her off. It turned out badly. No, we didn't think of stopping either one of the girls."

"You have another daughter?"

"We have a granddaughter who is like a daughter. She's away on business today. Actually, she's Helen's girl."

"But like a daughter?"

"We raised her," Jeri said. "Helen left her with us in Kathmandu. Eike thinks of us as her parents and sees Helen once in a while."

"What does Eike do?"

"She's a shaman." Jeri laughed at Thomas' expression. "So we have two nuns of a sort in the family."

"Helen left her behind?"

Donald looked directly at him. "It's rare, for sure. We were delighted to have Eike, though. Helen's choice was a great blessing to us."

Jeri interrupted. "Actually, Helen did go through a black period when she went back to the hills. I think a lot of it had to do with her view of the sad lot of women, especially in America. I don't know if her black period was triggered by initiation rites she was doing at the time."

Thomas, Jeri, Donald, and Dorje were all comfortably eating and drinking. Jeri seemed lost in her train of thought. "Psychologists describe a process of withdrawal from a situation you perceive as oppressive, even unconsciously, and coming back to a transformed state. It's the basis of a lot of myths, you know. Like Orpheus and Eurydice. Eurydice is attacked by a satyr and, in trying to get away, falls into a nest of vipers. She dies from a snake bite. Orpheus goes into the underworld to rescue Eurydice from death. Helen could have feared falling into a kind of maternal death. On the other hand, her black period could have been something caused by meditation practice, you know. Put her into a state, a new level of consciousness."

Donald added, "We heard that Helen had been sick for several months, but she didn't send a message for us to come and help her. She can send word anytime, and we're there. Same with Eike. So we don't know what happened. That is, we don't know how much of it was mental."

Both Jeri and Donald seemed eager to justify Helen's choice. "These days we may have different definitions of whether distress is physical, mental, or spiritual in origin," Jeri said. "If you see her again, you can ask her about it. I have to warn you, it may not be something she shares, especially outside the monastery. The meditation practices are very intimate and confidential. Religious people don't hang out in cafes and share stories."

"How are the two different? I mean Helen and Eike."

Donald laughed. "A difference between the two is that Helen is a 'Red Hat' monk who will circle a shrine keeping it to her right, and Eike's a Bon who will keep it to her left. Counterclockwise. They're contrary."

Jeri laughed too. "And Bons can marry."

"One gets lost in meditation and the other gets lost in ecstatic trance," Donald said.

"Ah. I'll try to remember that. Different rules."

"You don't sound like you've gotten too familiar with Buddhist ideas yet," Jeri said.

"No, not really."

"Seriously, Helen's practice emphasizes meditation and seeking enlightenment through consciousness and awareness," Jeri continued. "Eike follows what's considered a primitive form of the religion. It involves shamanism, sorcery, the occult, magic, healing. She specializes in healing rituals. She goes into a trance and engages the spirit world in lower levels of the afterlife called *bardo*, where the newly deceased dwell."

"Bon priests can kill a fetus in the womb or bring dry bones back to life," Donald interjected. "They can be like sorcerers."

"Wow. Do Eike and Helen have anything in common?"

"They have in common the basic beliefs of Tibetan Buddhism," Donald said. "You know, the moral logic behind all of life called *dharma*. Reincarnation. *Karma* as the mechanism that guides reincarnation. The need for a lama or guide."

Jeri added: "All Buddhists believe the world is a place of suffering and that we want to escape from the cycle of rebirth and suffering. They all use prayer flags and prayer wheels and make pilgrimages. But Helen's and Eike's daily activities and social activities are completely different."

"The two strands are really different," Donald said. "Maybe like Catholics and Baptists."

"What does Helen think of Eike's choice? Does she approve?"

"None of us here is prescriptive. That's our family. People determine themselves. Did your parents tell you what to do?"

"No. They just encouraged education. But no particular career."

"We're the same," Donald said.

"What about your beliefs? Do you subscribe to this?" Thomas was starting to feel like a family friend.

"We're probably Buddhists, but we don't have a denomination," Donald said. "We're not strict, as you can see from our food. We have to respect some of the more exotic practices, even if we don't understand them completely."

"Like what?"

"Oh, Helen learned the body-warming practice. It's a yogic technique related to meditation."

"How's that?"

"Yogis and lamas have a technique for heating their bodies," Donald explained. "That's why you see them bare-skinned in the coldest weather."

"How do they do that?"

"They picture flames rising around the whole body and over the head. They feel fire bursting out of their head and through the extremities."

"Well, that sounds handy. Do you think I could learn it?" Thomas asked.

"I don't think so. You might have to spend some years learning to control your thoughts and your breathing first. It's an advanced skill. You would have to do other things before trying that."

"Something to keep in mind. It gets cold where I live too."

"Another one is the 'rainbow body.' When certain lamas die, they can cause their body to be reabsorbed into the essence from which they came, leaving just a rainbow and hair and nails behind."

"Yikes."

"Eike's also known as a medium and oracle. She goes into a trance and can predict the future or explain something that's unknown through regular channels. She transmits messages from gods, demons, the dead."

"Have you ever used her?"

"No. We haven't asked her to perform any ritual. If Jeri's not feeling well, and Eike says 'She's going to be okay,' we don't think of it as a divine message." Donald laughed.

"My mother and aunt do messaging from the spirit world, too."

"Indeed! So what do you think of it?" Donald asked.

"I don't know. I don't know how much the power of suggestion and coincidence are behind the evidence for it. Don't know if it's true. I would have to believe in ghosts and spirits, wouldn't I?"

"Most Tibetans believe in them. The people we interact with every day have a lot of stories. If they live in small hamlets, especially, they're likely to be very respectful toward spirits. There were as many demons and ghosts in Tibet as people. They think they're everywhere."

"So what happened with the Chinese invasion? Did the Tibetans fight back?" Thomas wasn't a scholar at heart but he was thinking about his mother having to flee a hostile invasion of Lithuania at the end of World War II.

"They weren't equipped to fight back," Donald said. "They probably didn't even understand the threat. They had a long tradition of isolation from all foreign influences. Various foreign travelers tried to come in and discover them and Tibetans turned them back at the borders if they could. A few famous ones made it, and their books were best sellers in the West, like Alexandra David-Neel.

"A British incursion from India was sent up at the turn of the century and it resulted in the massacre of many Tibetans because their weapons were old muzzle-loaded rifles. They thought blessings would protect them. Their technology was at least half a century old. They didn't have roads, didn't even use wagons. The head monks refused to send young Tibetans to study in the West, fearing contamination. So when the Chinese invaded, the response was disorganized and ineffective."

Jeri added: "Nearly one-third of all males were in monasteries from the age of seven. Their knowledge of the world was limited. The people revered and supported them in every way. The monasteries depended on the work of the common people. Some of the monasteries were extravagant and filled with precious stones: gold, silver, turquoise and jade on altars, tombs, doors, and ritual objects. Sometimes, even common household items were inlaid with ornamentation. The Chinese called the system feudal and exploitative. Their view has some validity."

Donald pushed his dishes away. "The common people didn't live very well. They were like the common people supporting the monasteries in medieval Europe under the Catholic Church. They didn't get much education and a chance to get ahead. They were living a primitive, dependent and poor agrarian life."

"The leaders—the lamas who start out as infant *tulkus*, or incarnated ones—grow up apart from their parents and surrounded by men," Jeri said. "They're celibate, for the most part. And they're definitely not trained in political or military skills."

"Unlike most of Asia's Buddhist societies, Tibet never came under direct European control nor made any attempt to 'modernize' by establishing universities, importing European technologies, or sending elites to Europe for an education."

Both Jeri and Donald stopped talking in what seemed like shared sadness. Thomas realized if they had been in Nepal since 1986 at least, they probably knew the personal stories of hundreds of Tibetan refugees. They'd probably seen the personal toll of the Chinese invasion. He knew that the refugee camps had begun in the sixties, and thousands of refugees were spending most of their lives in exile, in temporary settlements. The tragedy was still unrelentingly present on a daily basis for many of the people Jeri and Donald worked with and cared about.

He thought about the irony that the artifacts of daily life in Tibet that refugees transported out—jackets, pots and pans, hats, holy manuscripts, cloth, pictures—were getting old, worn, broken. They were being replaced by Nike shoes, movie posters, neon, and plastic bowls. His mother Livia and Aunt Clara would find the situation painfully familiar.

***

Soon after Thomas found the Pilgrim Book Store, specializing in English-language books on everything Asian. He bought several books by Alexandra David-Neel and a famous travel account by Marco Pallis, her contemporary in the early 20th century. They were among the first Western explorers of Tibet and also expansive writers who loved climbing the mountains as much as discovering Buddhism. Both published photographs of their crazy journeys. Thomas was starting to get hooked.

BECAUSE IT WAS EASY for a tourist to get lost in Kathmandu, Thomas asked Dorje to spend another day walking around with him. Dorje could practice his English and Thomas would have a guide. Thomas' hotel was just north of the main tourist area.

"You're Tibetan, then, not Nepali?" Thomas asked.

"My parents are refugees. Escaped from Tibet. 1962."

"Why escape?"

"The Chinese came in 1950. In 1959, they started destroying Tibet. Trashing monasteries. Stealing things, taking ritual objects. Destroying books. Killing monks and nuns. Putting people in forced labor. Barbaric."

"How did your parents get out?" Thomas asked. "My parents had to run from the Russians on foot with just what they could carry. Roads were full of people."

"They had to get out at night. Chinese patrols were watching all the caravan routes. They didn't want these potential slaves to escape. They especially watched river crossings, any escape routes. They would shoot anyone, easy. It was winter. People had to walk across high mountains in snowstorms. They hid in caves during the day. Couldn't light fires or make noise. Carried a food bowl, a little food and prayer beads. Everybody on the way was afraid to help. My parents didn't have good shoes or good food, like trekkers have."

"Where are your parents now?"

"They went south to India, following the Dalai Lama," Dorje said. "Ended up in Assam. The Indians set up camps. We lost my father and my sister in the first camps, though. They got sick from bad water. India was way hotter than Tibetans are used to. People were made to do hard labor to keep them busy. Eventually, my mother moved to the camp in Kathmandu. I met Jeri and Donald here."

"Living in camps since 1962? That's forever. My parents were in camps for nearly five years. Five years made it a lifestyle. But it was a problem for the host countries in Europe. The Allies looked for ways to clear out the camps, because many refugees would not go back to their occupied countries. The Allies had to find countries that were willing to take people. Did your parents try to leave?"

"They had no choice. They're not going back to Tibet , and they didn't have the skills to go abroad by themselves. Small groups went to Switzerland, Australia, and America. Money comes in to support the camps. We're learning to make things to sell here."

"Did you learn Tibetan?"

"Oh yes. The schools teach Tibetan and Nepali and English. The monasteries teach Buddhism. Nepalis are Buddhists too, so it's not that strange."

"*Can* you go back to Tibet?"

"Too dangerous. The Chinese will put you in prison in a minute. They have big prisons. They don't want Tibetan culture. They've banned festivals. They allow only Chinese language in the schools. Not even folk songs."

"But *I* can travel there."

"Yes, they need tourists. But it's a police state. Full of Chinese people now. The Tibetans are the poor beggars and workers."

"It's true we could have travelled back to Lithuania, too. Once the Russians let visitors in, they controlled where visitors went. Same thing: Russian language in schools, Russian people moved in, the whole system favored Russians and collaborators. Locals were blocked from university."

"We're getting stronger now," Dorje said. "More of us are educated. The Dalai Lama goes all over the world."

"It's hard to get the country back. The Chinese are so much bigger."

"But your home country did become independent again, didn't it?" Dorje said.

"It did. It's beyond belief."

"We still wonder why Tibetan gods didn't crush the Chinese. Maybe they will."

As Thomas and Dorje walked the streets, Thomas still recoiled at the obvious poverty. Many on the street were barefoot, wearing only a dirty gray cotton shirt and shorts. They were wearing used clothes from all over the world. A fur-trimmed, tailored, red-wool coat on a child, or a Lacrosse polo shirt, or an Italian soccer jersey on an adult. Pedestrians were carrying small bundles of things from the market: potatoes, kerosene, a jar of butter. He knew an under-class existed in America but, in rural states, it was not as obvious. Here the poor were everywhere, sickly, skinny and dirty, with rotten teeth. They walked past the restaurants and hotels they could never afford as he might walk past shops in America selling Swiss watches and expensive luggage that he could not afford, behind an invisible barrier of wealth.

Dorje could afford clean, Western-style clothes and sturdy sandals. He could read and write and work in an office. He knew the laws, he knew history, and he knew where he was in the world. His parents might have had to survive snow-covered caves, infections, and dangerous boat crossings, but here he was. And here was Thomas, far from the miserable flight from Lithuania and from Seattle, touring Kathmandu. They were both within a generation of extreme displacement. They were like the early orchids plucked from China and South America, sheltered in artificial tropical greenhouses in England and other unnatural habitats, until they adapted. Now, orchids were common in hardware and grocery stores in America. What was once exotic, fragile, and nearly extinct is helped to thrive in new places, analogous to the many varieties of cannabis had been taught to grow in foreign soil.

"Do you resent the Nepal-crazy foreigners?" Thomas asked.

"We're used to them. They pay the bills. It's exciting."

"They've written a lot of books about discovering Buddhism." Thomas was thinking about some of the books he'd seen when he scouted the shelves of the Pilgrim Book Store in Kathmandu.

"Sure. The same thing happened to India. You need to be discovered."

"Except by the Chinese. Or the British. They want to take what they find and fix it to suit themselves."

"Jeri and Donald didn't," Dorje said. "They've stayed. They help. It's not all good or bad."

"Except when the invaders want to kill your culture, your leaders, your people." *Now, we're brothers in the tragedy of Displaced Persons,* Thomas thought.

"What to do. Pray."

"Have you traveled out of Nepal to go to school?"

"India. That was foreign enough. I have a lot of friends who went to England and America. They tell me about it."

Thomas and Dorje walked several miles back into town. They took a route through narrow alleys, bypassing the crowded market. By now Thomas was used to being surrounded by shops, beggars, pulled rickshaws, reckless taxis, polluting buses, air-conditioned government cars, and pedestrians carrying everything from chickens and goats to a massive stack of woven baskets on their heads. The sounds of bells and chanting, drums and cymbals came from back rooms and courtyards. People spat in the streets. Some of the back alleys were used as toilets. Walking through Kathmandu, now, was no stranger, thought Thomas, than walking through a mall in America, surrounded by overweight people who ate while they walked, surrounded by displays of extremely specialized luxury goods like electronic massage pillows and foot baths.

After Thomas and Dorje parted, Thomas passed a shop selling Tibetan artifacts to tourists. Dorje had explained to him the functions of the various ritualistic objects visible in temples and monasteries. He'd explained that the relics of famous lamas were often housed inside a *stupa* in an urn. Inside the shop were ritual daggers, conches, bone trumpets, bells, drums, skulls and singing bowls. Thinking about the cigar box that Paul currently inhabited, Thomas asked the shopkeeper if he had any special urns. Thomas was shown several. The one that caught his eye was about the size of a coffee pot. It was an old, brass container shaped like a *stupa*, with a round base surrounded by what looked like two necklaces of embossed squares. The lid had a square shape, then a stack of rings incrementally smaller, topped by a wide saucer. The urn was both a *stupa* and an urn and worthy of Paul, thought Thomas. He bought it, bargaining a little, but passively.

When he got back to his hotel, he carefully transferred Paul's ashes into the urn, pouring from the plastic bag that had been in the cigar box. Thomas wanted the old brass walls of the urn to have direct contact with Paul's ashes, so they would pick up ancient vibrations if such existed. Even though Thomas planned to scatter the ashes, he felt proud to give Paul, in the interim, a classy, Tibetan resting place that had meaning for him.

End of the Line

BACK IN JUNE, Livia felt faint with relief as she and Paul pulled up to her house in Seattle after flying back from Flagstaff. Thomas's pickup was in the concrete driveway. It was a fixture there. He had repaired and rebuilt so much of the house: fencing, patio trellis and stairs, deck, trim, gutters, and roof. Even though he lived in Winthrop now, he came back nearly twice a month. In her mind, he still lived in Seattle. Old clothes he'd never thrown away were in the guestroom closet.

Livia's younger sister Clara was home, as usual. For two years, they'd made a life together. As she and Thomas entered the living room, Livia saw her with new eyes: the short gray hair moussed into a stand-up brush. The artist from Sedona.

Clara should have gone with them to Arizona, Livia thought; it was Clara's home turf. Clara looked hip if you saw past her old age. She had been the thinner sister, but now she was heavy, too. She'd found a new scene for herself in Seattle. She had joined a group of fellow women artists who showed their work at craft fairs and galleries. Clara and Livia lived side by side in the ample house, their childhood competition long over and worn out. They had both doted on Thomas and Paul. Good days were precious, to be consumed like a particularly rich soup with delightful side dishes.

Livia's grief returned, as if she'd just witnessed Paul being dumped into a river, when she saw Clara. They embraced, and big sobs poured onto Clara's shoulder. Both Thomas and Paul were golden to Livia, but Paul had been her hope for a grander life. In her imagination, Paul had led her all over the world, with his lust for adventure and foreign sights and sounds. Paul was romance. Thomas was the steady homeboy, doing mundane chores on other people's property.

Livia understood why Thomas wanted to go right back to his place in Winthrop. He had work to do. He had never seemed to get over his tension with Paul. Having Paul in a box didn't make much difference. Paul had always been away, invisible. Memories kept their strained relationship going, even now.

***

Livia wasn't surprised when Thomas came back a month later. The three of them sat on the covered wooden porch, facing out. It was the third day of a heavy rain. Cold, clean rivulets poured from the cedar roof over the porch. The trio appeared to be under a gentle fountain, surrounded by soothing water music, the convergence of dozens of streams of water dripping independently: drip ... drip ... drip and drip-drip-drip and drip..........drip..........drip. Nature's calming machine.

It was routine for the two women to get together in the evening after a day of separate domestic rituals like having coffee on the porch, feeding cats, having toast with cheese and a cup of soup, tidying the living room, and checking the flowers in the yard. Clara spent some of her time painting greeting cards, which she sold through a local boutique. She had scaled down from large watercolors and acrylics. One thing was quite new for them, however. They had both developed strong spiritual leanings in their advanced age and had a group of friends who talked to spirits, channeled spirits and read the past and future for clients. It was a spiritual garden Livia and Clara cultivated together, which allowed them a very different and satisfying relationship in late life.

Thomas was smoking a joint at the far end of the porch and half-listening. Livia knew he didn't enjoy reminiscing about Paul.

"I think we're due for a cleansing. Take the bad stuff and wash it away," said Livia, pulling the fleece rug up on her lap, flapping her bare feet that rested on a stool.

"So much rain," said Clara, "We could be basking in cheerful sunshine, somewhere."

"God's way of purging our hearts. Water's simple."

A heavy tubular chime behind them sent out a deep drone under the eaves.

"I bet that's Paul," said Livia. "He used to say those chimes sounded like a Tibetan prayer bowl." Now the chime reminded her to grieve. Her cheeks were raw from frequent tears. Just ten years earlier, she'd lost her husband Nicholas. She knew that Thomas worried she'd be thrown back into neglecting herself. Except that now, she had Clara to make sure she got up, ate, went out in the yard.

On the sideboard just off the porch, Livia and Clara had set up a memorial space for Paul. In the space were candles, along with objects appealing to Paul: a liqueur glass of Cointreau, some Belgian chocolates (which Clara found at her special store), slices of mango, a plate with slices of Swiss raclette cheese and a Clausen's pickle. Livia and Clara had debated about including an Indian-style spicy chip called *pappadam* but didn't want to shop for it. In the memorial space, they had also placed a small amount of Paul's ashes in a Chinese snuff bottle with a picture of a samurai painted on the inside. *Paul would probably like being thought of as a samurai, fighting whatever,* thought Livia. *Waving a giant sword in the air. Making his mark.* He'd given the bottle to Livia when he got back from Japan.

The air outside was still misty, cool and quiet.

"I remember him chasing the cat in the back yard," said Livia.

"I picture him at my art show, sipping wine and chatting people up," Clara said.

"He was a good skier. He would skid to a stop just in front of me, rosy cheeks and snow caught in his eyebrows and hair. A fair-haired, confident boy."

"He repaired my sink once. He was down on the floor, laughing at the cat trying to squeeze under the sink with him."

From the stool beside her, Livia lifted a shoebox full of photos and notes belonging to Paul. She'd been through them many times. The guides had recovered his backpack from the trip. In it were gloves with the fingers cut off; a shammy cloth; a baggie with toothpaste, toothbrush, deodorant, wound-healing cream, Chapstick; and a down vest crushed into a small pouch.

Livia showed Thomas a jumble of things she had placed in a bowl. Paul's wallet with forty dollars in bills, two credit cards, a driver's license, a weathered photo of a red-head, and a weathered photo of a Japanese girl; a khaki Mao-style cap with a small rim; a Swiss army knife with a corkscrew; a few heavily creased maps of the Colorado River; and sunglasses like those worn by serious athletes.

"He didn't say much about the girl in the Peace Corps," Livia remarked, mostly to herself. Clara had known him well enough to know about the romance but had nothing to offer.

Livia and Clara had talked privately about Paul's accident. A sudden traumatic death could leave a soul stuck on Earth. There were ghosts who didn't realize they'd died. It could take an intervention to move them along. Somebody had to tell them they were "gone" and they should head for wherever it was souls congregated to consider their next moves.

But it was too soon to try to speak to Paul's spirit. She and Clara would bring it up with their spiritual group. Sometimes, the spirit of the deceased came to someone and talked to him or her, and that would help the living tell if things were all right on the other side. Livia's mind wasn't clear enough to work on the issue. Her grief was like a helmet of pain, giving her blurry vision and a constant urge to cry. She was in purgatory too, she thought. There was no pill for it. She knew from Nicholas's death that it took time to park the torment deep inside oneself, to start smiling, to relish her food again.

Bill, a marmoset monkey, sauntered out on the porch through the open door and leaped gracefully to Clara's chest. He'd probably finished a nap on the couch and was looking for company. Clara put her hand around him, covering most of his body. He nuzzled against her, reaching an arm to her neck. She'd named him after an erstwhile American lover, who, she said, had been slow, clingy, and laid-back. Long naps and tasty snacks seemed enough for Bill apart from his adoration of Clara.

The name "Bill" was awkward for Clara, and she continued the slight disdain for the original with her pronunciation of "bull" with a Russian accent. This Bill seemed to have her affections, however; they were inseparable. His low demands didn't seem to bother her. Livia had gotten used to seeing his fuzzy face next to Clara's most of the time. Even Bill's habit of grooming Clara's hair had become part of the background. However, his intelligent eyes were disconcerting to both Livia and Thomas.

After two years, Livia and Thomas were still bonding with the monkey. Livia wondered what the monkey was thinking, and if he was thinking. She was used to dogs but didn't understand what monkeys wanted. Dogs could be as smart as a two-year-old. What about marmoset monkeys? When strangers saw a furry ball with glistening dark eyes peek out next to Clara's left breast from a sling like a kangaroo's pouch, they actually stepped back. Bill did not seem to mind the rain, although if he were a dog or cat, he might hate it. He pretty much knew he never had to leave Clara's chest or shoulder if he didn't want to.

"We haven't done a good job of propagating the line," Livia said, looking at Thomas, then looking at Bill. "I wish Paul had had a traditional family. You, too, Thomas. A monkey doesn't seem enough. Ah me." Livia straightened in her chair. "Oh, how I miss Paul!"

The candlelight burned steady through the screen door. Clara sighed, got up, and walked inside to the memorial spread and took a piece of cheese. Livia followed her and took a sip of Cointreau. "I suppose we should go to bed. Thomas, please get the door." They blew out the candles, leaving the room dark. Each of the women leaned on the sideboard and pushed herself away. Neither wanted to ruin the mood with chatter. They left the room slowly, careful not to strain old legs.

Thomas sat on the porch in the dark.

Daikini

THOMAS FINALLY GOT A MESSAGE at his hotel that Helen was coming to town and could meet him in Durbar Square in two days. She hadn't forgotten his question about Paul's favorite places. He looked up Durbar Square in his guidebook and saw that it had five acres of palaces and temples, mostly with Hindu icons. It would be a great place to walk and talk.

They met at Kavindrapura, the mansion of the king of poets, as it was near fountains and springs. The day was cool, overcast. The square was packed with formidable architecture, a valley of temples. Walking there was like walking the streets of New York with your head craned upward. Fabulous detailed statues and wall paintings were everywhere. It was analogous to an outdoor British Museum.

"Helen." He saw her come around a corner.

"Thomas. Hi." She smiled in a formal way.

"Nice to see you again."

"You must be getting around easier now."

"What are you in town for?"

"Supplies. I stay only a day. As you know, it takes about a day to travel here." They stopped to look at a figure of the Buddha carved into a mud wall.

"You know, I went to an orientation on meditation for tourists."

"Oh?"

"Testing the territory."

"And what do you think?"

"I can see that it takes practice."

"Actually, a lot. But I don't want to discourage you."

They stepped over dogs sleeping on the pavement. *They seem to be loitering. Maybe the food is better here*, thought Thomas. "I've been thinking about faith. What makes people believe certain things."

"Like what?"

"Oh, ghosts and demons, for example."

"It's personal experience."

"I guess." They passed a crowd pressed up against a recessed statue he could see only part of. A priest was chanting, and the crowd was clapping.

"I think both Hindus and Buddhists put a lot of faith in intuition," Helen said. "You know some things without reading a book."

"I guess I'm programmed to be skeptical."

"Even Western scientists can be wrong. Once in a while, they think they have infallible evidence for something, and then it's wrong."

"Don't you worry about being wrong?" He was trying to stay respectful.

"Of course. But you have to trust yourself. Have faith."

Thomas was looking at her from behind as she walked ahead. Her reddish hair was short but glistened in sunlight. She was thin, fit, and walked with confidence and physical strength. His blood was racing. It took him by surprise. Was he hitting on a nun? They stopped at a vendor sitting on a stoop selling oranges and bought some, then sat down nearby.

"I read the famous travel stories. People have really fixed on Nepal and Tibet." He put the oranges in a row between them.

"Understandably. Me too."

"Have you heard of Diane Perry and June Campbell?" He handed her his pocketknife for the oranges, debating whether to do the work for her.

"Who are they?" she asked.

"They're Western women who became Buddhist nuns. Diane Perry actually spent time in a remote cave. She was

English. At the age of eighteen while travelling in Germany, she identified with Buddhism."

"I might have heard of her. My parents have books. I don't spend much time reading that kind of thing."

"June Campbell actually served as a sexual consort for a prominent lama. Did you ever hear of things like that?"

Helen flushed. "It's known to happen. It's a Tantric practice."

"She says it lasted several years. Only one other person knew about it."

"It's supposed to be secret."

"But then she publishes a book and tells the world," Thomas said.

"You're making it salacious. It's a divine act."

"Can you tell me what it entails, then?"

"I'm sure she told you. It's not the same as having an orgy. Western Puritans suspect it's all sex. Yogis fool with many bodily functions. Sex is one of them."

"She said it involves withholding the semen. The male is trying to be one with an 'other.' This transports him to a mystical state."

Helen changed the subject. "Did you know that during Durga Puja, on what's called a 'black night,' eight buffaloes and over 100 goats are sacrificed by Hindus?"

"Wow. A lot of blood!"

"In Pokhara, where I lived for a bit, there are nearly 40,000 sacrifices of goats during the festival."

"Do they eat the meat?"

"Yes, after it's offered to the temples. It's a very happy festival, actually."

"Speaking of food, let's go eat." They found a restaurant and had egg curry, cauliflower and radishes. He was starting to memorize her face, her neck, her ears, her hands. He wanted to touch her, even through those long layers of cloth she wore. Was he looking for the real Helen underneath? Or had he been possessed by the ghost of Paul?

When they left the restaurant, it started to drizzle. Thomas offered Helen his jacket.

"Oh, no thanks. I don't borrow clothes from anybody."

"Um. Why?"

"Your clothes carry your vibrations and the vibrations of places they've been. That's why Tibetans wear huge woolen coats and robes on their pilgrimages to India. They want to pick up the blessings of the place in their clothes, so they can bring them back home."

"What happens if you wear my jacket?"

"It interferes with my vibrations. My clothes, my self. My clothes are an extension of me and my spiritual state. Borrowing clothes is like taking in food that may not agree with you."

"You mean they would contaminate you?" Thomas was suddenly struck by how unromantic she was.

"No, I didn't say that. You could be quite all right, a good influence." She smiled. "The clothes of great lamas are placed in their *stupa* with them. They're an extension of the person."

"That sounds like Buddhists put a lot of weight on material things."

"Oh no. I think it's recognizing that things have powers, too. Westerners think all things except humans are dumb and inanimate. There are degrees of animation and vibration. Animals have more intelligence than we imagine. Things can be holy and precious. Things can hold memory. Don't you have things that mean a lot to you?"

"Yes, but my coat's not in that category although I do like it a lot. Very attached. Sure you don't want it?" He ran his hands along the Gortex.

Helen smiled. She seemed to be unused to teasing or making light of anything. He tried to imagine her with boisterous Western trekkers, whom he imagined to be happy outdoor types, for the most part. He wondered how often she laughed.

Thomas went back to his room and made himself a joint with *ganja*, the local name for cannabis. He'd found a supply easily. The police were not fierce about cannabis, which was refreshing to him. Finally, he was in a place where the situation regarding pot was as relaxed as he thought it should be. As he walked through alleys and bazaars, he could smell it as easily as he could smell cooking spices in the air. He remembered the quote by Dr. Meredith in Louisa May Alcott's *Perilous Play*: "I advise any bashful young man to take hashish when he wants to offer his heart to any fair lady, for it will give him the courage of a hero, the eloquence of a poet, and the ardour of an Italian." Thomas felt he could use a little extra power, under the circumstances.

"Mom?" Thomas said into the phone. "I want to stay longer. Can you cover my rent in Winthrop for another month? It's really cheap to stay. My room is ten dollars a night. A day's food is less than that."

"Sounds all right to me. What're you doing?"

"I'm reading. Started a meditation class. A lot of new things. Meeting up with Helen and her parents."

"I can imagine. Anything besides the rent?"

"Not really. I'll call Caroline about the dog."

"Okay. As long as everything's all right." She laughed. "You made such a fuss about going! Keep in touch."

"Will do."

***

Thomas got a message from Helen to come to Jeri and Donald's for tea. He was starting to know his way walking and went the two miles on foot just to enjoy the scenery.

When he got to the house, the tea was ready. Jeri and Donald asked Thomas what he'd been doing. He didn't mention meeting up with Helen, thinking she would have told them. He was now comfortable with them, Dorje, and even Helen as familiar people in an alien place—the camaraderie of expatriates, he'd heard about. Because they spoke English and were American, he could have a false sense of trust and kinship.

Helen was standing, leaning against a sideboard that had statues on it, making it resemble an altar. "I've got to tell you something," she said, looking at Jeri first.

"Helen. What is it?" Jeri said.

"Paul is Eike's father." Her lips were tight.

"What?" Thomas saw Donald shift position and look at her in surprise. His own mind went blank.

"Paul left long before she was born." Helen spoke as if she'd rehearsed the dialogue.

So Helen was Paul's lover, thought Thomas. He imagined the two of them hugging, touching, and kissing. He pictured a toddler at her knees. His mind raced to think of questions, to grasp the fact. He had to say something. "Did Paul know?"

"No." She clasped her hands to calm them. "He was headed to Japan. He wanted a carefree life. I didn't want to be a mother. We'd already parted, emotionally. I didn't think he would welcome the news."

"But you didn't give him a chance," Thomas blurted quietly, surprising himself. Now, he was channeling Paul, or what he thought Paul would feel. He tried not to sound angry. He'd never been faced with a baby himself. *Did Paul really die ignorant of this? His whole adult life, there was a secret in the foothills of the Himalayas. A life-changing secret that passed him by. Maybe keeping the news from him was a betrayal.* Thomas struggled to keep his own reaction out of it. *Would he care if it were him? How much?*

"Why didn't you tell him?" Jeri asked gently.

"I didn't want to be pushed in any direction, myself. We both wanted to be free. I was even willing to give the baby up for adoption."

Mother Kathmandu! thought Thomas. *Jeri's comments about Helen and family. Jeri became the mother.* Thomas tried to stay calm, but his distress was showing. He was still picturing a toddler. He tried not to look Helen in the eye. He tried to slow the conversation so he could remember it. "Can I meet her? You can imagine that my mother would love to know."

"Dorje knows where she is."

"Wow. I'm not sure I understand your logic." Thomas tried to keep any edge out of his voice. He'd just met her, and now he desperately needed her cooperation. *She was strange. Her life path was extreme. Abandoning her child was extreme. Was there more? She didn't seem like a crazy hippy,* he thought. *The Peace Corps would not have accepted a nutcase with a wild past.*

Thomas looked at Donald for fatherly solidarity but saw him looking at his daughter with sympathy and concern.

Donald finally looked back at Thomas, also with fatherly sympathy. "We'll have Dorje take you to meet her, of course. Thomas, I'm sorry. We're all shocked. We can't undo the secret from Paul. But we can undo the secret from you and your family. There's a lot of good in it."

"Yes. I agree," Thomas said, trying to calm his confusion. "Let's go from here. You know where I'm staying." He stood up to leave, looking forward to a long distracting walk back to the hotel. Suddenly, he was Paul's surrogate. *Paul's business again. Only not about ashes this time. Now, it's about flesh and blood, a daughter.* For once he felt sorry for Paul.

Grandchild

"HELLO?" LIVIA ANSWERED the phone. It was evening in Seattle and morning of the same day in Kathmandu. She and Clara were settling into an evening on the porch with sherry.

"Mom."

"Oh my gosh. Thomas. Is this costing you a fortune?" She looked at Clara with alarm and put the phone on speaker.

"I'll make it short. You know I've told you about a friend of Paul's from the Peace Corps, Helen Simons. And her parents."

"Yes."

"There's more."

"What do you mean?"

"There's a daughter. Paul's daughter."

"Oh Thomas!"

"In her mid-twenties now. Born after the Peace Corps. Raised by grandparents. Her name is Eike."

"Where is she?"

"In Nepal."

"Oh my! Oh my! A granddaughter!" Livia stood up, reaching to hug Clara.

"Not so fast. The girl's a shaman. I haven't met her yet."

"Oh. I don't think I know what a shaman is."

"I'll write soon. I just thought this was worth a call."

"Oh Thomas. What news! Tell us more!" Livia was exuberant. "It would be nice to have her with us, even in spirit. Another person to love. Someone alive. To replace all those people we lost in the war. Something good and sweet after those horrible times."

"Yes. I know. I know. Bye, Mom."

Livia looked up what a shaman was. She decided "medicine woman" was the most attractive description.

"Clara, I wonder if we'll ever see her. I'm so ready for a grandchild. Are you and Bill ready?"

"There are no guarantees, Livia. Hold your horses. Not all of our blood kin turned out just the way we wanted them to."

Livia was delighted to find new family, albeit in Nepal. She was too old to muster a long, taxing journey, but she was still alert enough to be fully engaged in life. She had long given up on legacies. From the comfort afforded by relatively modest means, she enjoyed the simple pleasures of family affections and watching the world change. A granddaughter opened the door to new stories and new delights. She was a deliverance of sorts from the miseries of the past.

Livia and Clara read up on shamans and tried to imagine the new girl. They sent her loving mental messages and speculated how she would react to finding herself in a long line starting in turn-of-the-century Lithuania with Ona the homeopath, the Baltics with Russian nobles, the suburbs of Seattle, Sedona with energy vortices, Nepal. How many times had death threatened this fragile line? Were Livia and Clara in the same world spiritually as this girl?

Neither Livia nor Clara had had a traditional family. They were Lithuanian refugees, displaced by World War II. They were part of the vast network of immigrants who were once elites, even aristocracy, in their homelands. They'd gone from privileged lives to refugee status, to eventually becoming struggling citizens with accents on the streets of the U.S. Like other immigrants, they'd fixed up their living rooms to resemble parlors in the home country, with carved Lithuanian masks, photos of old-country landscapes and flowers, native pottery, and colorful fabrics here and there—reminders of a good life in the past, decorating a humble living space.

Understandably, their sense of self was centered in the past, when privilege and luxury set them apart. Their relationships with others in America were colored by a reserved distance, as they tried to reconcile their fall from fortune with reality in a land that was oblivious, for the most part, to their culture and former status. But America had given them a chance to recover comfort and security, at least. Not knowing what to make of their accents, their novel clothing, and unfamiliar expressions, long-time Americans viewed them with curiosity and diffidence. Non-immigrants didn't know what to ask about.

Livia and Clara were not alone in America, but they did not identify with or even befriend many other immigrants. They were lost in their own personal stories and memories of a life few neighbors could comprehend.

Thomas's trip was giving Livia something Paul had given her in the past: adventure. She didn't want to suffer any new or strange places, languages, and people directly, but she didn't mind hearing about them. She was relieved, in old age, to be past many kinds of struggles. She and Clara could eat, sit on the porch, read, garden, and nobody would storm the place, drive them out or hurt them. There would be no more bloodshed, no more loss from savage invaders.

When the war encroached on Lithuania, Livia had just started the path to study medicine at Vilnius University, enjoying a student life of hiking, kayaking, and picnicking by rivers and lakes in the countryside. Clara was still at home with their parents. Livia's boyfriend Nicholas was a dashing architect, older and already established in a job.

Soon, they heard that the Russian occupiers were rounding up Lithuanians, especially those in leadership positions, like teachers, clerics, and government officials. It was primarily fear that drove Livia to Nicholas's bed. They were out one night, and she was too frightened to go back to her room. One way to avoid roundups was to be absent from your home.

Livia and Clara had grown up on an estate supporting about a hundred people. Their parents, well-known and well-regarded, were part of an elite community who felt they were in charge of their blessed lives.

Suddenly, the university was operating in fear of reprisals and controls, and Lithuanians were scrambling to continue their work and keep their families fed. Early in 1940 the estate was taken over by Russian officers who raided the livestock and crops without opposition.

Just a year later the Germans invaded and pushed the Russians out of Lithuania. Back on Livia's family's property, the family scrambled to bury valuables before German officers arrived and occupied the estate. Soldiers and transients stole art, furniture, farm tools, household goods, food stores and animals from the house and farm.

One night, Livia and Nicholas stole back to her father's village, where her parents had fled the Germans. Before they left, they begged her parents and Clara to join them in flight. Clara agreed to go.

In a matter of days, the three adults, young and fit, walked out into northern Germany. They scavenged and begged food along the way, competing with thousands of refugees along their path. Horse-drawn wagons and carts and people on foot filled every gravel road. They were heading east, away from the bombing and shooting. On the road, nationality didn't matter. Europe was small, and people fleeing from near and far converged into a flood of ethnic flotsam: people in pajamas, wearing several layers of clothing and shoes that didn't fit, carrying flags, pushing handcarts with bundles of pots and pans, teapots, and family heirlooms. Babies on backs, on carts, in buggies. Butter was one of the currencies. People at train stations gave out hot cereal, cabbage soup and bread.

After the war, millions of exiled refugees, including former soldiers, prisoners, and plain folk, started the long trek home, hundreds of miles on foot. In April 1945, Nicholas, Livia, Paul, and Clara were exhausted and hungry, but alive and hopeful now that the stench of death was lifting. At this point, they carried nearly nothing.

They ended up in displaced persons camps for four years. They were stateless. They moved between camps several times. It was a nomadic life, but no longer filled with terror. The main danger now was infection with dysentery, diphtheria, or tuberculosis and malnutrition. The staple, green pea soup, was barely adequate.

The Rusaks were among those who had no intention of going back to live under the Russian occupiers. People were committing suicide rather than repatriate. Finally, the Western Allies saw that forced repatriation was not going to empty the camps. Immigration quotas, for the Baltics especially, were increased by the U.S. After extensive paperwork, interrogation, health screening, and testing, Nicholas, Livia, and Clara made it onto a boat headed for New York City in 1949.

Their escape from death or torture had been successful.

Now Livia thought of her legacy: survival. "We've done very well here, Clara. Just think of what we have now. Think of the choices Paul and Thomas had. Think how old we are, how comfortable. Just think, Paul died having fun. He could afford to take a vacation in a spectacular wilderness after spending years travelling abroad. That's instead of death in the Gulag."

"True. But we always want to recover what we lost. We always want more."

"I don't know that I want all of it back. But I would have wished for more connection to it. It was getting thrown across the world that hurts. Getting cut off. The violence of it. The trauma."

"I know I should feel grateful. But I feel robbed," said Clara. "Paul got robbed of a longer life, but we were robbed of a lifestyle that was very comfortable. We wouldn't have had to work so hard. We would have had our parents, our cousins, our aunts and uncles."

"Oh, Clara. Nobody gets a whole life of good stuff, I think."

"Paul and Thomas had it good enough. They never faced getting killed by soldiers or starving."

"You just wonder how it all measures up," Livia said. "We raced for our lives. Were we just rats escaping a sinking ship? Isn't there supposed to be a grand bouquet for making it?"

"This is it, Livia. A box of ashes. The love of Bill. Your dear boy Thomas, visiting now and then."

Two doves were loitering on the porch banister. They were frequent residents, probably lovers. They cooed and danced toward each other occasionally, but mostly squatted, each in a big round poof of soft feathers, taking in the sun.

***

Because of the war, Livia and Clara grew into adulthood in exile. They could not contact their hundreds of relatives back in Lithuania. There were no large holiday gatherings, birthday and anniversary celebrations, celebrations of births and deaths. Because they had to work very hard to gain financial security in America, they did not have the energy to assimilate much socially. Livia and her husband Nicholas worked menial jobs first, and then professional jobs, moving to new locations to chase opportunity. Livia became a librarian, and Nicholas became an accountant. It took decades for them to reach a stable life: to own their own home and send both Paul and Thomas to college.

Both Livia and Clara struggled to find their feet in America. Their strongest instinct was to isolate and protect their children. Paul left home as soon as he could, to get away from the pressure to hide, travelling the world. Thomas lost himself in the woods.

The grown Paul represented another dramatic turn in the family's migration. After college, he travelled to France and then Nepal. Was that an escape from the sadness that he'd picked up from Livia, the tragic displacement from high to low? Or a quest for adventure, toward the exotic, fierce mountains and meditation bells of the East instead of the ringing church bells from tall medieval spires along narrow, cobblestone streets? Clearly, the

71

opportunities of America brought him, one generation beyond refugee status, to a position in which he had a choice to travel anywhere. He went into the Peace Corps.

***

Thomas was born just as Paul was entering school and finding his boy legs. Paul was soon roaming the cedars with other children in the neighborhood. They would disappear for most of the day, wandering dry forests until they got to a riverbed full of wonderful, large round boulders to climb and water for swimming. Paul learned to use a knife and compete with boys. They hunted bats at night, tossing up socks full of rocks, to get bats to collide with them and knock themselves unconscious. That never happened, but they never stopped believing it would. Paul was away playing in the neighborhood while Thomas learned to walk on the grass in the backyard, played in his inflated pool, ate carrots out of the garden in fresh air.

Nicholas took the boys fishing, an immigrant's cheap entertainment. He would leave them to wander trails and riverbeds while he mentally disappeared into the Zen of fishing. They were encouraged to climb rocks, cross rough water on fallen logs, and climb trees. Thomas was the tag-along but got left by himself often enough to become fairly independent, too.

When the boys were older, the family took car trips for vacations. Paul and Thomas lay in the back of the station wagon, staring at passing trees and sky, eating fresh fruit they'd picked in orchards. At home, when food was short, they ate ketchup and lard on Wonder bread and loved it. Once Livia started an office job, Paul and Thomas had graham crackers, apples, and chips as snacks. They visited the outdoor wonderlands of Idaho and Utah, including magical hot springs with sprawling, warm swimming pools and springs full of giant carp that liked to eat popcorn. They had all the basic camping gear. Like gypsies, they learned to work together and raise camp in less than an hour.

Livia saw how the boys differed. Paul was the explorer and adventurer, always somewhere else, doing something exciting and a little risky. Thomas liked to contemplate the grass in the backyard. He was attached to Livia and liked to help in the house. One of his greatest traumas was to be left with a babysitter before he started school, as Livia needed to work and augment the family income. He still found great comfort in coming home to Livia, just to see her. That habit hadn't changed.

When Paul joined the Peace Corps and went to Nepal, Thomas had just finished college. He had little awareness of his older brother's life. He'd been away from home himself for four years. He'd attended a local college but lived in student dorms in the era that followed the Sixties. The turbulence created by a lack of rules, rock-and-roll, drugs and social experimentation was more than enough for him. He didn't need to track Paul's doings and opinions. Thomas' own life was intense and confusing enough.

During college, Thomas made yearly trips to spend time with Clara and, because of her contacts, served as a counselor at a youth camp near Sedona. That was the extent of his travelling.

Thomas' parents and aunt, bearing the scars of a horrible war, had been forced half a world away from home into a foreign country, a foreign language. He was the beneficiary of their yearning for a quiet, simple life—a life in nature as much as possible, away from politics and public strife. A life emphasizing the present. His parents and aunt suppressed the past and didn't expect great things in the future, except survival. Whereas Paul wanted to be someplace else, a permanent expat, Thomas wanted to stay put, to be left alone and to cultivate his quiet garden. Now Paul's wishes had forced Thomas into Paul's world. And Paul's world had delivered a child, a grown child.

Soon AFTER THE BIG NEWS at Jeri and Donald's house, Dorje and Thomas took a trek to Eike's home village. Dorje had heard that Eike was going to perform a ritual there. The trip involved another long bus ride and a hike of several miles up winding paths and stone steps. Dorje walked the paths as if the landscape were his own property and he was checking areas he'd designed and installed himself. He pointed out a site where a yak had slipped and a place where an older German hiker tripped and fell down a slope. He called out the names of mountain peaks like favorite fixtures on his property. Thomas appreciated the steady walk with so much scenery to take in and could identify with Dorje's love for terrain. Like Dorje, Thomas liked to play guide in his home territory, too.

Thomas had just read in the guidebook how Westerners searched for Shangri-La in Nepal and Tibet. Nepal's terrain was beautiful and mysterious. It was easy to imagine a valley hidden and unreachable except with the help of an insider and guardian. He indulged a fantasy of following Dorje on such a journey. Then, Thomas realized that this hike had some elements of that fantasy. He was, indeed, being guided to discover the hidden, strange and unknown.

"Foreigner," explained Dorje, "is a dirty word among Tibetans. Over the centuries, Tibetans excluded the Mongols, British, Russians and Chinese as much as possible. Foreigners, Tibetans thought, were interlopers up to no good. Spies. Enemies by definition. People who helped spies trying to reach Lhasa a century ago could be killed."

"Thanks for the heads up," said Thomas. He thought he should get himself a Tibetan hat, although he was in Nepal.

"Foreigners bring the devil with them. Evil spirits are always trying to enslave or feed on people. A devil can get into the house on the shadow of a foreigner."

"Sounds reasonable, if you think of it as an infection."

"Not infection," Dorje said. "A blood-sucking devil."

"Thanks."

"They don't think so much that way in Nepal, Thomas. Tibet is different." Dorje laughed.

"But then the Chinese did become the invading blood-sucking devils in Tibet." Thomas was remembering a few things he'd read.

"Yes." Dorje stopped and looked at him with new friendship. "I guess strangers always wanted Tibet for something other than admiring and helping the people."

"Same thing with my family in Lithuania, Dorje. Other countries always wanted to take over the land and wished there were no people in the way, especially no centuries-long culture. But Lithuania didn't have these mountains as a barrier to foreigners."

"Even Tibetan mountains were not enough."

***

Finally, they arrived at a small cluster of stone houses with flat roofs, Tibetan-style, not Nepali. Children, chickens, and goats roamed the gravel around the houses, which were spread around the hillside, stacked on plots of flat earth. Dorje led the way to a particular house, obviously a locus of activity. It was small with whitewashed, clay walls. *It's like an adobe hut*, thought Thomas.

As they took off their backpacks, Dorje explained the event. "The shaman's doing the ritual of *Chöd*. The head of the family died last week. His soul will wander in the *bardo* unless the ritual is performed. His soul needs to be guided. The shaman will call on gods to show the soul to a higher place so the dead soul can be reborn. Souls of the dead can wander in ignorance and suffer interference from bad demons and spirits."

"What's *bardo*?"

"Like purgatory. Limbo. In-between. Stuck."

Thomas was wide-eyed as he took in the strangeness of the tiny hilly village. He pictured lost souls trapped in some cave.

"Normally the *Chöd* is done in a desolate place like a graveyard for energy. This one is in the family house. The shaman will call her guides and people to whom she owes a karmic debt and invite them to take the flesh of her body as an offering. *Chöd* means 'to cut.' She'll cut from her body. The shaman sacrifices herself to bring relief to the man who died. By facing gods, demons, nature, she generates a lot of energy for him. Then she releases the energy inside herself on behalf of the deceased, freeing his soul."

"How do you mean, cutting?"

"A female deity will spring from the top of the shaman's head. The deity will stand before the shaman, sword in hand. With one stroke she cuts off her head, severs her limbs, skins herself, and rips open her belly. She will blow a bone trumpet to call hungry demons to feast on the flesh. Her bowels fall out, her blood will flow like a river, as hideous guests bite and chew. The shaman tells them the deity gives up her flesh, blood, her happiness, her breath. The shaman imagines herself to be a small heap of charred bones. Adept shamans can see any form and create any kind of ghost. The point is to become nothing, give up the ego. This sacrifice gives the shaman power to heal or talk to unhappy spirits and ghosts who are interfering with the soul of the dead man."

Thomas and Dorje entered the house. Smoke from burning juniper filled the room and stinged Thomas' eyes. A few hanging kerosene lanterns and oil lamps provided the only light. He had to adjust to the dark and the smoke, both disorienting after many hours in bright, high-altitude glare. The shaman was at the far end of the room.

Following Dorje's gesture, Thomas moved to an open spot on the floor along the right wall, where he could see the shaman's face. Eike was pale and thin, with a burst of waist-length, white-blond hair in what he knew as dreadlocks, white-blond eyebrows, and deep-set eyes, making her look like a ghost. She wore a giant headdress—a broad band of red cloth with a dense row of pheasant feathers pointing upward—and a floor-length, maroon woolen dress wrapped in front and tied at the waist. Long necklaces of heavy amber, silver and turquoise beads were draped around her neck and swung as she moved.

Thomas looked for resemblances to Paul: her light coloring, for sure, and her height. He imagined her as an American, possibly a Peace Corps volunteer like her father had been, idealistic, out of graduate school, and bent on exploring the world. Except that she did not know about Paul, and she had never been to America. She was native here although her blood was not.

Thomas tried to imagine what Paul would have thought if he could have seen her now. Would he be proud of a wild, serious girl in a trance, the center of attention, speaking a foreign language, chanting and dancing with confidence, making dramatic gestures in what seemed like a complex choreography? What would she have become if Paul had brought her to America and raised her? Thomas could have been her doting uncle, the friendly sportsman who took her hiking in his native territory, the mountains of Washington State. Or Paul might have agreed to her growing up in Nepal, with him visiting from time to time, tied heart-to-heart across the world. Thomas was seeing her for the first time, and she was now in her twenties. It was too late for Paul. Thomas was surprised that he felt a pang of sympathy for Paul.

Eike's eyes were closed as she chanted, twirling a palm-sized drum so that the striker hit side to side, while ringing a bell with her other hand. Facing her was a small altar with three small mirrors and copper bowls holding water, grain, and butter lamps.

She would shriek, go limp, roar, jump up, and bend down as if wrestling an invisible creature.

Dorje had warned Thomas that interrupting a trance could kill the shaman. Thomas froze in place to stay unnoticed. After about an hour, when Eike seemed to quiet and sit in a contemplative posture, Dorje moved over to him and signaled that they should leave.

Dorje explained that she would need at least a day to recover. It was completely bad form to try to talk to the shaman. She was not a performer. Her very soul had been sacrificed to contact the deceased, to call up her patron gods and spirits and to fight off demons and devils who would try to use her trance to gain power over her or over the others involved. Thomas and Dorje left the room first. About eight other people had been crowded in the small space, sitting on the floor, on stools, and on a bench along one wall. Thomas was the only Westerner there, and he was grateful to leave in the dark and smoke without drawing attention. He'd barely seen the other attendees.

Coming into the bright sunshine outside was like leaving a noisy party in a bar and realizing the night had passed. "How do you know what exactly happened to her?" Thomas asked.

"We don't. The ritual is secret. Only initiates know it. Sometimes they talk about it. We know to stay out of their way. It's very dangerous. It's a struggle with powerful and unpredictable forces. The shaman does not always win."

"Oh?"

"Demons can take over. A shaman can fall sick or go mad."

"Who heals the sick shaman?"

Dorje laughed. "A more powerful shaman. You have to escalate, as you say. Power up. Like sports. Only the contest is deadly. Between souls and spirits."

"So how do I know I wasn't possessed by one of these bad guys?"

Dorje laughed again. "You don't. We'll just have to wait and see. Some people do bad things because they're possessed. Are you normally a good man?"

"Ah. Now we're invading my territory. Of course, I never do anything bad." Thomas laughed.

Feeling as if he had just watched an exotic movie, Thomas was quiet on the hike down from the village. He was frustrated that he hadn't learned much about Eike from watching her. They'd had no interaction. He still had no sense of her personality. The costume and activity were overwhelming, like a stage performance. But there was no back-stage visit with the person after she'd stopped acting. He saw her blond hair and some hint of Paul's genes in her face. She was tall and thin, clearly full of energy and health. Her cheeks showed the rosy glow of high-altitude living. He hadn't even heard her speak a word he could understand. The strangeness gave him a sense of foreboding, that she had been lost to his family until now, and she might stay lost in this foreign world.

What did Thomas' family have to offer her? He was an older guy, like the affluent trekkers who came through the mountains in a steady stream on their way to the pleasure of spectacular landscapes, with little more than curiosity about people living there. The trekkers were consumers of the geography of Eike's homeland, eager for photographs and souvenirs to take back, but rarely had any understanding of Nepal as a culture or peer relationships with natives. He worried that she would see him as one of the rich aliens invading this pristine world and bringing commercialism, global politics and exploitation. Maybe the Nepalis were not as simple as he thought, though. Maybe they were like his cronies in Winthrop, Washington, trying to cultivate their own gardens, their own sacred spaces, in the midst of the ugly modern forces in play around them.

***

A few days later, Dorje took Thomas back to Eike's home village for a social visit. Eike lived among several families who were related to each other. Dorje explained that she rarely came to Kathmandu and spent much of her time walking to neighboring settlements to conduct her business.

Dorje called into the house in Nepali. "Hello?"

A low female voice answered. Dorje and Thomas stepped inside. Eike was sitting on a bench next to a small temple area: an ornate picture of the Buddha, small mirrors, oil lamps, copper bowls of water, and flowers strewn over a silk cloth. There were a few pieces of furniture and cushions so they wouldn't have to sit on the ground.

"Hello," she said in English to Thomas, putting her palms together Hindu-style. She did not appear as wild as she'd looked the first time he'd seen her. She was wearing the wrapped wool dress again, a *chuba*. Her hair was still untamed but now rested over her shoulders in some order. Her face was clean, not streaked with smoke and sweat, and very pale in the dark room. Thomas felt relieved to see the girl behind the shaman, someone he might meet on the street near the University of Washington.

"Hello," he said. "I'm Thomas."

"Welcome."

"Have you heard why I'm here?" He knew there was phone contact with remote areas like this, but he had no sense whether the phone was used casually.

"Tell me."

Thomas and Dorje sat on nearby cushions. A few windows let in light and air. A fire was burning in the center of the room on elevated brick, with smoke going up through a hole in the roof above the fire.

"My brother was here in the Peace Corps, several decades ago. Up past Pokhara. He was a teacher."

"Ah."

"He died recently."

"And you want me to do the *Chöd* for him?"

"No, no. He was a friend of your mother, Helen." Thomas could not stop staring at her face, looking for Paul.

"Helen? This was a long time ago?"

"Yes. Before you were born. In fact, we think he had something to do with your birth."

"How's that?"

"We think he was your father." The idea was still novel to Thomas. It'd been only days since the news had taken over his mind. It was strange to use the word "father." It was strange to be speaking of Paul as a brotherly ally.

"I see. I don't think I can help you in that regard." Her face and voice showed little expression.

Thomas didn't know what he'd expected, but had hoped for some indication that she found the news significant. Possibly, he'd watched too many American movies and forgotten that she had not. He had no idea what this meant to a Nepali. "Well, there's not much to help. He left Nepal before you were born. You have a grandmother in Seattle, Washington, and an aunt." Thomas floundered for conversation. "They would be very happy to meet you. Your father didn't know about you. He would have wanted to, I think." Thomas was trying to create a drama, a backstory, and it wasn't working.

"Ah."

"I could take you to America to meet your grandmother, if you want to go. She would love to see you."

"I've never been outside of Nepal. My whole life is here."

"I know. But you might think about it." Thomas wanted to touch her arm, try to draw out a smile, but held back. He was disconcerted, trying to reach across chasms of emotion, geography, and his own vague idea of what he was supposed to do. He was not prepared for her cool response. Could she really be indifferent? He'd never been good at charming women. Eike was young and outside his experience as a fifty-year-old. Could he beguile her into wanting to become part of his family? He needed to think of something to hold onto her, a reason to come back and have another shot at a conversation with her. Looking around the room, he saw the ritual shelf. "Perhaps you can perform *Chöd* for him. I have his ashes in Kathmandu."

"When did he die?"

"Last summer."

"Yes, I could. We often do *Chöd* for foreign people. Did he suffer a bad sudden death?"

"As a matter of fact, he did." Thomas looked at Dorje for some clue as to where to go from here. They weren't in the city and couldn't just all go to lunch. He hadn't brought food or anything to offer as a gift. He wished he'd asked Dorje what was customary. It was too late. Eike wasn't helping him with the conversation. "Can I take your picture?" He pulled his camera from his backpack.

"Normally, I don't allow it."

Now, Thomas felt like a crass tourist and a stranger. Her remark felt like a rejection of him and his message. She was not seeing him as anyone special.

"But you might allow it now?" He looked into her eyes, pleading for sympathy, hoping for interest. He so wanted her to be normal, by his definition. He wanted her to understand her significance as a lost child.

"Yes, but no flash."

"All right." He adjusted settings on the camera. "Will you pose in the daylight for me?"

"Yes." She got up, and Thomas and Dorje got up with her. They walked out the door to the entrance. She stood in the doorway. Thomas stepped back and clicked the camera several times.

"Thank you." Thomas put his camera away. "Is there anything you want to ask me?" Now that he'd used the camera, he'd had something to do, and time to think.

"What was his name?"

"Paul."

"Come back in a week and bring the ashes." She smiled at him as if he were a passing stranger, a Western customer, and stepped back into her house. She came back and gave him a red, knotted string.

"What does it mean?" He looked at Dorje.

Dorje tried to smooth their way. "It's protection against evil. You can wear it around your neck or put it in your house."

Eike tied the knotted string around Thomas' wrist. It was the first gesture of warmth he'd received. He smiled at her, thinking she might find the visit awkward, too.

Dorje continued. "It's also a blessing. She put a protective spell on the string."

Thomas and Dorje waved good-bye and left her standing in front of her house. Maybe, she needed some time to think, Thomas assured himself. The visit was a beginning. An ice-breaker. Nepali ice.

Back in Kathmandu, he had the film developed. In the poses where Eike was looking directly at the camera, there was just a spray of light as if he had taken a photo of a flash or a mirror. Fortunately, she was looking away in one pose. He mailed a copy to his mother in Seattle.

***

That evening, he finally called Caroline for the first time.

"Thomas! What's up? It's been weeks!"

"I'm having a great time. It turns out Paul had a secret daughter. She's here. I've met her."

"Is she coming back with you?"

"Not likely. She's a Tibetan Buddhist shaman. Busy."

"Wow. What does that mean?"

"It means she heals people. Lives in a village. She's completely into it. I don't think she's interested in leaving for a minute."

"Does she look like Paul?"

"A bit. Blond dreadlocks, blue eyes. A witchy version of Paul."

"Bring some pictures."

"How's Sally?"

"Right now, rolling on her back by the fire. I don't think she misses you."

"Sure, you'd say that!"

"Kidding. We're enjoying spring. I've been riding a lot. Sally likes to run along. It's a great life. You should try it."

"I know. I should. You're good?"

"Blazing. There's a property up for sale that's got my eye. I hope you can help me fix it up."

"You know I will. You won't mind if I take another month?"

"No, no trouble. I'll make Sally look at your picture every day. You've never travelled much."

"Yeah. This is a big leap. I'll tell you all about it."

"Okay. Bye Thomas."

"Oh. Caroline?"

"Yes."

"I miss you."

"Devil!"

***

After he hung up, Thomas felt the shame of his split from Caroline all over again.

Things had blown up with her because of a stupid weekend, which happened to be her birthday. He'd gone off for a week with his buddies to the foothills of the Cascades north of Lake Chelan. One of them had a share in a remote hunting lodge. Four of them drove separately to meet behind a boarded up storefront just outside the national park, where they parked their cars out of sight and climbed into a Jeep for the last leg of the journey. The hunting lodge was at the end of a two-hour drive on overgrown, narrow fire roads that included a creek crossing. They would have to stop and remove any trees that had fallen since they were last cleared. The creek crossing with boulders of various sizes challenged the four-wheel drive. One of the men got out of the Jeep because it tipped so severely getting over the rocks. He scrambled across on fallen trees and large boulders right near the road crossing.

The cabin was a hunters' pit—all logs, dirty small windows, and grimy surfaces. The men choked when they entered, but that wasn't enough to inspire them to clean. An open door raised the dust, and an open window helped the wind carry some of it outside. Thomas was glad he had his sleeping bag, which he could put on top dubious bedding in one of the bunks. The plumbing and electricity worked, so the cabin was better than a tent. Thomas could wipe off the surface of a wood chair and put his feet up on a wood-burning stove. That was plenty of comfort. His friends had brought up a keg of beer. He had his stash of pot, which was certainly his favorite escape and not as caloric as beer. The men were going to barbecue steaks and throw potatoes into the stove. They would add a few condiments, including fresh tomatoes, pickles and sour cream, and they would have a feast.

They got to the cabin by mid-afternoon on Friday, allowing enough time to unload their belongings in daylight and start drinking while they set up target practice behind the cabin. Since they didn't have beer cans, they made sticks into little tepees that would explode with the right shot. It took the rest of the afternoon to gather enough sticks to create targets for many hours of shooting they planned. By the time they went to bed, they were high and happy, looking forward to days of decadence.

Thomas planned to hike out on Sunday to see Caroline that night, her birthday. Without a vehicle, the hike would take him four to five hours.

Saturday morning the men slept in and then hiked around the hillside, carrying guns to shoot rabbits and squirrels, if not bigger game. The landscape was summer-dry, with a clear sky. They were having a rowdy escape from jobs and customers and townspeople and tourists.

Hungry for a late lunch, they got back to the cabin to find another Jeep had arrived. Fred had a girlfriend who had a Jeep and three other girlfriends and knew the way. They were tough broads who could drive over the creek as well as any man. Thomas didn't know them as friends, but they were fixtures of the bar scene around Winthrop. In all, there were four girls, "one for each of them" in the minds of the other guys. This was awkward for Thomas who'd left Caroline behind, but he figured they were all "guys in the woods" where things were more relaxed, like Las Vegas. It would help to have women with some standards clean off the counters in the kitchen and wipe down nasty parts of the bathroom.

There wasn't any obvious pairing up until nightfall. Fred's girlfriend was clearly glad to see him and join in the drinking. Two of the girls figured out whom they liked apart from Thomas and the two guys helped them settle on mutual targets for the night. Another one, Mindy, clearly started bumping into Thomas in the small space, over and over. She was in her twenties and possibly liked older men. Also, he put out an attraction vibe that indicated he wasn't as wild and crude as most men.

Things took an embarrassing turn late in the evening when they finally had to go to bed. Fred, the host, had staked out the balcony for himself and his girlfriend. The bunks in the main room were less private, although one was behind a wall in the open room. Thomas had already claimed that space. Now, Mindy followed him there to share it.

"Ah. Mindy. I don't know."

"Where am I going to sleep, then?" she said, cocking her head. She could see that the bunk was narrow but wider than a cot for one.

"I have a girlfriend."

"I know." He was high, and she was drunk, and they had to concentrate to converse at all. "Side by side?"

"Okay. Side by side." He sat down to take off his shoes.

She jumped out of her shoes, took off her jeans, pulled up her sweatshirt with surprising speed for a drunk, opened his sleeping bag, and opened hers on top like a quilt. Then, she jumped in.

"Wait, wait," he said, finally aware of her maneuver.

"Oh come on, grumpy. You'll sleep like a baby." She held back the covering bag for him.

It was a frank seduction. She was younger and jumped him before he could close his eyes. They could hear others knocking about in the next room, but they were too high to sense much beyond their own bunk. He did sleep like a baby.

Sunday morning everyone stayed in bed until late again. This time, the eight of them wandered the hillside. It was another perfect, hot summer day, and they moved slowly savoring it. Thomas tried to cool things with Mindy, but she clung to him like a new conquest promising a repeat engagement. She was fit and confident physically, an outdoorsman's ideal mate. She could climb and jump with no fuss.

After about two hours, they stopped for sandwiches and beer. The party was turning out as perfectly as Fred had hoped: friends goofing around in the wilderness. Hangovers slowed them, but they were still up and about on the mountain. They weren't shooting much.

They wandered quite far from the cabin. Thomas was aware of the time but wasn't conscientious about pulling himself away. They were starting to head back, but it meant going off road and through a dense forest full of fallen trees. They had to get up on logs, walk them, jump to another log, climb down, and climb up. With eight people, the pace was uneven. Suddenly, Mindy slipped and fell off a log into a mess of other logs. She shouted for help.

"Hey, Thomas! Somebody! My ankle's hurt."

Thomas and four others were quite near. He quickly moved in her direction. "Don't move." He finally got down into the tight gap between logs where she lay. No one in the party knew he'd been a forest ranger. He checked her ankle.

"I don't think it's a break," he said. He was leaning into a mossy pocket where her foot lay. The others gathered around on nearby logs. "We'll wrap it. Anybody got a bandana or such?" One of the girls took a bandana off her head. He persuaded

Mindy to get up. They lifted her out of her hole and braced her on a higher log. Thomas wrapped the bandana tightly. "You shouldn't walk on that, though."

He knew he was in a pickle now. As Mindy's guy, he couldn't charge off. He was the ranger, the guy who knew the tricks of rescue. They would have to go slow. There was no way they would get back to the cabin soon, where he could then abandon them for the long hike down. It could be nightfall by the time they arrived at the cabin, which was too late for the solitary hike out and drive back to Winthrop for a birthday evening. He was cooked.

Two of them braced Mindy all the way back—over logs and then through forest underbrush for miles. It was Fred's short-cut back. It was indeed nightfall when they arrived. Mindy was in pain. They gave her whiskey and aspirin and made their steaks. She slept beside Thomas again, this time thrashing in pain all night.

In the morning, they packed up the Jeeps and drove down.

***

Word got back to Caroline about the party and even the sleeping arrangements. At least one of the people in the cabin knew Caroline, or had a best friend who did. Mindy's accident was bar news. Everybody asked, "What happened?" and got a story with colorful details. For most people, it was an innocuous event to be shared—guys and gals in the woods. For Thomas, it was a personal scandal. He was the oldest among them.

"You rat!" Caroline said, when saw she him at her door.

"Caroline, let me explain."

"Explain what? You landed inside her by accident?"

"It was a crazy situation."

"Yeah. Crazy and not my style."

"I didn't know it was going to go that way."

"Sure. You followed Fred, and you are so sad. Don't you know better? Did you even use protection? Do you know how old you are?" She gave him no slack.

They officially broke up. He'd become one of the jerks she saw around her and had long grown out of. He could see that. He wasn't sure how he could make up for the public mistake, and figured a long cool-off would be his strategy. Low radar. He felt sorry, sure, but also a victim of circumstances. He wasn't sure how he could have escaped sex with Mindy except by sleeping in a chair, and the pot had made him lazy and passive. The sex hadn't seemed serious at the time. He could see how Caroline thought differently.

He and Caroline were still friends, though. He arranged to leave his dog Sally with her while he went away. She said she still loved the dog a lot, maybe more than him, and said she didn't mind staying friends.

Mom, Clara –

I'd assumed that Helen was celibate, as most of the monks are. Apparently, there's a variation along this path. (Cover Bill's ears.) In tantric Buddhism, there's a belief that you can be realized in a single lifetime through certain practices that are not totally symbolic. As part of meditation practices, the monks learn to control body heat, breath and subtle energies. The final frontier is to control sexual energy and channel it into a kind of transcendent state of awareness or empowerment. Dorje says that Helen is or was secretly a dakini or consort with one of the high lamas. Lamas are, of course, thought to be celibate.

The sexual union teachings are rarely taught now because Buddhists think that these times are degenerate. Dorje says that you still hear of tantric sex being practiced. I certainly don't know the details, but they have to do with controlling ejaculation (or any sexual fluids) and routing them, as sexual energy, up the chakras in the body. Not exactly a romp in the hay. Doesn't even sound fun. I guess being chosen or choosing to do this puts you in a higher and more advanced group. And definitely secret. If the secret is exposed, it can cause madness, trouble, and even death to the lama.

Dorje says it's not something anyone will admit, and only very advanced yogis try it, because it requires tremendous control of the body, breathing, and the mind, and usually follows after years or even a lifetime of related exercises. I asked him how he knew, and he said that someone told him after the lama died, and that often the telling is meant to enhance the reputation of the lama. (Nothing new there.)

On the other hand, the early Tibetan Buddhists allowed marriage, so I don't know what to think.

As you know, there are reports of Indian gurus abusing their power and sleeping with nubile Western devotees. And we've heard of Catholic priests losing control with young parishioners. Much ambiguity. An outsider can certainly question motives and whether there's any coercion or manipulation. Is the Buddhist practice pure or corrupt? I dare not ask about it, but I thought you would find the rumor interesting. Nearly all of the Tibetan Buddhist teachers are male, so it's not usually a situation of social equality. I don't know about spiritual roles in the tantric practice, although I hear that the woman or dakini is by definition a powerful female guide and essential to bringing the practice to full realization.

There were supposed to be matrilineal societies in very early Tibet. Dorje says that male energy is the dynamic one, and female energy is associated with emptiness (a meditation goal) and profound knowledge. Some of the images show the female dancing on a reclining male. The classic tantric image is a male god embracing a smaller female mounted on his front. (OK, I will stop now.) Oh wait. I do hear that both women and men need a consort for ultimate realization. And either can become an advanced teacher.

Dorje says there are female lamas now. Nuns are getting access to advanced education in monasteries and to retreats, inside and outside of monasteries. Part of that happened because Buddhism and Buddhists migrated to the West, after the Chinese invasion, and some feminist influences took hold.

That's something that puzzles me: Why Helen would reject Western discrimination of women and enter a society and philosophy that says, "Yes, women are equal and powerful," but which excludes them, mostly, from advanced teachings and practices. Sadly, Dorje says most of the women in monasteries do simple rituals and work in kitchens. Same old, same old. My impression is that Helen is focused on the individual realization part of Buddhism and does not join the domestic forces in her monastery. Remember, she keeps one foot in worldly things through running the hostel.

Thanks for covering my rent in Winthrop for a few months. The money is stretching very well, and I am finding Nepal very interesting.

Love, Thomas

***

It wasn't long before Thomas had a new routine. He got up early to beat the heat, have coffee, and then go to a local temple that hosted meditation practice for foreigners. There, he joined the motley group of pale women in saris, funky men in cotton caftans, older travelers who seemed to know what they were doing, and people like him who looked like they'd just stepped off a tourist bus. The foreigners were taught how to sit and how to clear their minds, facing a modest platform in front of a Buddha painted on a wall.

Seeking innate wisdom was a strange concept to Thomas. In the past, he'd read or heard ideas from other people and tried to grasp them. What if nothing came during meditation? He thought of parallels to the high he got from pot, when his mind really did take over and reveal unconscious feelings and sensations. When he was told to contemplate impermanence, it seemed very abstract. He was thankful to be told to actually do something like repeat a mantra as a way of clearing his mind of distractions and wandering thoughts. Mostly, he was instructed to relax and focus on one thing at a time, by shutting out external and internal sensations and thoughts.

To his surprise, he came away from each session relaxed and strangely happy. He joked to himself that he must have been on the path already, through the release he got from pot. He was warned that meditation could give rise to vivid dreams.

After meditation, he walked around the town, found a reasonable restaurant for a good mid-day meal, and then returned to his room to read.

He found himself thinking about Helen all the time. He saw her in every female nun he passed, wondering whether her happiness really was wrapped deep in her *chuba*, keeping the hostel supplied, greeting strangers, and then disappearing into the monastery for meditation. It seemed so unfeeling to him. He thought of Paul and her as lovers. Had she been much different then? Had something happened to turn her away from her own child, from a marriage and family life? He, too, was fairly content as a loner, but knowing about Helen and Paul made Thomas even more convinced that he had a lot in common with Helen. Besides

Paul, they shared a love of rural, outdoor life and a social life that he had to admit, in his case, consisted of superficial, arms-length attachments. Her serenity was something he'd never seen in a woman. He definitely did not have it. Maybe those three years alone in a cave had made her serene. She seemed impervious to petty excitement, including visible delight. She was very serious. What kind of lover would she make now? Was he really attracted to her, or was he attracted to her composure?

***

Thomas decided to go visit Helen again. He went to tourist shops and bought a silk undershirt, a fancy Chinese silk scarf, a fleece blanket, dried apricots, Swiss chocolate bars, and a book by an American Buddhist nun who'd started a retreat center in the Southwest, living with her family. He thought Winthrop could be a perfect haven for such a retreat center. He would be glad to build it.

This time he journeyed to her village by himself. He told Dorje he was taking an excursion with a tourist group in the opposite direction. The long bus ride to Pokhara was fun the second time, because he was not as shocked by the steep roads and sharp turns. He went to the same hostel in Pokhara by following the paths of other trekkers from the bus to get there. Then he hiked three hours to Helen's village, again arriving in mid-afternoon.

"Hello?" He peered into the guesthouse. A Nepali woman greeted him in the reception area and beckoned him to sign a register. She pointed out the instructions posted around the table explaining meals, toilets, washing facilities, gave him a room key, and pointed in the direction of the rooms. She recognized him as a returnee.

"Helen? Here?" he asked.

She shook her head no and waved a hand in the direction from which he'd come. "Kathmandu," she said.

"When? She'll be back?"

She held up two fingers. Two days.

He was crestfallen. His anticipation had clouded his thinking so much that he had not imagined that she was not here all the time, or most of the time. He thought about himself being on hold in this wilderness. Fortunately, he'd brought a few books to read.

He woke to the sound of horns just before daylight, a call to early morning meditation. He got up and walked to the monastery. Only a few people were there. Hikers were already outside, geared up, preparing for an early start, heading through or out of the village to higher ground. He sat on the veranda in front of the temple. By now, he knew that it was acceptable for visitors to look through the entrance of the temple, and even stay outside to meditate or rest. But the temple was not a place where visitors walked in and looked around, flashing their camera at icons.

When one of the resident monks walked by and greeted him politely in Nepali, Thomas returned the greeting. He could not help imagining this monk as Helen's lover, too. A secret lover. He knew that the lama who had been her consort had died, but now, any monk stirred his imagination and jealousy.

After the mid-day meal, Thomas hiked the path heading up the mountain, following the trekkers. The path was exhilarating and reminded him of the Cascades. There were alpine flora, marmots, icy streams and looming ridges overhead, with trails that seemed to shoot up into the sky. He loved the surprise of new trails. He loved taking a turn in a trail and seeing beside it a cliff hundreds of feet deep. He liked climbing a difficult, steep path that hugged a giant rocky ridge and turning a corner into a golden meadow.

Two days after his arrival, he went to the monastery early and, through the door, saw more than twenty monks sitting in lines in the great hall, chanting. They were swaying and ringing bells. He sat outside on the veranda and tried to join them in spirit. Momentarily, he repeated a mantra to himself, as a pause from looking outward.

By late morning, he was reading a book in front of the guesthouse when Helen came up the path with a native man. They both carried loads on their backs in baskets strapped onto wooden frames, Nepali style. She looked surprised to see him.

"Why Thomas! What're you doing here?"

"A visit. I came for another talk, at least."

"All right." She seemed puzzled. "It'll have to wait until I've taken care of a few things. After lunch."

"Sure." He was relieved to see her and relieved that she was still welcoming. He looked closely at her face. He was greedy for familiarity. Now, his book bored him. To kill time, he went for a walk.

Lunch was served to six travelers. They chatted about their plans, the sights they'd seen that morning, the weather, the altitude, and their blisters. They had a Nepali guide who explained what they would see, how far it was, how steep. A few would take a day hike that afternoon to acclimate themselves to the altitude. They would leave on the next leg of their long trek in the early morning.

Finally, Helen came out and greeted all of them. She asked them if their rooms were adequate, if the food was good, if they needed anything. Much to Thomas' dismay, she avoided any private talk with him. He could see that she was putting off questions about who she was, what she was doing in this remote place, her robes, her life. She withdrew but motioned for him to follow her out the front door.

"In about five minutes, we can take a short walk toward the back. All right? I'll meet you here."

"Great." He left to get his gifts and water bottle.

They walked around the hostel, behind a few other washed mud houses and along a path toward a small upper meadow. There were rocks to sit on.

"It's great to see you again," Thomas started. "How have you been?"

"Just fine. How about you? Enjoying Kathmandu?"

"Very much. Started a meditation course. Reading a lot."

"How long are you planning to stay?"

"Maybe another month. I would like to see more of you."

"Me?"

"Yes. Get to know you better."

"I'm not sure I have a lot of time to spend that way."

"Here are some things I got for you. I hope you can use them."

She untied the knot of a cloth bundle. "Oh my." She took out the silk shirt, the fleece. She looked at the chocolates, the package of Nepali apricots, and bag of nuts. "You really don't need to bring me gifts. I have everything I need."

"Just wanted to be nice to you." Thomas gazed at her intensely, trying to read her face. More precisely, trying to find some warmth in her face that was directed toward him.

"Our gifts go to the temple first, actually. They're distributed there to those who need them."

"Oh. Sorry. I thought you were less in the monastery than the others. Is this a problem?"

"I can share these with the others. Then, it isn't a problem." She lay down the cloth and started to put the items on it.

"You don't accept personal gifts?"

"I don't see why. Maybe you don't understand my role."

"I'm trying to." He shifted, uncomfortable on the rock.

"My material life is minimal so I can focus on others. My comfort is not first."

"I see."

She tied a knot on the bundle. "I think you're seeing me as a lay person and a peer. I have more than a job. I have a mission."

"What about teaching me to meditate? Are you allowed to do that?"

"You said you were taking a course in Kathmandu."

"I am. But I could come and stay here if you were my teacher."

"I'm not equipped to do that. I have other responsibilities. And my own program. I think you're with the right setup for the time you're here." She stood.

He looked up at her. "What a shame. I really like you."

"Is this because of Paul?"

"No, no. Me. I'm not Paul. Here and now. I like you."

"I'm sorry, but I don't know how to respond to that. I'm a nun."

"I know. But there are other 'white nuns' who have gone back to the U.S. and started retreat centers and such. Had families. You aren't locked into this place."

"I am, though. By choice."

"Will you come and visit me in Kathmandu?"

"Thomas, I can't be your friend."

He started to get angry. "What about my consort?"

She flushed and finally showed some emotion. "Your what?"

"I've been reading about Tantrism. I would like to learn more. Would you show me?"

"Where did you get *that* idea?" She put the bundle down.

"I heard you knew something about it."

"I'm sorry you did. You have the wrong impression. In fact, you're perverting a sacred religious practice into casual sex." She turned to walk away.

"Other Westerners have taken it up. Without turning into monks."

"Not with me, they haven't."

"But you know the practice. At least, some of it."

"That's none of your business. We're done, Thomas. Go back to your pot. Find some playmates. Leave me alone." She headed down the path with fast, angry steps.

He didn't see her that evening or the next morning when he set out to return. He left the bundle of gifts with the Nepali woman in the reception area to give to Helen.

Lovers (1986)

HELEN SIMONS WENT QUICKLY to her tiny room in the teacher's dormitory and packed a small daypack with a few shirts, underwear, a book, and extra medicines that the regional coordinator for the Peace Corps had sent up from Kathmandu. Stationed in Pokhara, she was in the city that was closest to where Paul Rusak lay sick. She did not know him, but she was certain she would want a Peace Corps volunteer to help her if she were too sick to get out of bed. She also packed her more practical clothes, like a long skirt that would not tear easily and a padded jacket. She'd begun to wear native clothes because comfortable, warm Nepali attire gave her a feeling of belonging. When she wore them, the natives found her less strange and they focused less on her white skin.

She remembered Paul from the regional orientation. He was cute, charming, a world traveler. Before the Peace Corps, he'd spent years in Europe and spoke perfect French. He was blond, which really got the attention of Nepalis. His coloring gave him a magical aura that he wore with pleasure, like a fancy, flattering suit. Some might say he came across as overly confident. He was far more adept at learning languages than the rest of the Peace Corps volunteers. He consciously chatted up natives to practice Nepali and came to know them quickly. The other volunteers were shy and self-conscious about speaking. They used clumsy phrases and sentences, even in the market where people spoke in simple phrases. Paul was also more sophisticated than anyone else in the group. He was about five years older than Helen, she calculated.

The hike to his village was about six miles into the foothills of Annapurna. The path had a few river crossings and crossed Jeep and yak trails that went up and down stony hills and alpine-like fields. All of the villages where Peace Corps volunteers were stationed were at fairly high altitudes, starting at 6,000 feet. Helen had not done this particular trek before but had been assured that Paul's village wasn't a hidden place and that people would help her navigate the worn paths. She knew many stone steps and benches would be along the way. Nepalis had a preference for going straight up and down steep hills, not using switchbacks. Even the donkeys were used to it.

When Paul commuted from his valley to a sizable town, it wasn't an ordeal, just one day's journey downhill to Pokhara where there were places to eat, buses, hostels, and meetings with other volunteers when they gathered. Helen was located in Pokhara at the end of a bus line. She had been assigned to a boarding school, with comforts like plumbing and electricity, where it was safe for a Western female teacher. Working alone in a remote village, where most of the local teachers were young males, was risky for a Western woman. But because there were many tourists and trekkers on the paths, the presence of a solo female Western hiker wasn't odd. Being a foreigner provided implicit protection. You stood out, and, people knew that resources could be called on if there were trouble.

Helen planned for the possibility that she might have to sleep on the way. She packed a simple bedroll with a few Western amenities hidden inside: a super-light, down sleeping bag, a Gortex blanket, and a silk bed liner. Like many volunteers, she used Western hiking boots, a Western daypack, which had a lot of pockets and zippers, and a couple of ponchos for rain and shelter. Nepalis were hospitable and, in an emergency, invited travelers to sleep in a corner of their houses. So Helen's hike would not be into the wilderness. Some houses were built with extra rooms for trekkers. Many natives looked forward to the gifts and tips left by foreigners who didn't know the local practice of generously hosting travelers in the remote mountains. Helen also carried peanut butter and *chapatis*, her staple food.

As a gift for the unknown Paul, she brought cubes of chicken bouillon, chocolate, a jar of peanut butter, a package of oatmeal and powdered milk mix, and a bag of Fig Newtons she had scored in the market.

She never carried obviously Western toys like cameras and binoculars. The other volunteers didn't understand her habit because they wanted to capture every minute, every scene, in a photo. But Helen wanted to record memories in her heart. She thought holding onto experiences in the form of photos was an expression of worldly attachment, a notion she acquired from growing up around Buddhists in Nepal.

After locking her things in her dormitory room, she headed north.

When she set out, it was a reasonable day with some cloud cover, about sixty degrees. She was a hearty hiker and had become thin and wiry. She enjoyed the big stony steps, staircases into heaven. Sometimes, she could see nothing except sky past the top of a long ridge. Inevitably, the top of the hill revealed an entirely new landscape, and maybe a downhill path, meandering between boulders and dry gray rocks.

Once in a while, there was a burst of sturdy alpine plants, clustered in spots, or even a hillside covered with green, bright rhododendrons. Marmots whistled when they saw Helen. She imagined they were pleased to see her passing through. Privately, she thought of them as fat, hairy, little angels or fairies pretending to be animals and not very comfortable with their attire. Seeing their big furry backs lumbering to hide behind rocks was a delight and a reminder that the rocky green hillsides were a playground for a whole array of creatures.

She was thrilled by the occasional terrace garden behind a hut, or suspension bridges over small ravines with freezing, raging creeks. Patches of mist often hugged a small meadow and then dissipated, leaving a hint of vapor. This was to date her favorite situation: alone and safe with the elements on a high mountain.

She arrived at the village before nightfall. It was a cluster of houses in a pocket valley. Folks were very pleased to direct her to the back of the government-post building where Paul had a room. People travelled down the valley often and thought nothing of someone coming up for a visit. Paul had had other Western visitors and liberally introduced them as his extended family, as they were, virtually, through the Peace Corps.

The door of Paul's room was unlocked. She knocked and said "Paul?" and pushed the door open. He was lying on a wooden cot in a far corner of the room, with clothes hanging from nails over his head and beside the bed. He had a lighted kerosene lantern over his head, but was lying back, obviously not well enough to read.

"Hey," he said, leaning up in recognition. "I didn't expect a visit." He fell back on his pillow immediately, looking relieved.

"Greetings from the down side," she said. "How are you?" She put her daypack on a chair.

"Feverish. I can't seem to shake it. People are bringing me food and tea. I can't be up for long."

She took off her jacket and walked over to the cot. The covers were pulled up to his waist. He was bare-chested, probably hot with fever. She saw a thick crop of blond chest hair that resembled a mat of bleached moss. Her mind stopped temporarily, and she could barely look. Her breasts tensed up. His face was sweaty.

"What can I do for you right now? Anything? I have penicillin, ibuprofen, aspirin, and Kaopectate for diarrhea. Have you eaten?"

"No food. I'd like water and penicillin."

Helen got up to fill a glass from a nearby bucket, which the Peace Corps volunteers had been trained to keep for boiled water. She found the penicillin in her pack and handed him a cup of water with it. He fell back, looking exhausted, his eyes closing automatically. She put her bedding on the other cot, the one meant as a couch or a bed. She found the latrine and water pump outside. The cot was much like hers in the dormitory. She made herself some *chapatis* and peanut butter, lay down, and fell asleep. Paul wasn't dead. The penicillin might work overnight.

In the morning, he was awake but not alert. He was able to pull on a cotton shirt and make his way to the latrine in back, and he was able to drink tea with plain *chapatis*.

They talked very little because he had no energy. She knew she would have to stay a few days. She went to the water pump and carried in water to boil for drinking. She went out into the village and ran into the nearby neighbors who had been providing Paul with two meals a day.

She introduced herself as his sister, mentally registering "sister in the Peace Corps." Her sleeping in the same room with him would not necessarily be shocking, as whole families and strangers often slept in one room, and guests usually slept in a corner of the same common room. In Kathmandu, there were co-ed hostels for hikers and hippies. Privacy was not taken for granted.

Paul's neighbor, per regular arrangement with him, brought over plates of rice, lentils, potatoes, onion and eggplant. Helen found a supply of yoghurt and even some eggs among the few stalls farther down in the village. She could boil the eggs in Paul's room on a kerosene stove. Once he was able to eat, she made him a rice pudding. She spent her time reading and chatting with people in the village. His students came by out of curiosity and liked to stand in the door, looking in.

"Ma," they would say, using the local term for an adult woman. "Can we listen to the radio?"

"Not now. Your teacher is resting. Maybe tomorrow."

"Ma, do you need kerosene?" They knew they could get a piece of hard candy for the errand.

"Ma, can we look in your backpack?"

"Ma, can we try the flashlight?" This was repeated every day.

The irony of their typical diet was that, back in America, where she had gone to college, Helen had learned about trends of returning to simple, natural foods and rejecting junk and processed food. The Nepalis actually ate almost like vegetarians: rice, lentils, small amounts of vegetables (eggplant, tomatoes, potatoes, peas, spinach), small amounts of milk products (yoghurt, cheese), and small amounts of eggs, fish or meat (chicken, goat). Meat was risky for foreigners because it was not handled in sanitary ways nor was it kept cool and away from bugs. If Westerners stuck to the typical diet of this less-developed country, they would be eating healthier food.

By the third day, Paul was well enough to bathe. She hauled and heated some water for him, which was a luxury. She carried the bucket from the stove to a bathing area in the corner of the room, where soapy water could flow out of the house. The area was curtained with a colorful blue Indian cloth with mirrors sewn into the pattern. She was relieved to see him better.

"Do you want help?"

"I'm okay."

She saw him stumble to a low bench. He had stripped to his cotton boxers. Indians often bathed wearing something. "You soap up, and I'll rinse you off." Seated on the stool, he used a ladle to wet his skin and slowly soaped his whole body. She kept a discreet eye on him, just in case.

"Okay. Rinse."

She took the ladle and poured the warm water across his back, his face, his chest, his arms and legs.

"Wow. That feels good."

"Here, we can do your hair." She poured water over his head, put the ladle down and took liquid soap in her hands. She had not bathed many people in her life, but she could easily imagine what to do. She gently scrubbed his head. He relaxed and smiled, letting her go on longer than his hair needed. Then, she poured the rest of the warm water over his head and his body again.

"Okay, now I'm really glad you came up here." He took the small towel and slowly dried himself. She stepped out of the bathing area while he stood and got dressed.

She made tea for both of them, and they sat down to the meal that had been delivered.

"Helen, thanks. You never know how bad things will get."

"Oh, that's okay. You'd do it for me." She saw that he was eating normally now. "Have you made a lot of friends here?"

"Sure. A couple of teachers and I go hiking. We hang out. What about you?"

"Yes. I like most of the teachers. One of them studied in Kathmandu, in English. She's told me what they usually do in the classroom. It was strange to introduce new ways without knowing really well what they did before. She gives me that perspective." Helen picked up their plates and put them outside the door.

"I've been reading a lot of religious texts. Visited a monastery nearby. I might learn meditation, if they'll help me." She was shy about becoming too personal.

Paul told her he'd started a garden and was trying to get money to build a latrine. "Are your letters being opened? I've received a few that were sliced open and resealed. What do you think that's about?"

"I think that's customs people looking for money. One of the girls had a package from home harvested by customs. They took pens, razor blades, nylon panties. I guess that's their tip."

"One of my friends had a Christmas package coming with salami, beer, chocolate, and cheese. Just a little salami was left. And they charged one-hundred-percent duty on the declared value."

"Wow. Shameless," Helen said.

"Is anybody else getting sick?" He sounded guilty for causing a fuss.

"They said a lot of us are coming down with bronchial infections and dysentery, just as they warned. Nothing serious so far. Except you. And you made it."

"Sorry to make the record books," Paul said.

"I met one couple who were trekking through, looking completely Colorado. They were staying in Kathmandu for several months. Living well. Servants for everything. They couldn't stop talking about how cheap it was. They joined the swim club. They said they couldn't live like that back home, and they were going to enjoy it."

"Well, I met a few guys in Kathmandu who went in the opposite direction," Paul said. "They practically joined the beggars. If you consider that they hit on all of us for money, they're beggars. You know they can live on a few dollars a day in a place without plumbing and electricity. They were bringing the poor commune thing here."

"I hate having to be constantly on the lookout, though. People are so desperate. My parents in Kathmandu say you have to watch that the milk boy doesn't water the milk. If you don't know a shopkeeper, he'll slip a thumb on the scales if he can. The tailor may disappear with your cloth and come back with something strange, and half the cloth has gone somewhere else."

"That's going to happen everywhere. Capitalism."

"Oh, and a couple I know had their landlord move back into their building because he needed to hide from people who wanted to kill him," Helen said.

"Rough. It's not like that out here."

"My parents know some foreign families in which the trailing spouses couldn't take it anymore. Trouble with servants, disease, language. Mouse-droppings everywhere. The trailing spouses got ulcers and depression. Took tranquilizers. Ran to air-conditioned movies, or read magazines and drank beer in air-conditioned bars."

"A lot of that's just culture shock, "Paul said. "I love Kathmandu. Nepalis mixed with Indians, Chinese, Russians, Czechs, English, Americans, Germans, Swiss, and Tibetans. People pretty excited about touring, or some business they brought here."

"Yeah, they choke on seeing animal sacrifice for the first time."

"Speaking of mouse droppings. I'm trying to explain sanitation here and germs. They're very light on the concept. They have so many children because many don't survive. Even basic things would improve that."

"I heard of a teacher who got smallpox and kept teaching," Helen said. "He infected the whole village. The school was finally closed, and the children sent home. They scrubbed down a few rooms in the school. The exposed children went home over a wide area."

"Wow, that reminds me. I visited a place where a man showed me his daughter pocked with open sores playing with the baby. I told him he should isolate her. He said it was too much trouble."

"It's heartbreaking when they get sick because they have such a hard time healing." Although Helen had grown up in Nepal, she was still shocked about how primitive life was.

"At least, up here we don't have the rice fields they have in the south. The water running off the fields bringing human waste into the local streams, where they wash themselves, clothes, and animals."

"Ah. Hey, you know how they use one piece of cloth to wipe their eyes and brows?" Helen said. "Watch out if there's conjunctivitis, because that filthy pocket rag will spread it and keep it thriving."

"Evil spirits, Helen. Evil spirits."

Helen left with a bounce in her step. The day was bright, and the path was mostly downhill and now familiar. She could look forward to milestones along the way: certain stretches of steps, rope bridges, and marmot burrows. She returned to her school in almost half the time it had taken her to trek uphill.

***

Two weeks later she got a letter. The Nepali postal-delivery system consisted of people walking up and down those same hills and mountains. It worked surprisingly well.

"Dear Helen.

Thanks a bunch for helping me out. I'm feeling much better. Got back to the classroom. Eating normally again.

I didn't get a chance to ask you a lot about yourself because of the circumstances. I hope we can talk at the meeting next month. Would you write to me? How do you like your assignment? Are you having a good time? Do you feel effective? Have you made some special friends?

Your faithful servant, Paul."

He enclosed yellow petals from wildflowers. Helen was excited to picture him and to picture the two of them talking. The prospect of a friendship with a fellow volunteer had been far from her mind. Perhaps, it would be a romance, even more.

"Paul,

I'm having a good time, for the most part. My living situation is more comfortable than yours, with an indoor toilet and electricity. However, it's more confining. The other teachers are too curious, and I'm watched every minute of the day, when I'm outside my room. I try to use things exactly as they do, so I don't have to explain. For example, my toothbrush and toothpaste. The girls like to see how I manage my hair. The teachers want to try out my pens, can opener, and plastic bags. I have a kerosene stove in my room for heating water and some foods, like occasional oatmeal or hot chocolate, sent by my parents.

My parents are working with Tibetan refugees in Kathmandu. I'm an only child. I asked them to leave me alone so I could make my own way and have my own relationships apart from them and their politics and even good reputation. It's worked so far. People here can't imagine that my parents live so close.

I went to school back in the states, to Antioch College. It exposed me to a lot of cities, student-type jobs, and American culture, which was fairly new to me because I grew up here. When I came here, I didn't really 'get away' from America. I returned home and 'got away' from America. There are a lot of things I didn't like in America. The Peace Corps is giving me a chance to think about both places.

Where were you before this assignment?

Your shampoo girl, Helen."

Paul answered immediately.

"Dear Helen,

As you can imagine, I'm having some of the same experiences. The kids like to fool with my camera. Also, I have a short-wave radio that doesn't get a lot of stations but is pretty exciting when it picks up some. I brought a big bag of balloons, and they go a long way for laughs.

I'm finding it frustrating to get anything done here. Some of the teachers are very laid back. Mostly, it's a problem of resources. I've tried to get some science equipment sent from Kathmandu and, through headquarters, applied for a foundation grant to build a latrine. That may not happen even during my time here, but maybe another volunteer can see it through.

I'll be coming down the mountain for our regional meetings. Last time, I left early and caught the bus to Kathmandu the same day. Is there a place I can stay at your school, and we can take the bus together?

Thanks for your letter. I have more questions. I wish your hands were touching me right now.

Regards from the upper valley, Paul."

Helen hid the letter in her copy of *Introduction to Tibetan Buddhism*. She read it a few times every day. She wrote him a short, business-like reply about staying in the guestroom of her teacher's hostel, which had several cots.

***

Two weeks later, two girls came to her door, jumping with excitement. A foreign visitor! With white hair! Asking for her! Her own excitement jumped, and with some anxiety she checked her hair and clothes. She was wearing her hair loose, not braided, and a long-sleeved T-shirt covered her arms because of Nepali customs. She was expecting him. It was the day before the bus trip. But still, it was not a routine event. For the first time since she'd been there, she ran down the hall and the stairs to the front of the school, like a kid running home after school to play. He was standing in front with his backpack, wearing hiking boots, shorts, and a loose shirt. He looked like a trekker.

"Hey, Paul. You made it." He turned around and smiled, then stepped forward and gave her a fervent hug, holding on for a minute. Her heart was pounding.

"Hi. Great to see you. Thanks for the place to stay. I'm glad we can take the bus together."

"The guestroom is over this way. There's another traveler there, an official who's touring schools. They'll feed you along with us in an hour, so you have time to wash up."

"Super." He put his arm around her as they walked to the back of the school. She was totally unused to physical contact with a man and nervous about propriety.

"Maybe you shouldn't do that." She looked at his face just inches from hers.

"Why? It's socially acceptable. We're family, aren't we?"

"Oh. Yes. I forgot." She blushed.

"Is it okay?" He chuckled and pulled her waist to full contact with his.

She nodded and blushed.

Later, she went by the guestroom to show him to the eating area, a long table and chairs in a small room with a few posters of Hindu gods on the walls for color. Nepalis did not need to sit on chairs, but the teacher population was mixed, and chairs were a concession to their more educated, urban status. A woman brought out round trays with rice, lentils, and cabbage. Bowls of yoghurt were placed around the table, which the teachers passed and poured onto their plates. They ate with the right hand, Indian style. She and Paul spoke Nepali with the others, chatting about his hike, his school, the students, and the subjects they were learning.

After Helen and Paul ate, it was dark. He asked her to take a walk. The only privacy they would have would be outside. She led the way up a path into forest, where she knew several places to sit. It was still balmy. They found one of her favorite spots, which looked out over a dark valley surrounded by black hills and outlined by a sky of stars.

"This is nice." They sat down, Paul beside her so they were touching.

"Yes, it's an escape from being surrounded by people all the time," Helen said. "I can close the door to my room, but it's a dorm and you can hear everybody. This is my get-away spot."

"What do you think about when you sit here?"

"I think about things that happened during the day. Interactions with the teachers. Things the students did. What I'm learning. What I want to try to do differently."

"What do your parents think about this?"

"They spent their lives abroad, doing this kind of work. I think they like being expatriates. They like Indian culture. My dad likes the politics and watching the action. They're like missionaries without religion."

"They never took to religion?" Paul asked.

"No. They appreciate it and read about it. But they don't like religion per se. It's because of bad memories from their own childhoods. Both of them had missionary parents who were fierce proselytizers who got into trouble with the natives because of that. Saving the heathens, you know. They got kicked out of places like China. There was violence. I'm not sure I'm sympathetic to the messianic cause."

"Are you saving any heathens?" he asked.

"No. Like you, I'm helping a few Nepalis get ahead. Just a little bit."

"What will you do later?"

"I don't know," Helen said. "I majored in geography. I thought I would be a surveyor of new lands. Help capture the earth in charts and maps. What about you?"

"There's no clear path to anything," Paul said. "I might end up working for a non-governmental organization. International. Non-profits. Educational outreach. I feel some pressure, but I'm not sure what direction to go in. Maybe go back to school as a way of stalling."

"You can take French to a lot of places."

"Yes." He leaned into her and softly sang a French song. She went weak.

They held hands. When he stopped singing, he kissed her. For her, the kiss was like stepping under a hot shower on a cold day. Her body had never jolted like that. They lingered, prolonging the charge. He let go of her hand and turned her toward him. They kissed over and over. He made no attempt to take it further. She did not resist kissing and touching faces. In Nepal, it was generally taboo to touch a stranger's face, but it seemed natural and so pleasant. That night she slept with a smile on her face, restless and peaceful at the same time.

Helen and Paul walked to the bus stop to travel to Kathmandu in the morning. They were both glowing a little. It was early morning. There was a mist over the whole valley. They settled into a hard seat on the bus, side-by-side for the six-hour ride, swaying because of winding dirt roads that went up and down ridges and alongside rivers and through valleys. They both dozed, falling against each other, glad for the warmth and company.

To make good use of time, the regional meetings were busy. About fifteen volunteers were there. They talked about their assignments, action plans, and problems in the schools or communities. They went to restaurants in Kathmandu where they could drink cold beer and listen to Western music.

Helen tried not to cling to Paul and vice versa. They didn't want to appear to be anything but friends. But Helen felt like touching him all the time. Every moment she was aware of where he was in the room and longed to steal away with him. There were a few couples in the group, but to separate from the group in the pursuit of romance was considered bad form. Helen and Paul decided to spend an extra night in a hotel, away from the lodging provided to the volunteers during the meetings.

They put on their backpacks and walked as if they were heading toward the bus depot. Then, they detoured to a moderately priced hotel Paul had found that was not completely oriented toward pampered tourists and trekkers. They checked in as a couple travelling together, which was very common. The room was on the fifth floor with a small balcony overlooking a back street. It was modest, decorated with batik paintings. They went to an Indian restaurant for tandoori-style chicken. Meat was rare and a luxury in their diet.

Helen knew where the evening was headed but felt shy about it. She'd dated just a few men in college. She wasn't a virgin, but had very little sexual experience. In college she'd been surrounded by the hippy culture of casual sex, drinking and drugs, and she hadn't felt as strongly attracted to anyone as she now felt. She thought it would be nice to stay just good friends with Paul, but her own body was telling her that was a lie. As he unlocked the door to their room, she looked at the back of his head, wondering what he was thinking but felt too shy to ask.

After they went inside and took their jackets off, he turned to her and kissed her. He sensed her awkwardness. "Let's just get into bed together, okay?"

"Sure." Self-conscious, she put her jacket near her backpack, found her toiletries, and went into the bathroom. They had already spent several days in the city so she was less in awe of the comforts of having a bathroom with a shower. She changed into her silk, sleeping camisole.

"Hey." Paul got up and hugged her close. It was the first time he had seen so much of her body. They parted, and she got into bed to wait for him to get ready. He did not take long and soon climbed in beside her.

With no inhibition, he pressed himself to her, and they kissed. She was reticent and shy. "Let's just sleep this one. What do you think?" he asked, his soft hand touching her cheek.

"Yes. I'm sorry. I'm not experienced."

"It's okay." He turned out the light. He lay close behind her, ran his hand down her body, across her breasts, across her belly, and then let it rest, hugging her from behind.

In the middle of the night, extreme arousal woke them up. It was pitch dark, and the streets outside were quiet. Helen couldn't see Paul. Her body was flushed with heat. Almost simultaneously, they took off their nightwear. He moved on top of her. Her mind went blank with overwhelming pleasure. When he pushed inside her, it felt as if a large, gentle animal had enveloped her and taken over. They moved to touch as much skin as possible. Without thinking, Helen felt her body respond and swooned with lust. The sense of being swollen with pleasure did not subside after their explosive contractions stopped. They dosed off and woke the same way several times again.

Sunlight through the cotton curtains finally woke them into a world and room they could see again. Neither spoke. They were lethargic and blissful while their eyes opened and minds re-engaged. Paul stood up and walked naked to the bathroom. She watched him in wonder. When he came back, he smiled and got under the covers again. She rolled out the other side and self-consciously crossed the room to the bathroom herself. She also came back to bed, curling her back into his arms.

"The bus leaves at noon. We should eat before." She nodded. They took turns using the shower.

The six-hour bus ride back was uphill, full of the excitement provided by narrow dirt roads along steep ravines with sharp turns. The bus was old with a noisy frame and rattling windows. Helen and Paul talked little, trying to doze. He was to stay overnight in the guestroom again. They had dinner with the school staff.

"I'm going to that room with great reluctance, Helen."

"I know. I don't think we should rock the school with an incident, though. There's no way you can sneak into my room. I'll look for you at breakfast." They parted outside the school in the dark. At early dawn, he ate and said goodbye.

She got a letter within a week.

"Dear Helen,

I can feel all of me, alive, sensitive. The whole texture of the day has changed for me. Objects that were but surfaces have become solid, three-dimensional.

It's perhaps a bad time for me to write to you. I've been alone for too long, and it's hard to separate my desire and need for love from my desire and need for you. And now that I've begun to write to you, you're all around me. In a way, you overwhelm me.

There's nothing I want more than for you to be here. It'd be nice to lie here close to you, where I could just reach over and touch you. I think of you, I feel your presence. My heart has kept that time and place when you were in bed with me and waits to realize it again.

Can you come and visit? I think my 'sister' can stay with me the same way she did last time, only this time she can cross that huge space between the two cots.

My love, Paul."

She was quick to reply.

"Dear Paul,

I'm flying. My heart is happy; I've chosen the dream of you. I've leaped into space.   It's so pleasant to think of being with you again, even if it were just one more time. You're making every day disappear into euphoria.

I realize you've had more experience than I. I hope I don't disappoint you with my innocence. My inhibition. I've never felt the unity and intensity you gave me. It makes you god-like to me. I really don't want to come back to earth. Take me away!

I'll plan to hike up in two weeks. Must check on my brother.

Love, Helen."

The next time she paid him a visit, they hiked out from his village. The mountains were glorious and high, taking up most of the view around them. They trekked over rocky paths and green meadows. They stopped at a slow river for lunch.

"I never imagined a place this beautiful," he said, as he lay down on the wild grass.

"I grew up in it. And I went to college in the Midwest. For contrast."

"Not all of America is flat."

"I saw the Grand Canyon. I went to an outdoor camp in Vermont in the fall. That was spectacular. But mostly, I saw cities. I didn't have a car."

"Are you going back?" he asked. "It must be different to have your parents here."

"I'm not anxious to go back. There were a lot of things that put me off."

"Like what?"

"Women don't get respect. I probably couldn't get a good job. Women are not welcome in medical school. You can't get a credit card in your own name. It may be 'civilized' but not a good deal for me."

"Did you make some friends back there?"

"Sure," she said, "but no one who makes me want to go back. What about your friends?"

"Oh, I've been travelling so long that I don't have anyone in particular. It's hard to maintain a relationship that way. You have to explain so much. You can't stay close to anybody long distance. Let's take a swim." He started to take his clothes off.

The water was ice cold. He stepped into the water naked and mock-screamed. She watched his lean body. She took off her clothes and followed him. They held hands and gingerly stepped through shallow water, feeling every icy inch on their legs. The sun was blazing, but the altitude was high, and the air was cold. He took water in his hand and poured it over her buttocks. She jumped away and leaned down to splash him. Their naked bodies were still strange and intensely exciting to each other. The frigid water was a crazy contrasting stimulation. They ran out of the creek to their clothes. He put his shirt on the grassy ground and pulled her down. The heat of their bodies lifted the cold air away from their wet skin.

They continued to exchange letters between monthly visits.

"Helen,

Now that time is bringing you closer, I'm getting waves of anticipation that fly in spite of these present mundane duties. I've written several notes to you at times.

When I received your letter, I was actually shaking. I had to sit down. My heart and my eyes were full. I couldn't see. Nothing makes sense, but everything has meaning. When I awoke today, you were in my thoughts. You were there beside me, and you are here beside me now.

About the unity. It's not me, but life, giving you this gift. I'm so happy that it's me who gave you this experience. I promise you there's more to come.

I want to tell you many things. And they're probably very simple things. And I probably won't be able to tell them well anyway. I really don't know what they all are, but I do feel them. I want you to know how I feel.

To me, you're a promise of many things, an early springtime promise of what could come. But springtimes are certain and always fulfilled, while life is uncertain and many promises dry and wrinkle.

Because I care for you, I want the promise of your being to come true for you and in this way, it'll also come true for me, whether it be with or without me, which ultimately doesn't matter.

I wouldn't want to see you encrusted in the great social shell of predictable obligations. Nor would I want to see you disappear into the mass of hippies drowning in their first wet dream of escapes to Kathmandu. This is important: I feel that there are still things that you must do alone before you accept somebody else to do them with.

I hope you'll come to understand me. I do love you, your promise.

All my love, Paul."

***

Helen packed for the hike up to Paul's school differently this time. She packed her better camisoles, a blouse, and western pants in addition to her long skirt and thick wool vest. Everything along the walk glowed. She heard birds sing. The wind in the trees. Marmots whistling from every side and every turn, taunting her for her lover's secret. The water rushing downstream sounded like an endless waterfall bursting into the air after a long land-bound journey. She arrived while it was still light, stepping up to his door.

"Paul?"

"Hey! I'm thrilled to see you!" He jumped from his desk to embrace her. She was tired and sweaty from the hike, but energized. They hugged long and kissed.

"Remember me?"

"Sure do. Naked in my bed, too." She blushed. She put her pack down and sat down to rest. He had a bucket of water on the kerosene stove to heat. He left to get their evening meal. She'd brought some delicacies: dried apricots, chocolate, Western cheese, and Oreo cookies. They ate, sitting close at his desk, stopping to touch an arm, a cheek, a thigh, a breast or a belly.

When they were done eating, she carried the hot water to the bathing area and took off her clothes. She sat on the stool, naked, and started soaping up. "Did you think you were going to do that alone?" She started. He was naked now, too, and leaned over her to take her washcloth. She suddenly felt terribly shy but let him soap her. He wet her hair and shampooed it. Then, he got up and ladled warm water over her head and body. He rinsed himself, too. They stood to dry. She could see he had an erection, which was still not a familiar sight. They climbed into his narrow bed, and he proceeded to stroke and kiss her body everywhere, slowly. She closed her eyes and waited for her embarrassment to ease into mindless sensuality.

After the first trip, they found the one-day hike was a small barrier to a visit every few months. The euphoria of infrequent visits kept personal irritations at bay for a long time. Distance added pleasure to the isolation they'd expected with solo assignments. Together, they took the bus to Kathmandu, where they could book a room in a hotel and suspend the pretense of being brother and sister. Living in villages was like living in a glass house, where everyone watched and commented on their activities. In Kathmandu, they could eat well for a few dollars, joining others in the bars and clubs in town. They settled into the profound happiness of being in love.

HELEN AND PAUL'S ROMANTIC PASSION started coming down from its early fever. Six months before the end of their assignments, all the volunteers were thinking about their next moves. Suddenly, "here and now" was crowded by "where next?" Helen and Paul avoided talking about a time when they wouldn't be together in Nepal.

Helen talked more and more about the monastery, her meditation practice, and the texts she was reading. She was less the innocent, unformed woman whom Paul could relate to by showing her the world. He had wanderlust again and thought about spending several years travelling through Japan and French Polynesia, unencumbered by a romantic commitment. She worried that he was the kind of man who preferred to have a woman in every port. She thought he might like collecting countries and women for a long time.

> "Dear Paul,
> I think we assumed that we would go merrily along after Nepal, not keeping in close contact after we moved to other places, wondering what would come, and believing something good might come. I'm supposed to grow up and become myself, go on meeting people my own way, perhaps have romantic ties and behave as if you were not there, yet, paradoxically, remember you. And you were to go on exploring cultures, going to Japan and Tahiti, alone, and seeking me when you feel it is time. And I said, thought, or meant to say, that when you came back, I would meet you, no matter what my particular circumstances, because that was how you were to me and that seemed to be my place.
> I'm willing to leave it at that although I miss you already. We have so much in common in the way we think and in the way we love. How do other people reconcile the

different directions floating in their minds? Can we blend and sleep in the same bed going into the future?

Your little monk, with great attachment, Helen."

***

"Dear Helen,

I'm afraid that if I'm not holding you near, watching you, you might not understand. And right now, I think that for you to understand me may be one of the most important things for me. Shall I say that I'm unsure, afraid—afraid of what I would lose in seeking to lock you into my future, and yet afraid of what I would lose in losing you. Unsure, the first time I have been unsure in many years. You haunt me; you haunt me because you matter. I'd begun to wonder whether anyone could matter in that way anymore.

I also feel that there are still things that you have to do alone before you accept somebody else with you. And there are things I want to do—travel—with the same intensity and freedom I did in the past.

I'm always amazed to read your letters, to have you tell me things, where so often they parallel my own experiences, feelings, ideas. But we can't trap that familiarity and lock it in time.

Yours, Paul."

Soon after, Helen suspected she was pregnant. She and Paul had been careful with birth control most, but not all, of the time. The confusion posed by this fact was overwhelming. Her mind and spirit had been slowly spiraling into an ethereal world toward cosmic understanding, and now her body was growing a new physical body within it, grounding it. Pregnancy would bring hormones and non-stop demanding physical sensations that were completely antithetical to her spirit. She intuitively knew that her body needed to nurture the embryo and that the pregnancy would take her over. She had to give the rising spirit of the child a chance to grow without competing with her spiritual development. They would be bonded at the cellular level, each flesh surrounding the other.

A doctor in Pokhara confirmed her suspicion. Her first impulse was to keep it secret and digest the implications. Her cohort of volunteers was two months from leaving Nepal. Her friends were planning their travel, saying good-byes, visiting favorite places for the last time and turning homeward in their thoughts. She was in a private turmoil. Her pregnancy was not showing, which kept others away for now. She knew if Paul knew, she would have to respond to his reactions and wishes, and they might constrain her own. Paul knew she was planning to stay in Nepal. They might pressure each other into a decision they would regret later.

"Helen, you could come to Japan with me for a while," he said. "A transition before we part. We can see what happens with us in another country."

She looked at his familiar face and felt her body relax with familiar anticipation of touching him. The comfort of staying at his side was a tormenting temptation. He reached for her hand, coaxing her to warm to a future with him. But it was his idea of a future, and not hers, that he was talking about.

"Paul, this is spiritual for me, not another trip or hanging out in a country. I want to meditate and be around people who are meditating in Nepal."

He put his other hand out, pleading. She felt a shudder of withdrawal, like anxiety deep inside, hiding her secret. She wondered if the embryo registered her tension. She locked into her denial. She couldn't stand the intensity of the conflict she felt. "I like being with you but not enough to sacrifice this chance for me. We can write, but I think we're not interested in the same things." The minute she spoke, her counter feelings of longing and desire to cling to the pleasures he gave her intensified. She pulled her hands back, confused and hurt, but didn't take his hand back.

"I am so sorry," he said. "I am so sorry."

He got on the plane the next day, and Helen returned to Pokhara by bus.

***

In the following months, she rushed to see the face of every man she saw in Katmandu who looked remotely like Paul, hoping Paul had come back. She strained to peer into faces in pedi-cabs,

120

restaurant windows, and even trekking groups. Her nights were soaked in sleepless sweats as she remembered his body, his smell, his voice. She touched herself trying to remember the overwhelming passion triggered under his hands. Meditation barely began to calm the turmoil. She tried to picture life in the monastery without the Peace Corps community behind her. Her body was swelling, rounding, softening, and she was tired. She tried to imagine life with a baby. If she wasn't looking for Paul at every turn on the trails, she locked on the sight of women holding babies on their hips. She tried to guess the depths of their love and their burden. Were they exhausted but happy, or exhausted and steeled for the long years ahead, making sure there was enough food, enough love, enough luck?

She got a postcard a month later with a picture of Maneko Neki, the Japanese lucky cat, the beckoning cat, the cat of prosperity.

"Helen,
I found a job teaching English with a company in Tokyo. Lucky break. Living in a tiny but adequate space with tatami mats. Imagine soaking in a hot tub every night! Want to try Japanese Buddhism? Miss you.
Your biggest fan, Paul."

***

Helen's parents, Jeri and Donald, had lived in Kathmandu for nearly a decade, working with the Tibetan Refugee Center. They administered a school and social services funded by the Red Cross and the Swiss Development Corporation, in cooperation with the government of Nepal. They were settled within a community of relief workers and engaged with Indian and Tibetan culture. They had influenced Helen to choose teaching as her Peace Corps mission and to choose an assignment in Nepal.

Helen saw them regularly when she came to Kathmandu. She avoided them while Paul was leaving, to hide her emotional turmoil. She came back to the city a few months later, when her pregnancy clearly showed. Until then, her conversation with her parents was mostly about her simple life in the monastery, local personalities, and the beauty of the mountains. She and Paul had hidden their romance from her parents and the Peace Corps to protect their assignments, maintain face in their schools and villages, and stay free of interference and judgment.

When Helen passed through the gate, she knew that her softer face and fuller stomach would give her away.

"Helen! Oh, Helen. Why didn't you say something? Why?" Jeri said.

"I didn't want to worry you. It's a long story." She set her things down and went to wash up, running away from Jeri's disappointment and concern. When Helen got back to the living room, Donald rushed to hug her. His hand lingered on her thickened waist. The three of them sat down and clutched teacups on the veranda.

"The thing is," Helen said, "I'm not interested in having a baby. I want to be a nun. But here I am." She was wearing a long hemp skirt and a shawl in the orange-brown colors of monks. The shawl was draped over her belly to temper the shock of its new shape.

Jeri looked at Donald to see how he was feeling. They had worked together so long that their social reactions were usually in sync. He was an introvert, but he did most of the travelling and meetings with government officials and kept an intellectual perspective on their enterprise. His work required a cool demeanor. Jeri was steeped in relationships with local people, the school, and administrative work. She was more dramatic. Helen knew what to expect.

"How can you be 'not so interested in having a child'?" Jeri said. "What do you mean? What about the father?"

"The father doesn't know. It was an accident, of course. He's an American, now in America. It wasn't a deep relationship. Actually, I don't want him to know, and I don't want to get mixed up in his life again."

"How can you say that?" Jeri set her teacup down and clasped her hands.

"I just did. It was an accident. A fateful accident."

"But you need support from the father," Jeri said.

"And he has a right to know," said Donald with an edge.

"You don't know what this guy is like, Dad. I don't think you want to get him involved. Think about the types of guys travelling through Katmandu." Helen decided a white lie was needed, even at the cost of her reputation.

"But you slept with him," Jeri said. "You chose this boy or man. How could you pick somebody you want to forget about?"

"He's not a bad person. Just not the guy you want in your life forever after."

"So what are your plans for this baby?" Jeri was fidgeting with her teacup again and avoiding eye contact.

"I'm thinking of adoption," said Helen, slowly. "I'm thinking that you might help me find a Tibetan family or link up with the adoption channels for Tibetan kids."

"Oh, Helen." Jeri leaned into her with disbelief.

Donald's face got redder.

"Think about what's best for the baby, Mom."

"Oh, Helen! This is your child. Our grandchild. How could you even think of adoption? Is this the Buddhist way?" Jeri leaned back with a look of disgust unfamiliar to Helen.

"It has nothing to do with Buddhism. This is my decision, whether I can nurture a child and give it a wholesome emotional life. Think about the child. Isn't that what you're supposed to do? What's best?"

"I can't process this anymore," Jeri said, her eyes red. "Let's think and talk tomorrow." The sun was setting. It was a cool, clear mountain night. There were beautiful stars and bright reflections from snow in the far mountains. The serenity of the night sky mocked the messy emotions between them.

"The day we had you was the best day of my life," Jeri said as she straightened up again. She looked at Donald. "Remember the noise in Calcutta and the bustle in the hospital?"

"We were lucky to find good care," he said.

"You'll have good care here, too," she said to Helen. "But it feels like you're entering a convent."

"She *is* entering a convent," Donald said, putting a hand on Helen's arm.

"I never imagined you'd detach yourself from everything like this. From a child!" Jeri spoke quietly, as if thinking out loud.

Donald played good cop. "She's not detaching herself. She's always been a free spirit."

"Maybe it was growing up here, without any friends like you, and other families like ours," Jeri said. They were talking around Helen now. She let them vent.

"She just discovered meditation, Jeri," said Donald.

"It seems joyless."

"We've always improvised, Jeri. We can improvise here." He took Jeri's hand.

"Yes."

"Either way, we love you, and you are our daughter." Donald got up. "Let's sleep on it." They both hugged Helen long and hard, inevitably feeling the unfamiliar bulge.

***

Helen walked outside in the compound in the early light, looking at the garden her parents had populated with familiar plants amid bougainvillea and rhododendrons to remind them of home. There were custom-made wooden benches and brass statues in the midst of the pockets of plantings. The garden was a serene private setting that foreigners of modest means could afford in India and Nepal where housing was cheap. It was an oasis from the rough, poor, busy streets of Kathmandu.

The cook served toast and eggs for everyone with the rare treat of coffee instead of tea.

"I didn't sleep too well," said Jeri, getting up from the breakfast table to greet Helen.

"I know. I'm sorry." Helen sat down, eager to eat a rare American breakfast and just plain pregnant-hungry.

On hearing them, Donald came from the living room. He was wearing his at-home clothes: a loose white shirt and loose khaki pants.

Helen voraciously ate the breakfast and asked for more toast. Jeri and Donald's cook, like many others, was highly skilled in English cuisine, adapting it to the tastes of his employers.

"Helen, we'll take the baby," said Jeri, cautiously. "We can hire an *aya* for next to nothing. We know at least one Tibetan refugee who would be perfect to care for a baby. She is eager for work. You can visit when you can. You don't have to give the baby away."

***

Helen made arrangements to be away from the monastery.

After a chance to think about it, she realized that a child would give Jeri a new relationship with young Tibetan women and her peers. Jeri would have full control over child rearing and lots of help. Donald showed he was relieved that a problem had been solved. What could have turned into a painful crisis was looking like a workable new lifestyle for all of them. Helen realized that her decision was consistent with her family's culture of doing what you want or need to do, and not necessarily making conventional choices. Of course, Jeri and Donald had found each other and chosen to have Helen, but that choice was bundled with the idea of a small family in the role of missionaries abroad.

Now in her adulthood, Helen knew that Donald was a great companion to Jeri and had been a nurturing father. His main passions were intellectual—the politics and culture of Asia, and art—but he had a big heart and took pleasure in playing with children. He could be absent-minded and, on an art excursion, could forget to bring lunch or jackets or even that he had a child along, but his lust for life made up for it. He could launch into lectures about Tibetan *tonkas* and, shortly after, giggle about the antics of a goat.

Jeri's parents had a compatible marriage. They were both children of missionaries in China. They'd met in a boarding school in Hong Kong while their parents worked in remote villages and sanctuaries. Later, Jeri and Donald met again serendipitously in San Francisco at a conference about China.

"I never forgot him," Jeri said to Helen when she was in her teens. "He was an instant friend, and there was a lot of chemistry. When we met, we were not quite ready to lock in on each other, nor any one location. We knew we each wanted to travel all over. We were very independent because we had freed ourselves of American conventions while we lived so long in China. Then, we were in boarding schools that were outside the mainstream, outside suburban life. We were both raised for living abroad somewhere."

Jeri was part-Norwegian, with blond hair and blue eyes. Her weight was healthy. She was not slight and not really stocky, with full cheeks and a strong back. She liked to work outside and, wherever she was, walked long distances. She was cheerful and curious, often the first to start a conversation at a bus stop. She made fast friends in minutes.

Donald was what you would expect from a boy who grew up living in isolation abroad with parents who were serious missionaries. He was studious and sincere. He lost himself reading history and politics. He was clumsy socially, but so bright that people sought him out for his opinions and forgave the spilled cup of tea, the un-tucked shirt and khaki shorts with knee socks that were, in Nepal, reminiscent of British colonials. Like the clichéd colonialist, he even had a Scottish ruddiness in his skin and a fleshy, un-athletic body. In fact, he turned out to be very much a retro post-colonial. Instead of running the country, however, Helen thought, he was helping it in a supportive role as a capable administrator and advisor. He clearly cared for the fate of Nepal and India. To him, the festivals, street noise, dirt and crazy political movements were not obstacles or even frustrations. They stimulated him, and Helen had picked up that excitement from him.

Helen idealized her parents. They'd made her suspicious of compromising to American conventions—settling down in the suburbs and acquiring a house, car, and ambitious job. When her parents met in San Francisco again and figured out that the romance each felt about love and travel could be compatible, their relationship felt like heaven.

It did not occur to Helen that Paul was much like her parents, and that she and Paul were also juggling two romances.

Helen saw little of America until she was sent to college in the Midwest. Her parents guided her to an unconventional college that featured work-study and exposure to three-and six-month work experiences each year. She worked in New York, Boulder, San Francisco, and Washington during the four years of college. She found a peer community equally interested in doing good and saving the world.

While at college, she missed the mountains and the simplicity of life in Nepal, however, and never imagined she could stay in the States. She was already spoiled for a life abroad, around women who managed whole communities in foreign lands, travelled freely, and made their own decisions.

***

Many months later, after leaving her weaned daughter Eike behind with her parents, Helen continued her monastic life style in the Pokhara region. She did not shave her head, a symbolic renunciation of worldly life, but cut it short. She dressed like a Nepali and slept and ate simply like others in her community, although in her own hut and not in the monastery. Her material existence showed only a few remnants of her Western past, tucked away under a bench in the corner of a modest room: the nylon backpack, Gortex blanket, a fancy flashlight, and some Western clothes. She stopped missing Coke, corn flakes, peanut butter, and chocolate, although she ate them when visiting Kathmandu.

Unlike followers of orthodox religions, Helen didn't adopt social barriers to maintain a kind of theoretical purity, such as cooking and eating separate foods, or avoiding certain kinds of touching. She didn't want to assume a holy persona. Her spirituality was not something that needed to be expressed loudly, and especially not in any way that seemed superior. She continued to interact with Western hikers who came by the hostel, which only added to the allure of the hostel for touring visitors. She was a model for rejecting not only a Western lifestyle, but also a worldly life of any kind.

She thought about being in bed with Paul, of course. And while she was pregnant, her physical body was a sea of pleasure and pain, discomfort, urges, needs. It was impossible to suppress her earthly existence. She felt the echoes of extreme experiences of the flesh. But she also saw the misery that flesh wrought on most people: obsessions with sex, the bloated satisfaction and discomfort of pregnancy, the pain of childbirth, the fevers and fluids of sickness. She had climbed out of the sea like a lumbering fish to feel free in the air of contemplation.

Her mind could go anywhere. It could transcend sluggish appetites, pain, sleepiness, and hunger. It could seek a higher level of existence, unencumbered by flesh in this life, which would eventually free her from the encumbrances of earthly suffering. Staying stuck on Paul, her memory of touching him, opening to him, craving him, was a gauntlet, as was the gauntlet of hormones launched through her body by holding Eike.

"Don't you long for Eike?" Jeri asked Helen on one of her rare trips into Kathmandu.

"No. My mind is really elsewhere. Not many people choose to do what I am doing, and I should do it."

"What is that exactly?" Jeri still could not comprehend Helen's choice.

"Meditate. All of our meditation is raising the human race toward a state of grace—closer to truth. I like the chanting too."

"Doesn't the hostel get in the way?"

"It's a balance. I like that, too. It reminds me what normal daily life is like—the noise, food, money, petty passions. I like getting away from it. Getting lost in non-verbal thinking. Even contemplation without thinking."

"Do you try to teach the hikers about Buddhism? Does anybody try to join you?"

"Not really. They ask, but I don't explain myself. I don't have to answer their curiosity. They're very curious about me. We influence people by our example and leave them to their own journeys."

"I guess you have to be nice to them to keep the business going," Jeri said.

"We feed them and house them, but there's no need to round up more customers, nor to entertain them. They're here for nature. We don't seem to run out of visitors."

"Still, don't you enjoy the work of the guesthouse?"

"Actually yes. It adds variety to my day without taking me away from what I think is my important work."

Helen's goal was the middle path, as Buddhism practice goes, whereby she could work in a normal way, and yet advance her meditation practices without joining the regime—and taking a typical woman's role—in the monastery. There was in Buddhist history precedent for people who were realized beings but conducted mundane work in the world, like washing clothes, selling wine, or helping run a hiker's hostel. She knew about famous nuns who had combined spiritual pursuit with marriage and family. The famous nun Machig Lapdron left young children with their father, so she could meditate in a cave. Machig did not demonstrate any great attachment to them or to their upbringing. In spite of this distance, one of her children joined her in practice later and continued her spiritual lineage.

***

When Eike was four, Helen went on a three-year retreat, moving up the valley into a high cave. The cave had been occupied before, but villagers helped Helen make some renovations. They built a wall to isolate a food storage area that would not be exposed to heat. They built a wall that closed off the cave, leaving a door and window to the outside. Inside the cave, walls were "painted" with fresh clay, leaving them smooth like the inside of a house. Her furniture included a wooden platform for meditation and sleep, a stove, and stone shelves for belongings. Along the ledge outside the cave was a retaining wall that buffered wind, rain, and snow. She had a small stove to make tea and cook barley porridge. Water had to be brought up on a quarter-mile path from a creek. A nearby resident carried her food supplies and kerosene up the hill several times a year, weather allowing. This chore brought good karma to the resident and was common practice. Helen shared with him her stock of lentils, rice, cooking oil, salt, soap, milk powder, tea, sugar, apples, sweets, and kerosene. The retreat in the cave was a rite of passage for serious Buddhists, and Helen was now one of them.

A Head-Turning Child

EIKE WAS BORN in the Tibetan refugee camp clinic in the fall after the Peace Corps ended. She was healthy and big, reflecting Helen's diet during pregnancy and healthy lifestyle that included frequent trekking in high-altitude hills. Eike, named for one of Jeri's Norwegian ancestors, was mellow and sweet, with big eyes. Her dark, petite, Indian nanny Jampa immediately welcomed her with arms that rarely put her down. Eike could spend her energy looking at the many people surrounding her, who were light and dark and spoke multiple languages. They waved colorful cloth toys, mirrors and bells at her.

Eike's hair turned into blond curls. With blue eyes, she was a rare, head-turning child in Kathmandu. That difference garnered her much attention, which she returned with curiosity but not much emotional interest. Among Indians, lighter skin was envied. Among Tibetans, it represented despised foreignness. In fact, Tibetans and many Asians thought the white race was mentally inferior. They had seen the British take over India by force and use inventions to enslave people and spoil nature. To compensate, Eike's nanny Jampa introduced her to Nepalis as the child of the famous white goddess Ma-Chen. To Jampa, this white lie seemed like a natural way to make things easy for Eike.

Eike didn't recognize Helen as one of her significant caretakers, because, after the first six months, Helen visited her only once a year. Helen was just part of Eike's large extended family. Jeri was her primary mother, and Donald her dad. She was so loved that she did not pay undue attention to those who gave her affection.

Nearly every day, Jampa took Eike to her own home in Kathmandu to check on her grandfather and to bring him his mid-day meal. Carrying a stack of tin bowls locked together by a handle, Jampa and Eike walked from the refugee center through back alleys to a courtyard surrounded by two-story apartments and rooms.

There, on a balcony sat Jampa's grandfather, who'd been a cook in a Burmese restaurant but now rested his weary bones in the sunshine. Jampa made tea for her grandfather and Eike as they looked out from the small balcony at people coming and going to the market around the corner. The grandfather had taken up meditation, and a lama was guiding him in Bon practices.

Eike played with a cloth doll on the carpet in the living room. Occasionally, she woke from a nap and sat with her back braced against the grandfather, who often meditated for hours at a time. The warmth of her tiny body did not disturb him. The sight of a little girl with a blond Dutch-cut sitting with her doll content against a meditator was quite unusual and charmed everyone.

"DONALD," JERI SAID.

He was wiping his brow and getting a drink, having come in from a sweltering day of showing visitors around Kathmandu.

"Eike returned from Jampa's family village this morning."

"Oh? Where is she?" They hadn't seen her for months, as every summer she stayed with Jampa's aunt.

"She's napping now. A lot has happened." Jeri got herself a drink.

"Oh? What do you mean by a lot?"

"She studied Tibetan language as we expected," Jeri said. "Apparently, she's doing very well. Did you remember that the aunt is a shaman?"

"I remember we talked about that."

"She taught Eike how to prepare herbs and objects for rituals."

"Sounds good. A healthy exposure to work. Religious work."

"It went beyond healthy exposure, Donald." Jeri put down the drink.

"How do you mean?"

"She said she was dreaming about goddesses and ghosts."

"How did she sound talking about it?" Donald asked. "Scared?" There was no predicting how a ten-year-old might react to such an unusual experience.

"Not at all. She loved it. She really loved it. She said she wants to do more. She could not stop talking about it, telling me about the herbs, the people visiting, the healing."

***

When Eike was nine years old, a boy had taunted her: "You're a white demon!"

"I'm not!" She wasn't so sure.

"You drink the blood of dead babies!"

"Leave me alone!" She ran away. At home she sought out Jeri.

"Ma, why did he call me a white demon?"

"Because he's never seen someone as white as you."

"Why am I so white?"

"Your parents are light people. We inherit our coloring. It's quite normal. You see me. You see Donald."

"But you're not my parents."

"No, we're your grandparents. We're acting like your parents."

"Where are my parents?"

"Helen is your actual mother. But you're with us and Jampa."

"Who's my real father?"

"He went away. Far away. We don't know where he is."

"Will he come back?"

"I don't know. He may be gone forever."

"Do you know him?"

"Actually, I don't."

"Why not?"

"We don't always know our whole family. People disappear. You know the children in the orphanage? They're separated from their parents. Many people are separated from someone. It's sad, but true."

"When did he disappear?" Eike asked.

"Before you were born. I didn't know him. But you have Donald, Jampa, and me to love you."

"Am I separated from Helen?"

"Do you remember Machig Lapdron? She left her babies to meditate in a cave. Helen is like Machig Lapdron. She's a nun."

"Does she love me?" Eike asked.

134

"Of course, she loves you. She's your mother. But she's your distant mother. She's dedicated to meditation."

***

In her mid-teens, Eike stopped cutting her hair, and it turned into long, matted strands. Since she had never travelled outside Nepal or watched much TV, she had no awareness that matted hair was also a feature of Rastafarians in Jamaica and holy men in India. Her points of reference were local. Of course, her completely atypical blond hair drew much attention. Jeri and Donald did not know, but Jampa's aunt saw a pattern of a red lotus with three roots in a discoloration near Eike's navel. The aunt considered this a sign of a *dakini* or goddess.

Eike learned to read aloud the *Prajna Paramita Sutra*, a *Chöd* text frequently requested as a prayer for the dead by natives who sought the services of shamans and monks. Lay people invited shamans and monks to their homes for repeated readings. Each reading increased merit for the family. The readings had to be loud to attract gods and spirits living in trees, springs and rocks, who then shared the teachings with lower-level beings.

Eike also learned the melodic ritual of *Chöd*, or cutting. It is characterized by a particular chanted melody, ringing bells, and rapid drumming. *Chöd* originated in Bon, a pre-Buddhist Tibetan religion and exploits fear as a path to insight. The ritual is usually conducted in cemeteries and charnel grounds—where dead bodies are prepared for a sky burial in which they are left for vultures to devour. *Chöd* can be practiced in different places and with different deities. Tibetans often request that a lama or holy person conduct the ritual to help the dead move on to the spirit world. The shaman symbolically invites spirits and demons to cut up his own body and to take it as a surrogate for the deceased, as way of renouncing attachment to the world.

Eike's Lama Yeshi warned her that during the *Chöd* initiation, evil spirits and demons would appear to carry her soul to the underworld. There, Eike would watch them dismember her body. They would cut off her head and cut her body into small

135

pieces to be distributed to the spirits of various diseases. In this way, the shaman gained power to cure others of those diseases. She would depend on those spirits, so she was symbolically giving them her own flesh as a sacrifice. After her body's distribution, her bones would be covered with new flesh, and she would be given new blood. She would have terrible visions and hallucinations, see frightening storms and whirlwinds, as if she were having an extreme nightmare. At the end of the initiation, she would have new powers. The ordeal would test her ability to withstand possession and extreme spiritual pressures. She would learn to manage interactions with strong spirits.

She learned during initiation that four demons had to be overcome, each representing a weakness of the ego. The first challenge was to resist wanting to possess people or things she perceived through the senses. The second challenge was to resist allowing the mind to be distracted. The third was to resist wanting pleasure, like desiring more of something delicious or more of a good feeling. Finally, the fourth was to resist feeling that the ego is independent and separate from the world.

During regular, repeated practice, Eike was taught to use her voice, a drum, a bell and a human thighbone trumpet to make sounds. The drum had a ball on a string that could strike both sides of the drum, symbolizing masculine and feminine principles, and absolute and relative truth. The drum was turned from side to side to make a rhythmic, march-like beat. The bell was rung to evoke female energy. When the shaman's flesh was offered to the demons, the bone trumpet was sounded, making an eerie whining noise. Meanwhile, the shaman sang various chants. All of these were essential to create vibrations in the body of the shaman and to summon spirits.

The ideal place for *Chöd* is under a lone tree inhabited by demons or in a cemetery, so that fears can be directly encountered and transcended. Eike was warned that some people undergoing *Chöd* suffered fright that was so extreme they went mad.

After training in *Chö*d practice for five years, Eike would be called in by lay people to perform rituals when there were epidemics of cholera and other infectious diseases, or a need to heal some other disease. She might be called in for exorcism or to aid dying or dead person in their transition to new realms. Some *Chöd* practitioners cut up dead bodies for sky burial. The ritual was performed to harmonize human relations with nature. Thus, the shaman played an essential role in everyday life, and especially in deaths of family members. A frustrated death was a horrible fate, as the spirit would stay in an intermediate state in the afterlife, or *bardo*, wandering and trying to find relief. Finding a monk or shaman to perform *Chöd* for the deceased was highly desirable.

***

"Do you think shamanic practice is good for her?" Jeri asked Jampa. They sat on Jeri's patio with Dorje for a midday break. Eike was napping. "Should we keep her from doing it or slow her down?"

"I think she'll tell you," said Jampa. "A lot of shamans are discovered early. In that case, it's good for them to get initiated early and learn protections early."

"I hear that she likes talking with people." Dorje put his lemonade down. "Two weeks ago, a man came to the aunt's house for advice. He was being accused of taking another man's yaks and selling them. They were missing. The village was upset. Jampa's aunt was not there. Eike was there. The man thought she was an apprentice and asked her what happened to the yaks. She did what she'd seen the aunt do: She sat down and took up her simple strand of prayer beads, the one with wood and a few turquoise pieces. After she went through the beads, she took up some pebbles, threw them in the air and caught them. Then, she told the man that the yaks were in the next valley near the river. The man gave her a kilo of dried apricots and left. A day later they sent word that she was right: The yaks had been found!"

"Oh my," said Jeri. "Do you really think she knew?"

"She was right. She was right. That's what's important about a seer, even a young one," said Dorje.

"It only makes more people want to talk to her. She looks so strange, they think she's half-goddess," Jampa said. "If they accept her, and she's right, then it's true."

"She's already helping with healing herbs," Dorje said. "She's made teas herself many times now for common things like headaches."

"Well, I didn't know. Maybe I should consult her!" Jeri laughed.

"Don't laugh," said Dorje. "She's known for healing a sick baby. Again, my aunt was not there, and the mother was frantic. The baby had diarrhea. Eike prepared a tea and chanted over the baby. She told the mother to use the tea every two hours. After a day, the baby was fine again."

"And that's a girl!" said Jampa. "Jeri, it's your girl. She's a baby shaman. Don't send her to America. She has powers."

Eike walked in, carrying a cup of tea for herself. She sat down with the nonchalance of a teenager groggy from sleep. Her hair was becoming a fountain of blond moss, like a portable rain forest.

"Well, Eike, we're talking about you." Jeri smiled.

"How so?"

"I just heard that you're acting as an oracle. And using healing herbs by yourself."

"Sometimes." She looked unconcerned.

"It's a gift." Jampa leaned over and stroked her hair.

"Do you worry about being wrong?" Jeri asked.

"Worry is not a good feeling. I have to trust my instincts. I'm getting trained."

"Isn't initiation a risky time?" Jeri said.

"It's a careful process."

"'Opening the energy channels,' it's called," added Dorje.

Jampa added: "When my aunt channels, she starts singing a particular song. It's a signal that her goddess has entered her. Her voice changes. She wears a special coat and wraps prayer flags on her head. She lights a butter lamp and consults a couple of round mirrors that are held in bowls full of grain. Her goddess enters her through the mirrors. Then, people talk to the goddess directly."

"I don't have a deity yet," said Eike. "One will have to find me."

"This practice is forbidden in Tibet now," said Dorje to Jeri.

"My only authority is Lama Yeshi," said Eike. "If he recognizes the deity, then I'll be an oracle. Right now I'm doing intuitive readings."

"Again, what could go wrong?" Jeri said.

Jampa could sense Jeri's worry. "Spirit possession. But a lama can help a protective god push out a bad one."

"But that can mean bad visions, voices, fainting, weakness, and even something that looks like madness and dying," added Dorje.

"Dorje!" Jampa put her hand on his arm.

"My training is meant to help me manage the experience of possession. Jeri, I'll go into trances to help people. Spirits are already visiting me. I must manage them."

"What do you mean 'visiting you'?"

"I have felt them around me for years. When I'm alone in the hills, they pull on my clothing and touch me. I have to be initiated to work for others. Lama Yeshi has already introduced his goddess. I see her in the mirror, and I see her mountain and her lake, which is near us."

"My aunt actually sees things in the lake," said Jampa.

"I haven't been to the lake yet," said Eike. "But I see it in the mirror. I'm lucky to be surrounded by people who understand my experiences. You're not going to think I'm sick or mad. That happens with other mediums, and no one knows what to do. I'll have to learn to master spirit possession."

"But you don't *have* to do it," Jeri said.

"I want to! It's an astonishing world. A powerful world. I could heal people and answer questions that they have about serious things. Jeri, we can't be afraid. You see the good that Lama Yeshi and Jampa's aunt do."

"So if we see you shaking and yawning and breathing fast and jumping around and talking funny, we'll hold onto Jeri," laughed Jampa.

Jeri sighed. "Ah. Teenagers."

Back IN KATHMANDU, Thomas spent more time in hotel bars than he had previously. He wanted to take his mind off Helen and his failure to connect with her. Bar people were familiar to him from Winthrop and other places he'd lived. They were comfortable starting conversations with strangers who preferred to chat in public places rather than sit in the silence of their homes.

He'd already met several people who were old hands at bars like the Funky Buddha. They had jobs in Kathmandu with companies that supported mountain climbers and trekkers, taking care of incoming shipments, customs clearances, transport logistics, cultural advice and visas. Some who frequented the bars were unhappy about being in Nepal, while others thought Nepal was a dream come true. That made a difference in how well they tolerated the many religious holidays, misunderstandings, requests for bribes, exotic diseases, and discomforts of a noisy bedroom with bugs and mice underfoot. Only a few were interested in the local culture.

Thomas often smoked a joint in his room to avoid attention in public. Then, he went to the bar.

"Anybody know about Tantrism?" he asked his temporary family.

"Is that sleeping with the dead?" a woman asked.

"No. No."

"It's fooling with crazy energies," another suggested.

When Thomas got up to find the restroom, he passed the end of the bar. Jack, the bartender, leaned into him. "There is a woman teaching it," he whispered.

"What?" Thomas blinked away the pot-induced fog in his mind. "How's that?"

"She's like a private tutor. You have to swear to keep this to yourself. I like you. I don't like everybody."

"Where do I find her?" Thomas was alert now. His back straightened.

"A Nepali I know can give me the name. I'll ask him for you."

The rest of the evening, Thomas was like a man about to bungee jump from a tall bridge. He tried to imagine himself taking a step to the brink, then recoiled, figuratively, then stepped forward and froze again. He could feel terror tightening every organ in his body. Like a demon-*kundalini*. *Maybe this anxiety is legitimate preparation*, he thought. *It was waking his corporeal energy like a coiled snake. Taking it for a little exercise. Shaking it loose. Testing the connectors. Like a jumper cable bringing a battery to life. The jolt. Only terror, not pleasure. Would it go away?*

Thomas needed to smoke another joint. He saluted his new friend and made sure he would be in the bar during the week. Back in his room Thomas searched a few books for details that now seemed more relevant.

***

Thomas returned to the bar early the following day and drank ginger ale to keep his head clear. Finally, Jack showed up for work. He offered to buy Thomas a drink.

"Did you get the name?" Thomas asked.

"Sure did. Vanaja. She's here in Thamel, near the Internet café and the Kathmandu Guest House. Here's the address."

"I just go there and see her?"

"Sure. There's a sign on the door—'Religious Studies.'"

"Is it safe? I won't get mugged?"

"No, no. Tourist central. Watch your wallet on the street. She's for real. My friend knows her."

"Thanks, man." Thomas was too distracted to chat long and left after an hour of small talk.

***

Thomas told one of the people at the meditation center, "I'm dreaming a lot."

"Good. Your mind is relaxing and letting the subconscious work."

"The dreams are not very relaxing."

"They're letting out stress. Do you feel calmer?"

"Sure. Although I smoke pot too."

"Ha! That's cheating." The guide laughed.

"I like to cheat."

"You might be right. Meditation can reduce your heart rate and breathing, too. Your cortisol can go down. Don't know what pot does, in comparison."

"It's only been a few weeks."

"Five hours can change your brain. Eleven can rewire it, Thomas."

"What? I'm just doing the relaxation thing, counting breaths."

"Even so. Three minutes of meditation change your electromagnetics, circulation, blood flow."

"All right, is this a big sell? I'm not paying much for these sessions," Thomas said.

"Eleven minutes to nerves and glandular system. Thirty to affect all the cells and rhythms of your body. Gray matter after sixty minutes."

"Please. We reach nirvana how soon?"

"Two and a half hours to sync with the magnetic field surrounding you, in a pattern with the surrounding universal mind."

"So why does anybody do it longer?"

"Monks mediate many hours a day. You're unhooking the chattering mind." The guide was earnest.

"I feel pretty unhooked already."

"It's an adventure you haven't had yet, Thomas. Sit."

Thomas smiled. He was thinking of his dog Sally.

Thomas skipped meditation and, instead, went for an early run. Even at sunrise, the streets were populated. Natives were used to seeing tourists who ran to stay in shape for their big climbs and treks. Some tourists were wearing skimpy running clothes, which would be low-class for a Hindu or Nepali.

At mid-morning Thomas walked fifteen minutes to the Thamel area, which was already crowded with tourists shopping and eating. He had avoided the clichéd Kathmandu Guest House, suspicious for its obvious reputation as the place to be since the 1970s. He was staying just north of the Tibet Hotel, which was popular with tour groups heading north.

The sign on the door at his destination said "Religious Studies, Healing Therapy." The street was not entirely commercial. There was a money-exchange kiosk, a clothing stall, an open-air tearoom, and a small grocery. It appeared that people lived over the shops in the second and third stories. The door was locked, so he knocked.

"In a minute!" a female voice shouted in English. The door opened, sending out the scent of Indian cooking spices. "Hello," a petite, dark woman said. She appeared to be in her late thirties, Indian, with dark eyebrows and long, black hair. She was skinny and had on a bright, patterned *kurta*, the long shirt worn over leggings. She had ornate earrings and many bangles, Indian-style.

"I am looking for Vanaja."

"That's me. Come in."

Vanaja and Thomas walked into a small front room that looked as if it had been decorated in the sixties. Richly colored, Indian bedspreads covered a soft, low couch and two chairs. Tibetan carpets staggered across the floor. There were a carved coffee table, posters of Tibetan art on the walls, and large pillows covered in bright cloth from all parts of India. A hookah sat on the coffee table beside a few tourist magazines. "What brings you here?"

"To Kathmandu?" Thomas had taken his shoes off at the door.

"Yes. And to my door."

"I brought my brother's ashes to be scattered here."

"Oh, I'm sorry."

"I've been here nearly two months."

"How do you like it?"

"Great. Rich."

"Yes. A lot of people can't leave. The visa limit is five months. But they look for ways around that."

"I guess."

"And to my door? Religious studies or therapy?"

"I am going to a meditation class. Reading about Buddhism. I heard you were a tutor in Tantrism."

"How much do you know about it?"

"I've read Alexandra David-Neel's stuff."

"And that isn't enough?"

"I'd like to know more about the practice, the experience. The metaphysical explanations don't really cover that."

"It's not just a matter of positions, you realize."

"Sure."

"You build up to them, spending years learning to control breathing and other systems in your body."

"I realize."

"Ultimately you're doing an advanced Buddhist meditation, with your bodily functions involved."

"I know. I would like to try it. A tourist version."

She laughed. "Do you have a partner?"

"No." He held back, waiting for her to offer any ideas.

"For you, is this about having sex?"

"No, no. I've read that the goal is not to have an orgasm. Or, at least, control it."

"Do you think you're going to get more intense pleasure?"

"No. I read that the goal is a perception of oneness. Bliss. Erasing the feeling of separation and ego."

"That's right. It's a religious experience. Not lust. But you just started meditating?"

"Just started. I know it's asking a lot." He tried to sound respectful.

"You know that being with a stranger sexually for money is considered prostitution."

"Yes, I know." It had not occurred to him.

"I'll show you, but show you as a religious mentor would show a novice. You'll have to do a lot of exercises before actual union is involved. Do you understand? Hours every day for a week."

"I'm willing to do that."

"I'll charge you $500 up front. Whether you complete the process depends on how much you prepare. First, we'll spend some hours meditating together. I make the call whether you're ready. And either way, I keep the money."

"I see. That's a lot." He thought: a month's expenses. The cost of a guided trek for a week.

"No more than you'd pay if I taught you to speak Nepali in a week."

"That's true. But I would have a contract for that."

"You're going to have to do it my way. This isn't America."

"You've been there? Your English is very good."

"I've been. I prefer to keep my personal life private. We have to meet as Buddhists. In training, it's a spiritual exercise. We keep your personal life private, too."

"I'm feeling gullible, just giving over money."

"You have to trust me. In the end, I have to trust you with my body. And you have to let go of your conventions regarding women here."

"I can see that."

"Why don't you think about it? Come by tomorrow at the same time and tell me. Please don't pass my name around. You can imagine the kind of tourists I could attract. I have to judge people carefully myself. I accept very few people." She leaned over and put a hand on his knee. "If you just need a friend, or you just need something to do in Kathmandu, drop it. We should each meditate on the other, to be sure."

"I will. I will. I'll come back tomorrow, either way. Thanks."

They both got up. She put her hands together in a *Namaste* gesture.

"You know what this means?" She looked at her hands.

"Hello and goodbye?"

"It's the soul in me acknowledging the soul in you."

"I didn't know that."

They walked to the door where he put his feet in his shoes.

"Remember, hours every day for a week. Serious." She laughed.

"Americans like working out. Did you know?" He smiled back.

"Yes, I know. Bye." She closed the door.

He was on the street, dazed by the strangeness of the past half hour. He wasn't sure what to do except start walking through Thamel. Natives were doubled up on motorbikes, bicycles slowly weaving through the foot traffic, people carrying buckets, young whites and Japanese wearing fancy, small backpacks and down vests or jackets. It was hard to think. He'd forgotten to tell Vanaja he smoked pot. Would that get in the way? He didn't think so. What got in the way was doubt about a secret pact with quite a bit of money tied up in it. Did he have that much money? He needed to eat and nap. Finally, he decided one small thing: to turn in the direction of his hotel and go to his room and stare at the walls for a bit.

***

Thomas made sure he did not skip the meditation class. Ironically, he wanted to think about his dilemma, but not-thinking might work even better. For once, he shut out his awareness of others in the class. If he was really interested in spiritual insights, he needed to transcend the petty curiosity he felt about others. His head was spinning. *Was he about to do something wrong? Was he about to do something daring and spiritual? What would others think? What did he think? Did he care?*

Thomas took refuge in repeating the beginner's mantra he had been given, So Hum (I Am That/the divine), because simply not-thinking was impossible. The mantra synchronized his breathing and easily became rhythmic. When the hour of meditation was over, the leader engaged the class in a common chant. Thomas was relieved to feel calmer. To keep his mind from new digressions, he left the meditation room without speaking to anyone.

He made his way to a bank and took out a cash loan of $500 against his credit card. The financial transaction was large, even for a tourist. It took an hour for the money to clear.

Then, he slowly walked to Thamel again, this time aware of inhaling cool air and focusing on smells instead of people. That was an impulse he had, believing it would be the start of controlling sensations and reactions. The door at "Religious Studies" was unlocked.

He pushed it open. "Hello? Vanaja?"

"Come in." She was sitting on the couch writing in a notebook. "Come in and sit. How are you?"

"All right, I guess. Not too clear in my mind." He took off his shoes and swung himself into a low chair with wooden arms.

"Understandable. You're breaking rules." Vanaja smiled.

"I guess you're right."

"Not comfortable? I don't know you very well, so I can't tell."

"What makes it easy for you to break rules? Isn't this a secret even among Buddhists?"

"We're not talking about me. All you know is the sign says 'Religious Studies and Healing Therapy.'" She said.

"What're we healing?"

"Your soul. Is that enough?" She laughed and slapped his arm playfully.

"How do I know my soul is sick?"

"All souls are sick. Out of balance. Stuck in a feeling of separation from the world. Ego."

"Nobody's in good shape, then?"

"Some people are in better shape than others. But we try to realize the unity if we can. When we're reborn, we start from where we left off and try to evolve to a higher state of insight."

He looked at his feet.

"Do you want the tourist version, then?" she asked.

"Yes. Sounds good."

"Are you sure?"

"No, but it's hard to be sure about anything."

"Think of it as a meditation course. Three hours a day. We can both back out of the final experiment."

"True. True. Tell me what I need to do." He leaned over and handed her the envelope of cash.

"Starting today, your homework is to concentrate on your breath. Just be aware of every breath. What moves, what doesn't move. What it feels like to change the tempo. Register every sensation you can. Like a scientist, you're observing and manipulating your own breath. That's all. You don't have to take notes. You don't have to explain to me what happened. The goal is awareness. Your own. Check in tomorrow. Three hours. I mean it."

"Okay." He thought about smoking pot and decided his mind's natural state was already in a mild high. But he would smoke anyway. It usually intensified his intuitive mind. He got up, put palms together, and put on his shoes. This time the walk back to the hotel was normal. He had an assignment. The endgame was far away and could be cancelled. He would trust his guide.

***

On the sixth day, Thomas was clear that he wanted to experience the physical union with Vanaja. His body awareness had become so well-tuned that he thought of his breathing even while sitting in a bar. As he walked the streets, he would stop to sit and check his physical state. Vanaja had joked that he was becoming attuned to nature, only nature in the form of his own body instead of mountains and waterfalls. He was sleeping soundly. He could differentiate his awareness without pot and with it. He still preferred the stimulated version, because pot made him turn inward and intensified his sensitivity to his body.

"You're mastering your physicality, Tourist Version. There are a number of active energies in you at any time, and you have learned to parse them and redirect them a little. Our goal is to negate the difference between us. There's no subject and object. We'll try to feel suspended in time. There's no orgasm."

"No orgasm?"

"Anything you've gotten from the *Kama Sutra* is moot. This isn't about enhancing pleasure. This is about experiencing the divine, through the energies in your body."

"Why do people talk about Tantric sex as the ultimate orgasm?"

"Because they misunderstand it. Did you misunderstand?"

"No." But he had. Earlier. Now he was even more curious about the experience.

"It will be about breath, heartbeat, body heat, muscle tension and sexual response. All together."

"I thought semen was an important element."

"It's symbolic. Your essence and mine. They're metaphors. Hate to disappoint you."

"What if I can't control it?"

"You fail, Tourist Version. The point is we each echo the other's life forces and synchronize to a point of intensity that makes us forget time and separation."

"Life forces?"

"All of them, on both sides. My female energies and your male energies together. That's why you need a consort."

"Ah."

"Don't ponder it long. Today, we sit together and meditate, using all the channels you have developed, adding sexual response but without skin contact. You understand?"

"Ah."

"Sit back on the couch here and get very comfortable. I will sit on you, facing you."

Thomas awkwardly stood up from the chair and moved to the sofa. It was a novel interaction. Approaches to sex for him were usually a matter of swooning with lust and letting it carry him to greater arousal. It was hard to hold back sexual anticipation or even suppress it. He thought of Helen, how he'd looked at her and wanted to touch her, kiss her. That was suppression. Now he was aware of finer dynamics: the tension in his feet, the heavy feeling in his belly, the waking of his penis, his faster breath, heat around his ears, tingling up the back of his neck. If anything, he had discovered more of his own erogenous zones.

"Take off anything metal and put it to the side, away from us. You can put it out of sight, under that pillow." He took off his belt and put his wallet and belt under the pillow.

Vanaja was wearing a pale-blue *shalwar kameez*, a long cotton shirt and wide cotton pants. She moved toward him, facing him, leaned in with one hand on the couch near his shoulder, put one knee next to his hips and eased herself onto his lap. It was the closest contact they'd had. He could smell a light Western floral essence, probably from shampoo, not the heavy Indian scents he knew from the streets. Her black hair glistened down her back. She put her hands lightly on his chest. He immediately became aroused and felt ashamed to respond so automatically.

"Concentrate on your breathing first. We'll be breathing slowly and synchronizing for at least half an hour. Try not to feel emotions. Breathe. Only." She took his hands and placed them on her diaphragm. He was now conscious of her breasts but shifted his attention back to his hands.

"Your breathing and mine. Only."

They sat silent. He got used to her scent. It was hard to forget the gentleness of her hands on his chest, which did not move. Gradually, they slowed their breathing and tried to have the same rhythm.

"Now hearts." She moved his hands to her chest and placed both of hers over his heart. Again, they sat long while sensing heartbeats that gradually also calmed down. He could not tell if they were in sync. But there was a kind of feedback loop that might have influenced his pace.

"Now heat." She took his hands and placed them on her lower neck. He could feel her skin now, cool and moist. He could also feel her hands on his neck, like a healer's touch, not resting fully but hovering lightly.

"Now sexual energy. Think about my body and let yours respond, slowly. Think about where and what is responding. Savor the energy. Keep in mind your breath, and heart, and heat. Have it rise up your spine, not down. Not your penis. Go out the top of your head." She moved his hands to her breasts. She put her own hands flat against his lower belly, in front of her pubic bone.

He pictured her naked and tried to imagine her breasts. They were soft masses, not shielded by a bra. He wasn't sure he was allowed to move his hands so he kept them still, pressing against her slightly. At this point, he found it nearly impossible to sit still and not move his hips up or touch her urgently all over.

"Energy. Let it move inside you and up out the top of your head." She was looking him in the eyes intently, trying to help him register control and direction. He felt his whole body engorging with lust, like a leech blowing up and ready to explode. He lost any awareness of her actions except for her eyes calmly directing him to concentrate and control himself.

"I can't," he whispered.

"You can," she whispered back. "Release it up."

After what seemed like an endless dream, his lust eased like a fever tapering off. He could see her again and feel his breathing. His body was sore from the long-fixed position. She held his shoulders and moved off his lap. They both stretched to give their muscles relief. He felt tremendously sleepy, as if he'd had sex. His penis was back asleep.

Vanaja moved to the chair and sat down. "Do you need to sleep?"

"No," he said, groggily. He stood up slowly. He walked around the room, looking at the posters to diffuse the physical intimacy between them and get his circulation going.

"Come back tomorrow. After your three hours."

"Okay." He looked at her, acknowledging the invitation. He tried not to smile. Not friends. Not girlfriend. Not intercourse. But very interesting.

"You'll sleep well. Don't stimulate your body. You know?"

"Yeah. Thanks." He retrieved his belt and wallet from under the pillow. "See you tomorrow." He gestured good-bye. She was calm and looked concerned as she tried to read him.

As Thomas walked back to his hotel, he tried to sense whether anything was different, besides his fatigue. *Were colors brighter?* He did feel calm, as if he'd accomplished a long run and triggered masses of endorphins. He decided not to go to the bar that evening. And smoke no pot. He would not have another shot at this. He had to treat it with at least the same respect as a triathlon.

He wondered about Vanaja. Everything had seemed to be about him, but then, he was the novice being led. He had nonstop curiosity about her. *Was she Hindu? Buddhist? Nepali? Indian? She seemed very comfortable with American slang. Who else was seeing her? She was a younger woman he might meet anywhere. But she was a therapist. You didn't usually know what your therapist had for breakfast. What they did at night.* Just because there was a sexual dimension, she became a woman and a potential friend and partner. He was sure she was not going to cancel on him at this point. She'd acted like a therapist the whole time, not a local, desperate for an income. She'd persuaded him to meditate every day as if it were normal for him.

***

153

Thomas arrived on time. The door was unlocked. He pushed it open and called out. He was feeling fresh, rested, eager. *Let the adventure begin.* The feeling reminded him of the first times he'd visited Caroline: anticipation, happiness, energy.

"Hello, Thomas." Vanaja came in from the hall. She was wearing a long kimono, which was odd now that he had gotten used to seeing saris and *shalwar kameez* everywhere. The kimono was Japanese style—light-green cotton with white cranes. "Would you like some water or a *lassi?*"

"*Lassi* sounds great."

"I'll just get you one." She left the room as he removed his sandals and sat in one of the armchairs. His mind flashed back to the previous day. The intensity, the tension. His body tensed up at the thought of the challenge. It was as if he were anticipating a long run, projecting the discipline to embark, to start, remembering the feeling he would have when he got into the run and forgot time, distance, even temperature. The feelings he would have when the run became difficult and he would force his mind to suppress discomfort and doubt about his ability to finish. His determination to continue, persevere. Was there a warm-up exercise for tantric sex?

Vanaja brought him the cool, mango *lassi,* and he drank it slowly, as if it were fuel rather than food. She sat in the other armchair.

"How are you feeling today?"

"Rested. Fine."

"We're going to do the same things today, but without clothes."

"That's not easy. Given yesterday, I mean."

"I know. It will be very slow." She got up and took the glass from him, carried it down the hall, and came back immediately. "If you want to stop, just say 'stop.' Okay?"

"Why?"

"Your body might tell you something's wrong. Your heart, for example."

"Heart's good. I understand."

"Remember the point is a higher consciousness. Think about energy hovering over your head, and think about our energy hovering over us together. We're both on the journey."

"Yes."

"Together. Neither is an instrument for the other."

"Yes."

"Take your clothes off when you're ready. You can put them on the chair." She picked up a dark blue woven cotton throw from her chair and draped it over the center of the couch. "You can sit here like yesterday."

Unlike kicking off for a long run, this was awkward. He was self-conscious. They were strangers. She was not a female doctor wearing a white coat. They were not drunk with lust. She stood, waiting. He unbuttoned his cotton shirt and folded it neatly. Then he unbuckled his belt and dropped his khaki shorts. He had a lean, tall body, with little chest hair. He and Paul had different body types. His brown hair was long now that he'd been in Kathmandu more than a month. Without his shirt, his hairy head with a beard looked too large. His hands looked giant and rough next to the soft, smooth skin of his chest. He was wearing navy boxers. He turned away from her while he dropped those and added them to the neat pile on the chair. Then, he moved to the couch and sat in position. He avoided looking her in the eyes, which he would do if this were a seduction.

Vanaja pushed the kimono away from her hips and climbed onto his lap. Without layers of cloth to soften them, his long lean legs were hard and bony. When she moved the kimono aside to sit on him, he saw she had inserted a female condom. He had seen one before, but not often. Its latex circle dropped below her vagina. He wondered how other men might react. He was still looking down when she sat back and removed the kimono from her shoulders. Her breasts were nicely rounded and full. Not exaggerated like those on erotic Indian statues, but normal and arousing. His automatic response was taking hold. He could feel her skin against him. Control was going to be impossible.

She put her hands on his cheeks. "Breathe. Deep slow breaths. Look up." Then, she took his hands and put them on her diaphragm again, and put her hands on his bare chest. He could feel his erection pushing against her leg. He could feel his body tense up and swell with lust.

"Breathe."

He felt as if he had been brought to a simmer and left on the stove.

Every ten minutes or so she escalated the contact.

"Breathe." He almost laughed but stopped himself. Stopped himself from moving. Took slow breaths. By now, he could redirect his focus. It was magical to separate from his body like that. It was a struggle to pull back from thinking about the sensations of their sexual contact. His mind went back and forth from "don't move" to "breathe."

After another long adjustment to being coupled, she coached him through different functions. He had to suppress the urge to touch and kiss. Therapist. Stranger. Beauty and softness. Temptation only intensified his desire.

When they moved to focus on body heat, he was trembling with arousal. His rough hands on her delicate skin were unsteady. He could not feel heat on her skin. He could feel heat all over himself. He felt flushed. He tried to feel whether she was flushed, but he had lost sensation in his hands.

After a long adjustment again, she finally said: "Sexual energy." His mind obeyed, and now he could dwell on the infusion of electricity from toe to head. He was shaking with tension. "Top of your head. Together, over our heads. We're together." She was looking at him eye-to-eye, trying to pull him into controlled focus.

He lost it. His body convulsed into an obvious orgasm. He stopped, his head against her shoulder.

"I am so sorry."

"I know you tried."

"I failed." He pulled back from their near embrace.

"It's okay, Tourist Version. You tried, honestly. Real yogis need a few lifetimes of practice."

He closed his eyes, disappointed and ashamed. *He'd failed the race. The triathlon. Never made it to the finish. Wouldn't know what the finish looked like.*

"Did you get close to something new, spiritually speaking?"

"Yes. Yes, I did."

"Well, that's it. A training run." She moved off him and quickly pulled on the kimono while he got up.

"Thanks. Thanks for giving me the chance."

She stood, tying the kimono. "You're welcome. You should keep doing the meditations by yourself. For years."

"Ah. I will think about that."

"Take sex out of the picture."

"No fun. But I get it."

He straightened up and looked at her, this time to remember. Her long, black hair flowing down her back, stark against the pale, green-and-white cotton kimono. She had brown eyes. Her hands were folded in front. He thought of their insane gentleness.

"Bye. Good trip back."

"Thanks. I really appreciate it." He didn't know whether he should kiss her and remembered the *Namaste* just in time. She gestured back, slowly, leaning down Japanese style, as a deep honorific.

***

Thomas stopped at the bar for a beer and something to eat. He slinked into a chair as if he'd done something forbidden and didn't want to talk about it—a crime, a love affair. In it, there was shame and secret pleasure. He had both the urge to talk out his mixed emotions with a friend or even a stranger, and the strong sense that they were taboo to admit under any circumstances.

Most people would hate him if they knew about his mixed emotions. You couldn't trust people to think as you did. He knew that from pot. Many years in the marijuana business had trained him to keep secrets. He'd learned to bury the urge to talk about what was really on his mind. He laughed to himself: the mix of "high" and "low"; the parallel universe of sitting here appearing respectable and at the same time hiding a possible sin. The mix of external control and internal impulse he'd experienced was like a combination of lust and spiritual journey. She was right: he was a tourist.

Hadn't he read that Tantra was about breaking ordinary conventions, breaking taboos, in order to transcend them and see them as silly? Kathmandu was a strange land, and he was doing the best he could to explore it and stay out of trouble. He was not going to give in to the myths of respectability, however. *Being respectable is not a sufficient agenda. We're all sinners,* he thought. *Just like Vanaja said, all souls are sick. We wouldn't be here if we didn't have something to work on.*

He wondered what Paul's secrets had been. *Did Paul have transgressions? How bad were they?*

"CLARA, LET'S HAVE A PARTY for the girl." Livia was chopping fresh vegetables for a giant pot of soup. She was rocking her Alaskan *ulu* knife vigorously over a pile of onion. Arranged on the counter were matching plastic bowls, with beets, cabbage, carrots, white beans, chopped chicken, chopped sausage, and potatoes. She was hypnotized by the rhythm of the knife.

"Well, of course! What an utterly stirring idea!" Clara exclaimed by pulling her shoulders up and clasping her hands, which made for horrible napping for Bill in the sling. He woke up from his hammock-under-the-arm and climbed onto Clara's shoulder. It was afternoon, and she was sitting at the table in the kitchen drinking tea, a time when Bill usually took a long, warm respite, with a little sun shining in through the window on both of them.

"An Easter feast. We must introduce her to her roots." The imagined Eike was starting to take on a reality for Livia even though she hadn't even seen a photo yet. Her intuition was in high gear, and she was starting to feel a passionate attachment to the girl. Possibly, she'd been drunk on grief, and now she was ready to be drunk on love.

"You don't think this is jumping the gun, as Thomas put it?"

"Oh, let's jump. I feel pretty sure it's okay to jump, don't you?" Livia said.

"Yes. Life is short. " Clara could hear Livia coming out of a long fog of gloom.

"We'll do our traditional cakes. Herring. Dyed eggs. Beet salad. Chocolate. Champagne." The foods were familiar, old-country and traditional in the family. They brought back memories of what had been lost.

"The sweet yeast-cake with the cross on top, the *pashka*, a German layered cake, the American coffee-cloud sponge cake." Clara nearly sang the words as a refrain in a favorite opera.

"Clara, you get out the recipes and start a shopping list. We can divide the shopping."

They were completely unified, joined in their wish to recreate the part of their youth that was delightful, rich, and childishly oblivious.

"I want to make the cakes," Clara said. "You do the other food."

"Fine." Livia knew she was better at cakes, but it didn't matter. It was all going to be good and fun.

"Let's invite Nancy and Victor. We'll need extra power to reach our little Eike, don't you think?"

Livia heard the phrase "our little Eike" and didn't mind. She and Clara both needed all the happiness they could muster. Finally, they could share. Old grudges were so stale. Companionship so rare. They were together in their final struggle for dignity in the face of aging. "For sure. In fact, we could use Phil. And Alice too. Let's ask Michaela to come and help with the table and serving, don't you think?"

"Okay. You make some calls," Clara said. By now, Bill was hanging on through serious jostling. "We have a few weeks."

She quickly found three of the most important recipes: a beet salad, a sweet cream dessert, and sweet Easter bread. They sat making a grocery list as if plotting a sacrament.

***

There was a flurry of activity over the next two weeks. Michaela, the cleaning woman, came to help shop, clean, and prepare. Livia and Clara dyed boiled eggs and set up the dining room. They bought flowers and cut flowers from the garden. They planned their clothes. It was their favorite annual ritual. Each of them did part of the kabuki.

160

They worked well in tandem. One cooked potatoes, while the other gathered the other vegetables. One diced vegetables while the other prepared dressing. Clara manned the Kitchen Aid mixer, while Livia delivered to her, on call, dry cottage cheese, butter, sour cream, sugar, eggs, vanilla, and whipping cream. Livia put together a wooden mold and pressed the mixture into it so that the sign of the cross would appear on the sides when the mixture was taken out. Then, they put the ingredients for the Easter bread into the mixer. That was an ancient ritual, a kitchen dance, repeated for centuries. They watched the dough rise in a coffee can lined with wax paper to create a tower. The finale was to take the coffee can out of the oven and see that the dough had indeed risen over five inches, and the cross made of dough on top was more visible after it had baked brown.

On Easter, Livia and Clara got up early and greeted Michaela. Nearly all of the foods would be served cold and had been prepared the previous day. Flowers were in vases. Bill wore a tiny yellow vest with turquoise accents. He actually seemed to like wearing special clothes. Livia put on her pink silk shirt, a long multi-colored beaded necklace and a lavender scarf. Around her neck she put a special leather strand holding a large, Maori greenstone *tiki* that had particularly strong energy. Among her Sedona clothes, Clara found a green-and-purple kaftan, which she wore with a dramatic, rare, watermelon-tourmaline bead necklace.

The guests arrived about eleven in the morning and had coffee while the Livia and Clara explained Thomas' travels in Nepal and the history of the people he was seeing there. They had no photographs except a few pictures copied from library books: a Tibetan shaman, the Dalai Lama, monks in Tibet, pictures of Kathmandu.

Nancy, Victor, Alice, and Phil were part of an informal club that experimented with spiritual communications and readings. Nancy channeled a spirit guide and had published a book on the topic. Clients paid Victor to do psychic readings for them and gave him more business than he could handle. Alice communicated with departed loved ones and had written a book on the subject. Phil used his intuition to help people with business and personal plans.

Of course, the informal club members liked a day off, a holiday gathering and the adventure of this meal. Victor wore a fine dark-gray felt hat, a light gray wool suit with a dark shirt and a gray tie. Phil was more comfortable in his usual scruffy dress and came in khakis and a teddy-bear sweater with a pattern of gray lines on dark green. Nancy was used to dressing for crowds and wore a flowing, light-blue pantsuit with a colorful, pink-and-purple blouse. She wore no jewelry as it interfered with spiritual communications and energy flow. Alice liked to wear long vintage Victorian dresses on appropriate occasions, and a Victorian dress was certainly a good choice for this celebration. Serving tea, she would have looked good next to the Mad Hatter.

"Let me explain the foods," Livia said. "The columnar risen bread and the pashka are Orthodox Russian traditions. They have crosses and celebrate the resurrection of Christ. We like the symbolism, regardless. Rising is always good. The other foods, including the Easter eggs, are chosen from Lithuanian traditions. Don't eat anything just to be polite. And save room for cakes. There will be take-home cakes, for sure. We just must indulge to celebrate properly. Please do your part."

"We're so glad to have you," added Clara. "Please leave this chair for our new granddaughter Eike. This is kind of a resurrection for our family." The seven of them seated themselves at the round table, with the eighth chair empty. Bill stationed himself on Clara's shoulders. "Let's first bless our gathering and issue an invitation." They joined hands around the table. Several candles were lit. Flames are sensitive to drafts and thus good signals of spirit-visitors.

"A minute or two to energize ourselves." Livia bowed her head and squeezed a hand of Alice on her right and, across the empty chair, Clara's hand on her left. The sun shone through the large window, which looked out on a giant, flowing birch tree, bird feeders, spring-green grass, and budding bushes in the yard. They paused to sense each of the others, mentally absorbing the personality and presence of each person. They tried to transmit good feelings and communion. This was not hard since they normally enjoyed each other's company with little friction.

"Now I would like us all to call Eike in Nepal, and invite her to join us. She is a serious young woman with long blond hair, possibly sleeping right now, possibly meditating, or possibly in a trance and traveling in the spirit world. We ask Eike to join us here, to meet her grandmother, her great aunt, and our powerful kind friends. Eike, come see us. We love you. Come see us." Livia paused. For several minutes, the friends around the table concentrated on picturing Eike, and each called to her. Some of them knew Eike might not join them soon, if at all, and would take coaxing. After a few minutes, Livia said, "Eike, come and join us. We have a meal for you from your family past. Please come."

They looked toward the empty chair to see if they could perceive a spirit presence there. "Well, let's eat this good food." Livia reluctantly let go of the hands she was holding and looked up. They passed the dishes around.

Victor passed the herring. "You know, I read that advanced yogis can project ectoplasm across long distances. Like a second body that materializes in a different place."

"I'm not sure she's that kind of holy person," said Livia.

"I think yogis have to initiate the transport," said Phil.

"But we invite people from the afterworld all the time, Phil," Livia said. "We pull them to us. They have to agree, of course," said Alice.

"Ah. So much seems possible."

Clara and Livia put token amounts of each traditional food on the plate for Eike. They poured champagne for everyone and started to eat, talk, and enjoy a relaxed Easter meal. The colored Easter eggs were subjected to a tradition common in Lithuania and Greece, that came from possibly common ancient Indo-

European roots: striking the smaller tip of an egg against another to see which one would break. The winner would go on to strike another egg and so on, making for new winners. The eggs were yellow, green, blue, red and purple. There was no predicting a winner. It was a playful lottery, celebrating the randomness of luck.

"I bet they don't get herring in Nepal," said Victor. "What do they eat there?"

"I think their festive food is something like beef dumplings," Livia said. "It may be like our *kuldunai*, I think: ground beef and spices wrapped in dough and then boiled. We should make some soon. We should look up an authentic recipe."

"The beet salad is totally eastern European," said Clara. "You could make it anywhere you have beets and the other vegetables. Oh, except it needs good garlic pickles. I guess everybody doesn't have those. Do they have vinegar in Nepal?"

"Here's a toast to Eike," said Nancy, raising her glass. "She may not drink, but we can pretend this is mead or something ancient and Indo-European. Eike, Eike, here's to you." The celebrants around the table looked toward the chair, smiling and enjoying each other.

Suddenly, Bill screamed and jumped crudely, with harsh nails, from Clara's shoulder onto the sideboard that held the cakes. He bounced against the frosted, coffee cloud cake and then leaped down, ran to the drapes on the far end of the room, and jumped up them. Several people dropped their forks. Bill was staring at the empty chair or behind it. There happened to be a large mirror behind the chair. Most of the mirror was above the guests' seated level.

"Hello. Hello, Eike. Hello," said Alice, used to this scenario. "Tell us you're here. We're so glad to have you." They all stopped breathing and waited. Nothing. Bill was wide-mouthed and wide-eyed, clinging to the top of the drapes, staring in the direction of the mirror.

The flames of the candles swayed to one side, together, as if blown from the mirror.

"Ah, Eike. My dear." Livia faced the candles and didn't turn toward the chair. "Come and stay with us. We so want to be with you."

The others looked toward the mirror. Victor said he saw a cloud-like apparition but could not be sure.

"Well, let's enjoy ourselves," Livia said. "We're not expecting more than a visit."

They continued to eat, ignoring poor Bill. Clara left him alone, so as not to disturb any dynamics near her. He seemed out of harm's way, albeit in a state of panic.

They were nearly finished. A yellow egg had won the last round of striking. Livia placed it to one side in the near-empty bowl of eggs. The guests passed the last of the herring, beet salad and cheese.

"Livia." Phil looked at Livia. "Livia. Look at the yellow egg." The bowl was in front of him. The firm egg, having won out over the last egg to be eaten, now had a dent in the top. "I think Eike brought an egg to the party. And she holds the winner now."

The friends at the gathering leaned in to take a look. Phil picked up the egg and passed it around. They were pleased with themselves.

Victor set up a camera on a timer, and they posed around the table with the mirror behind Eike's place in the center.

Michaela got up and starting clearing away plates. She made several trips to the kitchen while everyone else continued with champagne and coffee. After Michaela had removed all of the lunch food and plates, she stood behind Clara. "Shall I take away Eike's plate?"

"Why yes," said Clara. "That's fine."

"Oh look," said Michaela, staring at the plate. She pointed at a long, blond hair that had fallen over the beet salad.

"Aha," said Clara. "What we have here?" She pointed at the hair, rather than touching it.

"Oh my goodness."

"Is that real? Touch it," said Victor.

Clara touched it. "Yes, it is." She was a little giddy.

"Now, that poses some interesting possibilities," Phil said. "You could do DNA on that, couldn't you? You might have a little piece of Eike right here." Phil leaned back in his chair, taking the role of lead analyst. "Didn't I tell you about ectoplasm?"

Livia teared up. "Oh my. Oh my." She wiped her eyes with the cloth napkin. She wasn't so jaded from psychic successes that this wasn't special.

The guests passed the plate around, putting it back at Eike's place at the table to savor the surprise.

Clara got up and coaxed Bill down from his perch and wiped the frosting off his little outfit. He was calmer now and glad to be in her protective arms again. She put on her sling and let him disappear into it.

Michaela went back to the kitchen for the coffee pot and refreshed cups at the table. She got out dessert plates and passed them to each guest. Then she got one cake at a time, brought it to her place at the table, and cut portions for those who wanted a sliver or more. That was a way of delighting in each cake, as a celebration of the effort involved, because some of them took hours and many steps to bake. It was a communion in the sharing of confections. The coffee cloud cake had a huge spot where Bill had smashed into it. Michaela saved the pashka, the triangle of cheesecake-like white mousse, for last.

"Who would like *pashka*?" she asked, looking down to carve off a spoon for them. "Wait! Look. Someone's taken a bite!" She pointed to one side with a dent.

"That was nowhere near where Bill went," Livia commented, quietly.

"No, definitely not," said Alice.

"It sure looks like a bite," said Victor.

"Well, I guess we are sharing this," Clara said with glee.

166

They each took a spoon, as if this were a routine ceremony.

***

Back in the mountains of Nepal, Eike woke from a deep sleep and pulled up her covers for a slow wakening. She'd had a vivid dream. A group of swans was feeding on the green shore of a lake. She'd been to a large lake near the national park and had seen swans there, so she recognized them. They appeared to have found food scattered on the shore and were eagerly nibbling it, strolling around comfortable as if no human or animal were in sight. They moved in the sunshine, pairing up to go after the same morsel, then strolling away. She could feel the breeze from the water. She was curious what they were eating and walked closer. Rather than scamper away, they raised their orange-marked beaks in unison to stare at her. They acted as if she, too, were a swan and were part of their family. Swans pair for life and are often joined by offspring from previous years, so a large companionable group is common. She reached out to touch a swan. It jabbed toward her hair and pulled gently, as if grooming her. She reached down to pick something up from the ground—a bizarre oversized yellow egg. It slipped from her hand. Suddenly, there was a scream outside her vision. She looked and saw a very small monkey, wearing a vest, holding tightly to the branches of a bush, glaring at her.

CLARA WAS TAKING DISHES out of the dishwasher.

"I'm a little worried about Thomas," said Livia, sipping her evening sherry at the breakfast table.

"Do you think he's in danger?"

"No. But he might be a little gullible." Livia pushed the things on the table back into their proper places.

"What could happen?"

"The wild mix of Kathmandu might have bad guys in it. Robbery. Extortion."

"He's not a young man, Livia."

"All the worse. They might think he has money because he's older. People are desperate when they're poor."

"Were we desperate?" Clara asked.

"Actually yes. Nicholas stole potatoes to feed us."

"But did he rob people? Hurt people?" Clara knew the answer but was making conversation.

"Never. But he would have, I think, if he'd had to do it to protect us," Livia said.

"Thomas is more likely to be conned than Paul would have been."

"He doesn't have a lot of money. Not much to lose."

"Sure. What if he gets sick? Some ungodly parasite or something?"

Livia knew Thomas lived outdoors and crawled under houses much of the time and was as hearty as a cedar tree. "He wouldn't be the first. I'm sure doctors have seen those things before. He has Jeri and Donald to watch over him."

"What if he takes up with some religious nut?"

"Clara!" laughed Livia. She was talking to a lady from Sedona. "You're related to a few religious nuts."

"Right. Did you read *The Razor's Edge*? The title refers to the annihilation of the ego in Buddhism. That annihilation is like riding on the edge of a razor. Violent metaphors. Picture Thomas playing with razors. Maybe picture him about forty years ago playing with razors."

Livia knew Clara was making fun of her motherly instincts.

Clara finished the dishes and sat down. "The only worry I have is that he might too much enjoy a place where he can smoke pot freely. I can see him getting lost in that idea."

"But he can do that here with his own stuff," said Livia.

Clara put her hand on Livia's. "I didn't realize we both knew about that."

"We apparently do. I'm proud that he can grow it himself."

"How did you find out?" Clara stood to put dry dishes away.

"His girlfriend Caroline and I were drinking alone once. We were talking about places to live, and specifically his barn. And you?"

Clara turned around. "He gave me a joint."

"Clara!"

"I was in the dumps. He came to visit in Sedona. He was being kind. Sharing."

"I see. And did you make a habit of it?"

"I would have, with a steady supply."

"So?"

"Medicinal. It's good for arthritis. It's good for the dumps of aging."

"I'm drinking sherry." Livia lifted her glass.

"To each his own."

"So we don't need to send the militia to Kathmandu just yet?" Livia asked.

"No, Livia. We can only hope for some good stories."

***

The two of them puttered around the kitchen making coffee. Livia was obviously still thinking about Thomas. "Clara, let's ask Victor to come by and give us a reading on these children."

"What a good idea. Let's have brunch. You call and ask him to come over next weekend." Clara looked around the room for her cookbooks. "I'll plan the food. We'll sweeten it for him with some good food. We should have Nancy over, too, for fun."

"I have to wonder what this child adds up to. Is survival our family legacy? Is it everyone's?" Livia wondered.

"You mean, as opposed to leaving something behind like a work of art or a building? What crass achievement do you have in mind?" Clara liked to goad her.

"Yes. What is lasting, with all these people scattered across the world, trying to find a place to live and do whatever is meaningful? Is there such a thing as a family legacy when we're basically a bunch of people with shared DNA but, sometimes, little else in common?"

Clara was already opening cookbooks and marking pages. "I guess if you think DNA carries with it some values and personality, then there's continuity, whether we know it or not. We can always leave cookbooks."

"I wonder if instinct drives us to identify with each other because of our DNA. Would Eike know me if she passed me on the street? Do we smell the same, somehow, or have the same expressions?" Livia said. She thought a lot about what all the survival was for.

"I've read that people find similar personalities repeated in the family after several generations, even when they don't know about the ancestor. There must be a common spirit—a spiritual family underneath it all."

"I would like to believe that."

Clara found her notepad and started to make lists for their lunch. Because Victor was Jewish, he especially liked whitefish salad and good pickles. She would get some sunflower-seed pumpernickel from the Swiss bakery and choice olives from the gourmet market. An imported Swiss Gruyere. Lapsang soochong tea for an exotic, but dark, complement to the heavy, thin bread. A fruit salad of mango, raspberries and blueberries, with tangy, but sweet, vanilla yoghurt as topping. A small Boston lettuce salad with vinegar and oil. For dessert, she would make small individual pots of crème brûlée.

***

Because Victor had emigrated from Europe too, Livia and Clara set the table with nice china. The table looked refined and colorful. The guests arrived around noon on Sunday.

"So what have you been up to, Victor?" Clara asked.

"Oh, I've had a few executives asking about business deals. A woman contemplating a divorce. A young woman desperate for love. A parent frustrated with her teenager. I'm pretty busy."

"And, Nancy, how's business?"

"Too much travel. I've had weeklong bookings at several spas. They're nice for me because I'm given free services. I had a fantastic massage and facial last week. The spas are odd settings for the types of serious questions I'm asked, though. Clashing experiences. You know, 'Let me indulge myself with hot water and hot rocks, but wait, why did my father cut me out of his will?' I'm not sure what my guide Cepheus thinks of my entertaining the rich. But it pays the bills. And some of my clients do navigate tough issues."

"Well, spa goers are just another audience," Clara said. "Maybe they concentrate better when they're on a retreat. Nothing wrong with that."

"Shall we do the reading before or after the meal?" Livia asked Victor.

"Before. I can't guarantee a clear mind after eating what I see on the table. Let's go to the porch."

The four of them, with Bill riding in his sling, moved to the porch and took favorite seats.

"Let's begin. I need a few minutes of quiet." Victor leaned back and closed his eyes. He knew they were going to talk about Paul. His face relaxed and softened. After turning their chairs to face Victor, the others settled calmly, looking down to privately summon their own guides to help.

Victor opened his eyes. "What do we want to know?" he asked.

"What's behind Paul and Eike?" Livia asked. "Did they know each other in a past life?"

After a pause, Victor spoke slowly as if information were coming to him across a noisy frontier. "Yes. They were lovers. He was a soldier in medieval Japan. They were very young and very much in love, but he loved battle more. He left her behind to seek personal adventure and personal glory. She was devastated. He never came back. She died pining for him, without a family."

The women raised their collective eyebrows. Clara spoke. "What's the meaning of this life, then, for their relationship?"

"It's punishment for him. He was denied joy and love, in the form of his child in this life. He abandoned her before, and this time she was taken away from him."

Livia's maternal protectiveness rose up. "He's still leaving women behind, I admit, but not Eike. He didn't know about her."

"That's right. The opportunity was taken away from him. And now in the afterlife he realizes that. Now, he himself regrets being left. He was intended to have love stolen from him this time."

"What about Eike and the rest of us?" Livia asked. "Are we close in some way?"

"Yes. She was the mother of Ona, your grandmother, the healer. Eike's still in your family circle, you see, although you may think she's too far away in this life. You have a relationship with her now, don't you?"

"Was anyone else close before? Who's repeating a close bond?"

"Yes. Thomas was Paul's father at one time. That's why, unconsciously, he doesn't mind taking care of things for Paul. He wants Paul to be set right and to do right for him. Also, Helen and Eike are repeating a bond. But in reverse roles. Eike was Helen's mother in one life. She died young. Helen did not experience her as a mother and felt little attachment. That theme might be playing itself out in this life, with Helen letting go of Eike and renouncing motherhood."

"Oh, dear," Livia said. "It sounds as if Eike suffered a lot of loss before. Cut off from love. But she does have those lovely grandparents."

"Yes. Because they are her actual loving father and mother, she's not as abandoned as you think. It's just that the family does not follow the traditional model."

Victor closed his eyes for a moment, signaling silence from them. Then, he opened them again. "There's more. Thomas and Helen have a connection. Unrequited love. They were like Romeo and Juliet, children in opposing families. They were taboo for each other. Kept apart their whole lives, but passionately aware of one another."

"Oh my," said Livia, wondering how that had played out between them in Nepal.

"Victor, do you see the four of us together in past lives?" Nancy asked.

"Actually I do. We were soldiers together. I see us wearing sandals. Armor-like suits on our bodies. Swords. All men. Sleeping around a fire. Eating. A pleasant camaraderie. Nothing terrible. A lot of fun." They laughed at the image of sweaty soldiers.

"Victor, what about Bill?" Clara asked.

"Bill has been your child many times, Clara. He likes being a child. That's why he came back as a monkey this time. He doesn't want to grow up." Everyone laughed. Bill was fast asleep in his sling.

"Oh good." Clara laughed. "This time I won't have to put him through college."

"On that note, let's eat!"

Three Mothers

SOMETIME AFTER THE REVELATIONS with Thomas, Jeri told Eike that Helen would be coming into Kathmandu. For Eike, it was welcome news. She'd been well-sheltered by three mothers. Jeri, Jampa, and Helen had all taken care of her in different ways. None had been harsh. She had no reason to believe it wasn't normal to be surrounded by caring women. When her Lama Yeshi initiated Eike, the care of her soul was transferred to him.

She'd had little experience by which to judge Helen. Jeri and Jampa were her warm mothers, and Helen was her cold mother. Most of her friends had one warm mother. She saw their attachment and loyalty to one mother and felt lucky to have several. Some of her friends had themselves become mothers and disappeared into kitchens and houses with babies strapped to their backs or hanging onto their legs.

She only vaguely remembered distress regarding Helen. She remembered running down the road as Helen walked away with very fast and efficient steps, carrying a cloth bundle and using a walking stick. Helen didn't look back. Eike ran after her crying, begging her to slow down. But Jampa, who had chased after Eike, stopped her, picked her up, and slowly walked back to the house, holding her close and soothing her.

In later memories, Helen was sitting and talking with Jeri and Donald in their living room or in the garden. Eike was not aware that Helen had arrived at the house because no one came to get her. When Helen saw Eike, she did not hug her. Helen leaned down to touch her arm or her hand but did not run to grab her up like Eike's friends' mothers did. Eike was not aware when Helen left because she simply disappeared. Helen did not like to be asked about her things. Helen did not like to be touched. The people who ran to lift and hug Eike were Jeri, Jampa, and Donald. They hugged her spontaneously many times a day.

Now that Eike was grown up, she was accustomed to Helen's coolness. She hadn't seen her in more than a year. They never talked about Eike's life or Helen's. Intimacy never became a habit. In fact, Jeri did not push them together. It was unusual for Jeri to tell Eike that Helen was coming.

"Has Helen met Thomas?" Eike asked Jeri when she heard about the American.

"Yes. He went to her monastery at least once."

"What did she think of that?" Eike was in her early-twenties and suddenly looking outside herself. It was strange to remember that Jeri was both her mother and Helen's. She'd never thought of the two of them that way. She and Helen shared a mother, like sisters a generation apart.

"I don't know. We'll have to ask her." Jeri responded quite naturally although Eike was breaking a subtle, long-standing taboo against talking about Helen. In shielding her from Helen's disinterest, Jeri and Donald had acted as if Helen did not exist for Eike. It might have been painful to them to think of Eike's distance from her own mother, and, they thought, potentially painful to Eike.

"And what do you think about Paul being my father?" Eike asked. Jeri flushed. Eike sensed that they'd protected her from any sense of rejection, but now she was old enough to control the conversation. "I would have liked to meet him. Did you know?"

"Know what?"

"Know about him?"

"We didn't know who your father was. Helen didn't want to tell us. She said he went away."

"Thomas said Paul never knew about me." Eike's voice was tense.

"That's what we heard."

"Paul might have wanted to see me."

"I imagine."

"He might have wanted to keep me."

"It's possible."

"But Helen didn't want to give him a chance to take me?"

"I guess," Jeri said. "I don't know."

"Do you think it was right?" Eike usually asked about Helen with detachment, forgetting that Jeri was talking about her own daughter and might not want to put Helen in a bad light.

"We'll never know what we all thought and felt at that time. If you have your own children, you might appreciate the dilemma Helen was in. Sometimes, we make decisions without knowing everything we wish we knew. Sometimes, you don't have time to think very long. It's natural to want to control the consequences of our decisions." Jeri stood up to walk around. "Helen was young. She might not have trusted Paul, or known him well enough to talk to him. Maybe she didn't want to know what he thought about a baby. He might have chosen to travel on, even knowing about you."

"True. I didn't think of that." Eike tried to imagine a young man walking away.

"We're all clouded by what we think we should think and do. We think 'Paul should have known.' 'Paul would have been a great father.' It could be that the best answer is 'We don't know.'"

"Did he ever marry?"

"No, he didn't. Thomas says he loved travel and his work and never settled into a family."

"You and Donald liked your travel and work, too."

"We did. And we loved Helen and you. Living here, we could have you and have our work, and stay in Nepal."

"Thomas said something about so many 'white nuns.'" Eike changed the subject. She rarely talked with Westerners to hear what made them curious. Unlike Helen, she was not around trekkers.

"What did he mean?" Jeri said.

"Western women, converted to Buddhism. Alexandra David-Neel, Helen, me, others."

"There are as many 'black Christian nuns,' Eike. Christians converted people all over the world and welcomed religious people from all cultures. It's gone both ways."

"True."

"Thomas was telling you something about his own experience," Jeri said. "He possibly hasn't known many women or men who fell in love with a different culture. Or a different religion. He's just discovered Buddhism himself."

"What's his religion?"

"I'm not sure. He seems thoughtful. He believes people should be able to smoke pot." Jeri laughed. "Does that count?"

"It doesn't."

"You'll have to ask."

***

Helen arrived at the house and settled into a guestroom.

Eike spent some time thinking about mothers and how they behaved. She realized she habitually treated Helen like a distant friend of the family rather than a mother. More precisely, she didn't treat her like her own mother. Now that Helen was a nun, she was honored and supported as a holy person in the community. Some Buddhist nuns had had families. *How did nuns with children behave?* Eike wondered.

Eike knew that Alexandra David-Neel had adopted a Buddhist monk as her son. She treated him like a fellow-traveler and an assistant, however. When she took him to Europe in her later years, he was miserable. Did she worry about his happiness? When she put her name on novels he wrote, was he truly ego-less? They shared a cause in common: the export of Buddhism, manuscripts, texts, concepts. Was that as good as love?

"Hello," Eike said as she entered Helen's room. "How are you?"

Helen stood up and turned toward her, surprised. She was even more surprised when Eike tried to hug her.

"Eike. Fine." Helen pulled back.

Eike could see her awkwardness. Eike had broken their habit of silent distance.

"I've learned about Paul."

Helen's face tensed up. "Yes. Well."

"Why didn't you tell him?" Eike decided to go with the theory that Paul was, in fact, her father.

"He was an unlikely father. A father by accident. I didn't think it would be good for you and me."

"People are not always the way you think. You didn't know." Eike was just beginning to think about the adults in her life as people. Flawed people.

"The one thing I did know was that I was not a willing mother. I'm sorry, Eike."

"I know. Not telling him did close off any relationship I could have had with him, though."

"I didn't want to bargain across the world."

"We are bargaining across the world now." Eike tried not to look defiant.

"I know. But you're an adult now. Not a child who can be torn apart."

"I realize."

"Look what a home Jeri and Donald have given you. You flourished without people fighting over you."

"Paul's family could have loved me, too." Eike abruptly turned and left the room.

Family

DORJE TOLD THOMAS that Eike was coming to Kathmandu and would stay with Jeri and Donald. Thomas said he would like to drop by, and Dorje said he would let them know. He wanted to take every opportunity to get to know her.

Dorje was Thomas' friend now and had sympathy for him. The last time Thomas saw Eike had been awkward. Taken by surprise, she'd given him the protective bracelet and treated him as she would a Western stranger or a client, not as an uncle with news of a father she'd never known. Thomas was worried that she was as cold as Helen, and he felt reluctant to impose on her again. He was glad for a second chance.

Jeri, Donald, and Eike greeted Thomas at the door. Surprisingly, Eike was wearing Western-style clothing: an orange shirt over pajama-style cotton pants and flip-flops. Dorje had told Thomas that Buddhist religious people wore mainly red, maroon, and yellow: the palette of saffron. Again, Thomas felt as if he were in a movie set, but the scene had changed. *Was this switch between lives easy for Eike,* he wondered, *or schizophrenic? With long, blond dreadlocks, she looked like an artist from Sedona. Doing performance art, perhaps. Light shows, somber music composed for Japanese Butoh in the background. Native American chanting.*

Again, he searched for Paul in her face and body. At the least, she had Paul's confidence and sense of purpose, which Thomas had always found irritating because he didn't share it.

"Thomas, how are you?" Jeri was playing hostess.

"I'm great." He shook hands with Donald and hugged Jeri. He wasn't sure about hugging Eike so he stepped back awkwardly.

"How's your mother? And Clara?" Jeri asked.

"They're very well. Healthy. Loving my stories."

"Dorje says you're staying another month."

"Yes. Living here sure is cheap. The only thing I've left behind is my dog, and she's in good hands." Thomas smiled to think of Sally.

"How are you passing the time?"

"Meditation class. Reading. Did Alexandra David-Neel, thanks to your suggestion."

"Oh great! Another fan, I hope," Jeri exclaimed.

"For sure. Just reading her is an adventure." Thomas looked at Eike's expression. She was quiet and pleasant.

"Donald and I have to meet with somebody for about half an hour," Jeri said. "Can we leave you two to talk, and then we'll have lunch?"

"Sure."

Jeri steered Thomas and Eike to the garden where they sat on teak armchairs. A servant brought them squash, a lime-and-seltzer drink that was another British legacy.

"Your great-grandmother was a medicine woman, you know," Thomas said to Eike. Somehow, knowing they shared genes gave him a sense of familiarity. They were insiders, yet he could not shake the feeling he was talking to someone in a movie. If she was dreamlike, did he seem the same way to her?

"How so?"

"She was a homeopath, treating people near her village in Lithuania. Nobody was licensed in those days, of course. She must have been self-taught. Actually, I don't know how she became one."

"The herbs must be the same all over the world although I don't know for sure. I never studied it really."

"I dabble in supplying the herb marijuana. Self-taught too!" Thomas laughed. "That's because it's illegal. People take it as medicine. Your great-grandmother was dealing medicine at the turn of the last century. She died when my mother was fairly young. My mother studied medicine, but she had to stop because of the war."

"What did she end up doing?"

"She became a librarian in America, eventually, after some years raising my brother—your father—and me. She wanted a quiet corner. Had enough drama during and after the war."

"When did she leave her home country?"

"Around 1943. The Nazis and the Russians invaded, in near sequence. All kinds of killing. Our family was at risk of being deported to the Gulag by the Russians. They would have died, for sure."

"So they emigrated?"

"In 1949. My father Nicholas took the family west and found work in construction. He got certified in architecture. Eventually, they were out of poverty."

"Where did you grow up?"

"Paul and I grew up in Seattle. A very nice city. Rolling hills bounded by the sea on one side and mountains on the other. You'd like it."

"I haven't travelled much."

"Did you ever want to?"

"No. Haven't thought about it."

"My mother was very disappointed that Paul and I didn't have families."

"Why not?"

"Hard to say. Paul was on the go."

"And you?" Eike was again assuming her adult mode, entertaining a stranger.

"I never met someone who stuck. Or stuck with me, I guess. Anyway, that's why my mother and Clara are excited about you. You're the end of the line. After all that displacement, the war, leaving people behind, losing family and country. You're a blessing. A reward."

"We make our families, I believe. Spirit can be stronger than blood."

"I never thought of it that way."

"We can be related in past lives. DNA is not everything. There's DNA, and there's spirit that may not be carried in linear generations." Eike did not know that Livia thought the same way.

"Still, I think Paul would have loved you. He was a warm person."

"You're guessing."

"Regardless of past lives, there's biological identity and human instinct," Thomas said. "I think those bonds are pretty strong. Most fathers fall in love with their children. Forever and deep."

"The relationship between Tibetan Buddhists and their lamas can be the strongest."

"I wouldn't know. Are you not allowing for family? Do you feel like you would do anything for Jeri and Donald?"

"I would, on many counts."

"Then, we have many bonds. We can cultivate bonds." Thomas thought of the irony of his own life: Most of his cultivation had focused on plants. He was pressuring her in a way that he would not pressure himself.

"I agree," Eike said.

"Here's something I brought that you might like." Thomas gave her the cap that Paul wore.

"It's not a cap I would wear."

"I know. But it's a piece of Paul. A piece that isn't in the form of ashes, anyway. He wore it on his fateful trip."

"I see."

"Here's a photo, too. That's my mother Livia, her sister Clara, and Bill, Clara's monkey."

Eike put her finger on Bill. "I've seen him." She laughed.

Before Thomas could ask her what she meant, Jeri and Donald came through the gate to the garden and invited them into the house for lunch.

"Thomas," Donald asked, "Have you looked at the *Tibetan Book of the Dead?*"

"No. Should I?"

"It describes the afterlife in the *bardo*, which is a kind of purgatory. I can lend you a copy." Eike gave Donald a warning look, but Donald did not see her signal. "It was very popular in the West after it was published in the 1920s by Evans-Wenz. People were interested in spiritualism after World War I. They wanted to know the fate of all those soldiers who died in the war."

"How does the book fit in with Buddhism?" Thomas asked. He thought the conversation was indirectly about Paul but wasn't sure.

"It's a mortuary text, read aloud in the presence of someone who's dying or just died. It describes the process of death and rebirth. *Bardo* means 'in-between state.' There are three states, starting with the moment of death."

Jeri added, "The Christian last rites prepare a person for death. Buddhists prepare the dying for rebirth."

"Do you think Paul's in the *bardo*?" Thomas asked. It hadn't occurred to him to worry about Paul's soul. Their childhood dynamics, their mutual past, occupied his mind.

"We don't know. It's likely. Sudden death."

"He can be helped along," Eike interjected. She was suddenly engaged in the conversation, looking at Thomas with sympathy for the first time. It was, he thought, her healer role that had kicked in, not the role of the child of the father.

"That's the *Chöd* ritual she's going to do," Donald explained. Jeri and Donald discussed a date for Dorje and Thomas to bring the ashes to Eike. It seemed like a momentous plan. Thomas felt aligned with Jeri and Donald and their family for the first time. They were all going to help release Paul from his life.

***

Mom, Clara –
You asked me what Eike actually does. She's a cross between a medium and a medicine woman. She works by becoming possessed by her patron deities or spirits. She goes into a trance to find out how to cure someone of

something, exorcise an evil spirit, or predict the future. The dangerous part is that the trance leaves her vulnerable to evil spirits and demons that might try to take possession of her and turn her to their purposes. She has entered the spiritual realm and has to operate there by its rules. Her own will is involved in choosing how to negotiate battles there.

I heard that she's served as an oracle of sorts, too. She can be the voice of a god, passing on blessings and advice. Shamans in her school of Buddhism—Bon shamans—are more skillful than nuns like Helen in dealing with demons that harm living beings or the spirits of the dead. Tibetans, similar to animists, think that every part of the environment is alive with sentient forces. Except they're not all good. They have to be pacified and respected. Bad spirits can cause leprosy, abscesses, consumption, ulcers, itches, sores and swelling of the limbs.

Eike's purpose is not final liberation or meditating "on behalf of living creatures." Her purpose is practical—healing by fighting demons and getting good forces to help, maintaining balance in this world of demons and spirits. She's supposed to care for the living and the dead, protecting their life forces, and to bring back the spirits of the dead.

She uses sound and incantations to go into a trance. The ritual is very noisy. There's a drum, and bells, and a horn made from a human femur, sometimes, although I didn't see her use one of those. She gets a spacey look in her eyes.

I think you've seen mediums channeling a certain spirit do the same thing. Except here, there are a lot of traditional costumes, smoke, drums, bells and special recitations. I bet the rituals here are noisier than your sessions!

Photos of the live action are forbidden because they interrupt the flow of energy and can jeopardize Eike's safety.

By the way, departed ones who appear in the dreams of their relatives are probably unhappy and calling for help. The lamas are called to quiet and comfort unhappy spirits.

Similar to your beliefs, the Tibetans think we each have a life force within our physical and mental constitution. It can depart the body and wander off, or get carried off, leaving the original person sick or unbalanced. There are rites to call the life force back into the body.

Hey, you two should talk to Eike. I will try to get her to call you.

Love, Thomas

Spirits

THOMAS RETURNED to his routine of going to meditation class
in the morning, having lunch, reading, and visiting the hotel bar
at night. In its furnishings and service, the bar catered to
travelers. It had enough space to accommodate about a dozen
people.

The bartender Jack spent much of his time at the bar. He
was an American in his twenties, a little heavy-set, but very
congenial. Perfect bar buddy. Thomas thought the bartender
might have had trouble with high-altitude and been forced to quit
rigorous work leading trekkers. He knew the guy had a brother
who was brokering craft exports to Chicago.

"So how did it go?" the bartender asked.

"Vanaja? Good." Thomas suddenly became shy.

"Did you get the experience you wanted?"

"I learned some meditation techniques." He tried to look
bored.

"Like what?"

"Can't say. It's holy. You know."

The bartender moved closer to him. "Like hitting on a
nun?"

"Actually, I *am* hitting on a nun." Thomas was drunk but
nevertheless tried to steer the talk away from his now-taboo
subject.

"You?" The guy looked him over to note his age.

"Why not?" Thomas gave him a wait-and-see-what-
happens-to-you look.

"How does that work?"

"You appeal to the woman inside."

"Oh. Sure. And how did you meet this nun?"

"She was my brother's lover. Long ago."

"So you're going after his ex, even though she's a nun? What does he think of that?"

"He's dead."

The bar started to fill up with people, interrupting the conversation with Jack. The jovial talk around him gave Thomas an empty feeling, as if he'd been left behind on a dock.

Jack came back. "Sorry, bro. What happened?"

"He drowned last summer."

"And the girl?"

"She's here." He thought of how far she was: the bus, the hike into the valley.

"So you like her?"

"I do. But she's not having any of it."

"What did she say?"

"Told me to get lost." Thomas pushed his empty glass forward.

"Do you think she'll confuse you with your brother?"

"Have some respect. She's committed to her religious practice."

"But you want what your brother had?"

"No. I don't think so." Thomas drank another beer and turned away. "I think I need to stop drinking for tonight. See you around."

"Yeah, see you."

Thomas stumbled out the door into drizzle. He tried to remember if he had a joint to smoke back in his room. Thinking about Paul and Helen together had pushed him over the edge. *Was he trying to be Paul? Going after Helen to punish her for cutting Paul off from his own child? Or was he trying to get what Paul had in Nepal—a lover, a partner, a companion? Or was he simply lonely and, therefore, found it easy to focus on Helen, one of the few women he'd met here?* In his mind, he'd put Vanaja into a secret envelope and tucked it in a fat book inside a deep box. He was sure that someone would think his relationship with her had been sinful. It was hard to sort out what he thought about it. The experience with Vanaja was a legitimate pursuit of advanced meditation, but he was a tourist. It was analogous to taking communion, as an atheist, to see what it was like and whether it had any interesting effects. Except the time with Vanaja was worse than any wafers he might have illegally tasted inside or outside of church. But didn't holy people want you to take communion?

***

In the bar, Thomas overheard two guides planning for a commercial trekking group that would be hiking from Pokhara and going past the hostel Helen managed. He asked the guides if he could join the tour, since it would last only a few days in the hills. Beds in hostels were hard to come by, but the guides had an extra space and took Thomas on. That gave him transport to Pokhara and access to guides, porter, room and food. Although Dorje had taken him there once, Thomas knew a lot of Dorje's arrangements in the near-wilderness had been invisible to him.

The trekkers left for Pokhara, spent a night, and a van dropped them at the trailhead. The ages and nationalities of the group were mixed. There were a few retired couples from the U.S., a woman from Germany, young people from New Zealand, and an older man from France or Switzerland. Porters carried the bulk of their belongings, leaving them with daypacks to manage on their own.

Thomas knew the first teahouse on the tour was next to Helen's monastery and arranged to stay there three nights while the group hiked farther into the mountains and returned.

Helen was not there when the group arrived around lunchtime. Thomas stayed on the patio, reading a book, while some of the trekkers took an optional afternoon side trip to a nearby waterfall. A few of them chose to stay at the hostel, as well, drinking lemon tea and basking in the sun. The morning hike had given them enough exercise.

Mid afternoon, Thomas spotted Helen heading to the kitchen. She was carrying a basket of herbs. Her short hair and dark saffron clothes set her apart from the locals who tended the hostel in fancy boots and clothes.

He tried to intercept her: "Helen!"

She turned, surprised. "Thomas. What are you doing here?"

"Joined this trek. To see you." He got up from the plastic chair. "Can you spend some time?" He'd approached many women in his life, but few who were busy nuns. Her appearance made her seem inaccessible. He'd already misread her badly on his last visit. The gift package. The question about Tantric sex. *Keep her speaking to me*, he thought.

She looked as if some emergency had grabbed her attention. "Barely. I don't really hang out. Maybe a cup of tea once the dinners are served." She was already turning away.

He knew that dinner was hours away. She'd put him off. "All right. Then. Tea. Thanks." He sat down, wondering whether her response was harsh or normal for her.

It was still bright daylight so he got his camera and took a walk down the path they'd come up, because he could judge distances and the time it would take him to get back.

***

His group of trekkers reconvened. They'd hung socks and towels on lines strung between poles in front of the rustic rooms facing the courtyard. They were asked to order food so that, after about an hour, the cook could supply what they wanted.

They ate dinner around a large, square wooden table surrounded by benches that filled the small room. Afterward, Thomas sat with his book. He hadn't seen Helen again. The kitchen was out of sight, and behind it were paths that led up to the actual monastery. The hostel was like a station right on the path. Trekkers passed its patio all day long. The private village and monastery, located up on a plateau, were nearly out of sight.

Finally, after most of the tourists had gone back to the patio to take pictures of the sunset or retire to rooms, Helen came out of the kitchen area.

"Hey," Thomas said. "You didn't forget."

"Of course not." She carried a tray with two lemon teas.

"Do you grow your own herbs?" he asked, thinking of his herb cultivation.

"Yes, we do. Some. Peppers, coriander. Onions. It's not easy to get water up here," she said. She sat down.

His only connection to her was Paul. "Paul carried a photo of you, you know."

"Oh?"

"Holding a yellow flower. I found it in with his things. The kind of things you keep to remember, you know." He wished he'd brought the photo. He hadn't imagined he would ever meet her. *A girl, in love. With long hair. Attractive.*

"Nice. But deep in the past, Thomas."

"I'm sorry about last time." He sipped his tea to pace his speech. "I guess I'm an idiot about your lifestyle."

"Understandable." She, too, sipped to leaven the awkward silence.

"I hope we can be friends," he said, looking up. "I hope you'll give me a chance to get to know you."

"Thomas, you're still misreading me. I don't hang out. I have few relationships outside my family and the monastery."

"Still. I'd like to leave on a better footing with you." He felt like putting a hand on her arm and resisted.

"It's not that important." She stood up, putting her half-full cup of tea on the tray and picking up the tray.

"I'm here for a few days. Another tea?" He pleaded. He was used to women brushing him off. He wasn't sure what the stakes were now, however. He watched her walk away as if she hadn't heard.

Back in his room, he lay down on the cot to read by a flashlight mounted on his head. *What was he after? Paul left her*

191

behind long ago. She kept a big secret from Paul. Was she going to give Thomas anything? Was he really after a sense of how Paul was in his young days, when Thomas didn't know him at all? Did he want her? How?

***

At breakfast Thomas looked toward the kitchen for any sign of Helen. There was none. His group was leaving for a night at another hostel higher in the valley. He had chosen to stay put and had two days to kill. He looked at the row of daypacks parked on a concrete wall, as the hikers got ready to depart.

He decided to hike halfway up with the trekkers and then return. That would occupy one day. He got his own gear ready and locked his room.

Later that afternoon, when he returned from his hike, he put his pack away and walked behind the hostel. Narrow paths and stone steps led up between concrete structures and wooden barns. Goats were sitting on hay, chewing as they looked out over the picturesque valley. Even the goats had a great view.

He saw the monastery, painted yellow and larger than the other structures. It was decorated with a stenciled line that outlined the wall and the door. In front, flags, mounted on tall vertical poles, beat in the wind. Only women and children were walking around neighboring houses. He went up the hill to the side of the structure, looking for gardens.

There, Helen was kneeling in a vegetable garden, gathering something into a basket.

When she saw Thomas, she again looked up as if some emergency had just come to her attention. She had an expression of concern, surprise, dismay and focus.

"Hello again," he said cheerfully, walking up to the fence by the garden.

"Yes," she said, sitting back on her heels.

"Tell me about the stuff you're growing."

"It's nothing special, Thomas. You've seen it before."

192

"Tell me, have you ever doubted your choice? I mean being a nun." He still didn't know what he wanted, but maybe some insight was a start.

"I don't really want to talk about my choice. What about yours?" She smiled with a touch of warmth.

"Which one?" he asked.

"Coming to Nepal. The ashes. Why?"

"For Paul, I guess. He never asked me for anything. In fact, he never showed much interest in me." Thomas was not used to talking about his feelings or about Paul.

"You're doing it out of love?"

"That wouldn't be my word." He shifted uncomfortably, looking up the valley toward the hills.

"Then service. Maybe. Taking care of somebody. What they need." She took up green branches of coriander and arranged them in her hands before placing them in the basket.

"I guess. One last thing Paul wanted from somebody. Maybe he wanted me to meet you," Thomas said in another attempt to draw her out. Flirting usually worked for him.

"No, Thomas. You just made that up." She laughed. "I have to go." She got up.

"Can I see you tonight again? Tea?"

"Tomorrow, after dinner." She spoke over her back again, as she had the day before.

"Sure," he said. Another day to wait. He would hike again. Clearly, she was not going to give him a lot.

***

It was pouring rain. Thomas felt sorry for his fellow trekkers who would be returning in rain. Wet boots, wet socks and wet rain jackets, if they had them, the chilly, cold water washing their faces. He knew the paths were mostly open to the sky. At this altitude, trees did not grow tall and offer shelter. His own plan for a jaunt up the hill was spoiled. He moved a chair under the awning in front of his room and read.

Other groups came through at lunchtime, and Thomas sat beside them for his lunch of lentils and rice, again. The hostel did not offer much variety because all the food had to be transported up the hills on the backs of porters. And Nepalis never tired of lentils and rice. He did not buy himself a can of soda. This hostel was one of the first on the long treks up the valley, so it could offer more luxuries and have the cans and bottles carried out.

Finally, the sun came out, and his group arrived. The hikers immediately took to their rooms to unpack and find dry clothes. The patio was covered with wet clothes on lines and wet boots optimistically placed in areas of sunshine.

He was eager for his last chance with Helen, at least, as far as he knew on this trip. He had started to imagine her in Western clothes. She had the confidence of Clara and Livia. She could run a temple in America: a room full of Buddha statues, oil lamps or candles, flags all around, the sound of chanting monks piped in for atmosphere. He knew the cliché. There, she would drive a car. What kind? Maybe a modest Honda Civic. Beaten up. Big enough to carry herbs and vegetables in the back, which she would transport from her garden to the temple kitchen.

After dinner he stayed in the dining room again, watching for her. The dining table was nearly bare of tourists when she finally walked in from the kitchen.

"Hey. Thanks for coming." He tried to stand up from the bench, but the table held him down.

"Your tea," she said, placing the small tray in front of him. She climbed into the bench beside him, but a few feet away.

"Your garden got water today," he said, picking up a cup.

"A good day if you're not hiking," she said.

"Did you and Paul hike around together?"

"No. It was a means of transport." She was slow and curt again. "Although I think Paul did some trekking toward Everest. Just one trip."

"I worked outside a lot. Forest ranger."

"But not anymore?"

"Now just odd jobs. Lots of them, though. I do a lot of work outside." He suddenly missed his routines. His dog. His dinners in the bar.

"You didn't follow Paul into the Peace Corps?"

"He was more adventurous than me."

"He was idealistic."

"True. He basically stayed in the Peace Corps." Thomas thought of the decades when he rarely saw Paul except during an occasional meal at his mother's house.

"What do you care about? Do you have family?" She said.

Her question was a point of personal interest. But he could not think of an interesting answer. "I'm not driven. No family except my mother and aunt."

"Thomas, we're very different. My whole life is serious. My parents are serious. Taking care of others."

He picked up the implication. *He didn't take care of anybody.* "Well, there is the thing of just enjoying life. With other people who enjoy life." He could tell they were losing each other.

"True. We make the life we want if we have a choice."

"I would like to enjoy being with you. As a woman, I mean. I would choose that." He grinned and reached to put his hand on her arm.

She quickly pulled her arm out of reach. "You're not Paul, Thomas. This isn't some fantasy life where you just entertain yourself." Her voice was raised and tense. She got up abruptly, clumsily extracting her legs from under the table and over the bench. "Enough!" She grabbed the tray with her cup on it, again half full.

"Wait!" He tried to stand up, again leaning against the table. Only two older hikers about twenty feet away were in the room, not paying attention. "It's all right. Let's just talk." He watched her back disappear through a cotton curtain covering the door to the kitchen.

He'd been rejected before. This how it felt: embarrassing, dark. *She wasn't going to warm to him. She was Paul's girl. Was he trying to get back at Paul? He was a big, tall guy from America. In this job, she must have run into others like Thomas. But I brought back the memory of Paul,* he thought. *And she quit Paul, and quit Eike. Maybe all that meditation was an escape from some pain.*

Electric Flow

IN HER SECOND YEAR in the Peace Corps in 1986, Helen started frequenting a monastery on the hill behind her village. About thirty residents were there, male and female. The lay monks, alongside their religious practice, ran a hostel for travelers and hikers. Helen had been reading Tibetan and Hindu texts in translation, popular paperbacks left in the hostel by Westerners and serious texts she could buy in bookstores in Pokhara and Kathmandu. She liked the cycle of daily routines designed around meditation, communal eating, chanting, and individual retreats to personal rooms.

In the monastery, rows of butter lamps lit the main hall, giving it an ethereal atmosphere. Constant subtle drafts made the flames unsteady. Their flicker revealed fragments of gods' and demons' faces on the walls and illuminated silver and gold urns holding the ashes of former lamas on shelves near the floor. The sounds of chanting mixed with the sounds of bells, drums and trumpets. The effect was mystic and brought a sense of convergence: god, demon and man; past and present; spirit and flesh; light and dark; words and music. The concert could be heard every day, a simple reminder of the presence of harmony and non-material spheres.

Helen's conversations at the monastery led her to start meditating, sitting beside her small home shrine. She had not chosen any particular mountain god, and none had chosen her. But she had a poster of Ma-Chen over her shrine, which consisted of an incense burner and small colorful pots for flowers. Ma-Chen is a light-skinned and beautiful goddess, who rides a snow-white stag. Her hair is braided with colorful ribbons streaming down from a golden, jeweled crown. She wears a pearl necklace, bracelets and anklets, and a shining bell is fixed to the belt around her silk coat. Helen felt a little guilty about the ethnocentricity of a white woman, but found the image more accessible than the ornate faces of demon-gods, who were purple, red and angry. She preferred the image of a benign female rather than images of evil or feared warriors.

Her daily meditation of nearly an hour became normal, like bathing and eating. It became an essential function in her life.

Helen started to feel anxious about leaving Nepal. She felt a deep bond with the culture. One night she went to sleep, restless and disturbed. It was raining. A cool breeze ruffled the square cheesecloth cocoon of mosquito netting hanging from a wooden frame over her bed. In the middle of the night, she bolted awake and saw the image of a large Buddha at the foot of her bed. Her body felt charged and immobilized, not as in sex, but as if it were in dramatic suspension, with pleasurable waves of energy flowing through every limb. It seemed as if her whole body was tasting a bite of warm chocolate. She tried to cry out, to wake from what she thought must be a dream, but she couldn't control her voice. The Buddha was glowing and out of focus like a ghost. Through bewilderment and amazement, her thoughts registered a message: "He is here and everywhere, within you, regardless of where you live." It was a sign that she could go anywhere in the world and her exploration would not stop.

***

She struggled to replay the vision. She found a passage in an ancient text describing a similar vision as a "sweet flow of nectar" through the body. The meaning was not ambiguous; it didn't require dream interpretation. She felt that she'd had a spiritual experience with physical dimensions. No external evidence of the experience existed outside her mind, but she had no trouble reconstructing the vivid physical suspension that had lasted minutes.

She thought about Moses seeing the burning bush or people having visions of Christ. The most important aspect of her vision was really Buddhist in essence: a realization through a representation of the universe of which she was a part and a microcosm. The Buddha was not someone to appeal to, who might reach down and bless her, but a symbol of reality of which she was a part. She'd felt a connection to all reality, and she longed to feel the connection more strongly. She felt actual passion for this connection.

In late morning after classes, Helen hiked up to the monastery and sought out Lama Lobsang, her favorite monk, to tell him about the vision. He was interested and reassuring. The vision was an outcome of her meditation practice, he said, and a sign that she was learning and advancing in insight.

After that experience, the idea of leaving Nepal was completely alien to Helen. She felt she'd arrived in her home and found a spiritual mission. She continued teaching but increased her meditation time to several hours each day.

The thought of returning to life in the U.S. was anathema. She couldn't warm to its endless shopping, gadgets and pressure to wear makeup and dress in uncomfortable sexy clothes. She couldn't warm to the idea of perpetually driving a car with the need to give full attention for what seemed like hours to the inanities of traffic lights, signs and noise. In Helen's mind, Americans seemed to succumb to a stupor of rushing from one setting to another, squeezing their lives with parking, walking through gigantic grocery stores, choosing foods from millions of products, cooking in haste, talking in haste and working long hours. For her, urban life, impersonal relationships, and traveling long distances to see friends were not appealing.

Her thrills were in nature and simplicity. Watching chickens in a yard. Playing a simple game with children. Smelling the air and trees. Every day, feeling the massive weight of high mountains in the distance. It was the constant turbulence of American daily life that grated. The thought of returning made her feel choked, clouded, smothered and tormented. The complexities of advanced civilization did not appeal to her. Modern life, as she had seen it, seemed pointless, like putting your soul in a blender. There were no blenders in Nepal, at least not in the hills.

Early on, Jeri had introduced Helen to Alexandra David-Neel, the woman who sneaked into Tibet in 1924 by crossing over mountain ranges in winter from China. At the time, Alexandra was middle-aged and travelled with the young Lama Yongden, whom she claimed as her adoptive son. They were disguised as pilgrims, wearing thick, wool robes, with belongings in bags and tucked into the pockets formed in the front folds of their robes. She learned Tibetan as suggested to her by the Thirteenth Dalai Lama himself. Her pockets contained two cameras, gold jewelry, a compass, a pistol, a cooking pot, begging bowls, two spoons, a Tibetan necklace of bone, and gemstones to use as currency. They carried no food. They depended on alms given to travelling monks. They made tea by starting a fire with a flint.

Because foreigners were absolutely forbidden to enter Tibet, Alexandra used soot from the cooking pot to darken her face and hands. This worked for months while she and the young Lama were in Tibet. They endured terrifying snowstorms, high-mountain passes and tense encounters with dangerous locals. The entire journey took three years and covered thousands of miles. The Lama Yongden gave readings and performed blessings and rituals to win over farmers who shared their food and huts or barns. After Alexandra David-Neel returned to Europe, with a 1924 photograph of them in front of the Potala Palace, the chief residence of the Dalai Lama, as proof of success, she wrote thirty books about Tibetan Buddhism and her travels.

British officials were furious about her transgressions, but she had many allies among monks and native officials. Later, thousands of readers were enthralled by the secrets and stories she told. She was one of a handful of Westerners to enter Tibet and write about what she'd seen. Unlike the others, she had become an ordained nun and stopped at many monasteries in her travels to learn new teachings and practices, just as other Buddhist monks did as a way of life. She did not die until she was 101, yet another testament to her extraordinary stamina and vitality. Single-handedly—or rather, with the help of her son Lama Yongden—she was a significant conduit between Tibet and the West and helped spread Buddhism to Europe and America.

Jeri and Helen worshipped Alexandra David-Neel as if she were a goddess. If there were a *tonka* for her, they would have had it on their walls. Instead, they carefully cut from books a few photos of her, which they displayed in simple frames. They did not place her framed image in a Buddhist-style temple, but they put it on top a dresser with rose petals, incense, and a *kata*—a white prayer scarf. As a child, Helen liked to light a small lamp as a warming icon to acknowledge Alexandra's victory over blizzards and warm the long, cold journey she had endured.

When Helen got into difficulties with Nepalis or Tibetans as she was growing up, Jeri, to inspire her, would say: "What would Alexandra do?"

***

After her fellow volunteers had left the country, Helen went back to the monastery near her village and lived in a little stone hut close to it. She moved her meager furnishings and settled in, now as a citizen with a long-term visa and not as a Peace Corps volunteer trying to get people to do something. In the beginning, she could hear the chanting of morning rituals as the monks had their first cups of tea. A rough *stupa* stood near the back of the temple, and she sat there, looking out at the valley below, feeling the baby grow. She began to sit outside the doorway of the temple during morning meditations. Soon, the monks began leaving a little carpet on the patio at the doorway with a cup of tea, every day. They had entertained Westerners before, although none who intended to stay. Lama Lobsang became Helen's Lama.

Many of the routine rites were conducted to ward off bad luck and attract prosperity and virtue for the people who supported the monastery. Most people in the village were dependent on farming, subject to luck with weather and markets. There were rites and festivals for specific days in every month, and many required preparation. Some festivals required ten days of activity. Helen began to learn the rhythms of village life this way and find jobs to do, such as gathering juniper sprigs, collecting ritual payments and offerings of food, preparing ritual items, repairing costumes, and such. The communal part of Buddhism, the *Sangha* was her adopted community and extended family. Personally, she assumed the more subdued decorum of Buddhists in monasteries, moving slowly, without hurry, feeling the present in the air, under her feet, in her hands. Soon Lama Lobsang gave her permission to participate in rituals in the main hall.

The monastery maintained a hostel on the near hillside, and Helen began to help, as it served travelers, especially Western hikers. Her English and familiarity with the guests' perspective was a great asset. Word got out that her presence made the hostel especially easy to navigate. It had special accommodations for trekkers, such as foods like fried potatoes that Helen introduced. Some of the guides brought small groups regularly. Thus, she began to contribute to the monastery in a way that was compatible with meditation and, at the same time supplied her and the community ample access to butter, cheese and yogurt. Most monks were supported by their families of origin who sent them food, cloth and utensils. Helen's parents were willing to sponsor her, but she was in a rare position to participate in commerce, albeit modestly, and did not need them to provide for her. Her pregnancy was disguised by loose wool tunics and did not draw attention.

***

Thomas' arrival brought back the memory of Paul. Helen had chosen between the sweetness of romantic love and the profound peace of meditation and religious community. She could not imagine combining them, or combining a religious life and raising a child. She would have preferred to have the sweetness of Paul a little longer, but the Peace Corps program ended. The pregnancy also forced decisions she wasn't ready for.

Thomas was no temptation. He wasn't Paul. Thomas' shallow efforts toward flirtation were like sneezes in the blissful wind and sun of her spiritual life.

Community

JACK, THE BARTENDER, was living in a group house on the other side of Thamel. The house was a hive of international volunteers, both short-term and long-term transients. Thomas was starting to tire of hotel living even though it was cheap. Since he and Jack got along and the house needed a tenant, Jack offered a small room to Thomas. The house was a run-down former mansion with rooms for about ten people depending on sleeping arrangements. There were old and young residents. The group house appealed to Thomas as more congenial than the hotel with its mix of transient strangers that changed nearly every day.

When Thomas and Jack arrived at mid-day, Thomas met Finnish and Dutch girls in their twenties, sitting on a wooden settee in the living room. One was teaching the other a song on a small guitar. The Finnish girl was covered in beads: through her hair, around her neck, hanging from her ears, and wrapped around each arm was a stack of Indian and Tibetan-beaded bracelets. Except for her very white skin and flaxen hair, she looked like an African princess from the *National Geographic*. She had obviously collected a lot of Tibetan bead necklaces, too, draped over her embroidered, yellow-cotton, Indian-style shirt and long, black skirt. The Dutch girl was wearing jeans and T-shirt with a deep-cut neckline. To Thomas, her looks were European—intense eyes, bushy unplucked brows, curly brown hair bouncing into her face, an easy sexuality. They shared one of the rooms and planned to stay only two months. They were working in a nearby orphanage.

"Here's Thomas," Jack said to them.

"Oh, hi," they said almost simultaneously. "Welcome. Know any songs?"

"Rolling Stones. Beatles. Maybe not your style."

"Oh yes, it is," said the Dutch girl. "You're on." He felt like he'd broken the age barrier a little bit, even though hers wasn't a serious invitation.

"What do you do here?" asked Thomas.

"Orphanage. We teach hygiene."

"Hygiene?"

"Washing hands and face. Toilet habits. Keeping yourself clean. Brushing teeth."

"You'd be surprised," said the French girl with a heavy accent. "They're just learning about germs."

"They think if you put water on something, it's clean," added the Dutch girl.

"Anyway. We're in a room on this floor. We see you, yes?"

Thomas laughed. "Yes." He'd forgotten the confident lightness of young women.

In the kitchen, he met a dark-skinned, long-haired, intense guy from Poland, probably in his thirties, who was making himself an omelet on the hotplate. "Borys is one of the lease-holders," explained Jack. "Long-time resident." Borys' clothing included a Tibetan wool vest, jeans, and flip-flops, all of which looked very lived-in. Having seniority, Borys had one of the better rooms on the upper floor in a corner. Jack told him that Borys worked intermittently with one of the tour companies, leading hikers on day trips. He spoke English, French, Russian, and a smattering of Nepali.

The house was functional, with many sparsely furnished rooms, and windows on most sides. Jack gave Thomas a small room on the first floor with a wooden cot, thin mattress, and bedding that looked clean. The room was lit by a single bare bulb overhead. Jack warned of frequent blackouts and recommended having a flashlight on hand. The door to Thomas' room could be locked with a padlock. He'd seen padlocks on various doors. The house was like a hostel, with friendly camaraderie and trust mixed with wariness about petty theft and respect for the fact that most of the residents were strangers. They were strangers from many foreign countries who might not be predictable in what they did and said.

"Am I the oldest guy here?" Thomas asked Jack.

"Probably. It doesn't matter. All kinds of people come through. Retirees, for example. Not everybody wants to sleep on a hard cot, though. Cold showers, too. No real kitchen."

"Cold showers?"

"There's a tank on the roof. It can run cold. Usually runs cold. Really bad in the cold season."

"At least, there's plumbing."

"Yeah."

Four roomers lived on the ground floor: Thomas, the two girls he'd met, and a burly dark Israeli. Jack was upstairs, as was Borys, another Israeli guy, and an Australian couple.

Most of the residents were away during the day. The Australian couple worked at a small Tibetan refugee camp in the city, where they tutored a lama in English and taught children English or supervised their exams. The couple, who were in their late twenties, were not stereotypical Aussies. Both were shy and slight. They said the camp was much like a boarding school, with all the usual jobs of supervising students, repairing things, cooking, and supplying it with essentials. When Thomas heard about the camp, he knew his handyman skills could contribute to many of the projects and he could join the volunteers, but he didn't want to compromise his current vocation of meditating and experiencing Nepal.

"I usually get a plate of curry at the bar for dinner," said Jack, who was American. "Shopping for your own food here isn't like at home. It's a lot of work. Meals are so cheap, it's nuts to cook. You can get scrambled eggs or an omelet any time of the day, nearly everywhere." Jack was probably in his thirties. He didn't look like a heavy beer drinker, but Thomas knew from observing Jack at the bar that he always had a few. Still, Jack was congenial and comfortable in the ways of Kathmandu and didn't appear to be a drunk or troublemaker.

Moving out of the Tibet Hotel gave Thomas the opportunity to explore new neighborhoods, consisting of two and three-story buildings where Nepalis lived. He could still walk to his meditation classes, taking a different route. He was starting to understand the context in which Jeri and Donald lived. They were long-term, assimilated expatriates, with a garden and servants. Now, strolling from his new house, Thomas passed locals carrying their own groceries and riding bikes or bike-rickshaws to work.

That night, he met more residents of the house. One of the Israelis, Gideon, was a long-term roomer who was in the business of support for climbing groups—gathering supplies, packing, arranging for drop-offs and pick-ups along routes that covered miles of territory. He was a weathered climber himself, in his late thirties, who saved his money to finance personal expeditions higher into the mountains. His room was full of ropes, axes, boots, and boxes of energy bars. He bought hiking gear from transient trekkers who came with the best stuff for their big trips to Nepal.

Thomas saw the two girls in the kitchen area. The French girl was eating a rice-and-lentil dish. He could smell spices in the air, like incense, but more appealing to the stomach. There were only a few cooking pots. The girls seemed resourceful and knew how to use what was available. Living in the house was much like camping, but no one was in charge.

During the next week, he kept his schedule with the meditation class and continued to have lunch in Thamel on the way back. In the afternoon, he continued to read in his room or sitting on a stone wall, if he could avoid being bothered by children. Inside, he could hear his housemates coming and going, up the stairs, down the hall to the bathroom with a shower on his floor, out the front door.

Now and then, he went out into the common room to see who was there. It was furnished with a few random pieces: wooden armchairs and a settee, a few beat-up tables, a crude floor lamp. The concrete floor was cold and ugly. None of the residents was interested in decorating or cleaning. Cleaning was a matter of who got disgusted first. The cooking area was so small that it had no room to set anything down. Bugs were a problem. The house was mainly a place to sleep and leave belongings safely behind a padlock. The lease-holders had hired a Nepali servant to clean the common areas once a week.

Thomas had transported the urn in his backpack. Now, it sat on top of a low wooden stool near his bed. It looked like a shrine and could be mistaken for one by a foreigner, although there were no accoutrements, such as incense, flowers, bowls, silk cloth, or candles. Nepalis would see the urn as quite normal, except Thomas was treating it as a decoration, not the center of a personal shrine, as they would fashion it.

***

The unfamiliar bed, covers, room, air, sounds and lights on the walls made it hard for Thomas to sleep. He was a long way from Winthrop, the warmth of his dog Sally and a large clean room with windows on two sides, a down comforter, and the quiet of living on the edge of wilderness. One night, he got up when it was very dark to find his way down the hall to the bathroom. It had a concrete floor with a large drain in the middle. There was a tub with a shower over it but no shower curtain, because it would get moldy. Everything in the room was concrete, metal, or porcelain. It could be hosed down if needed. A glass window was open, with bars in the frame to keep out intruders. He flipped the wall switch.

Swarms of giant cockroaches, on every wall and all over the floor, jumped in panic. They ran stupidly in all directions, seeking shelter. They were about two inches in length, and Thomas got a good look at their numbers. Some of them charged in his direction, when actually they wanted to escape. He screamed and

208

jumped back out of the room. He was in flip-flops, which he'd worn in his hotel room too. His bare feet felt the cool air and, worse, anticipated the onslaught of giant insects.

After a few minutes of shock, he could see bare walls and floor again as the majority of insects had scampered out of sight. But when he looked at the toilet seat, he could see two-inch insect antennae waving from under the seat. Apparently, the underside of the seat could be a good hiding place for cockroaches. Urgently needing the facility, Thomas stepped toward the seat. He took a hanger someone left in the bathroom and used it to lift the seat. Three roaches jumped away and disappeared behind the toilet. This was not very reassuring, but he knew they would stay out of sight. Wide-awake now, he used the toilet. He backed out of the room and switched off the light. *Next time, a warning flashlight*, he thought.

***

One day the Australian couple was waiting in the common room, hoping to seeThomas. "Thomas," the man said, standing up. "You said you were a handyman." He turned to start a conversation.

"Sure."

"We've got a situation. Thought you might help?"

"What's up?" Thomas was heating water for instant coffee.

"A storage room at the camp has shelves that collapsed. Nepalis don't use a lot of wood, and need to reuse wood, but the shelves are a mess. Would you mind taking a look at them? Even if you just told some students what to do, that would help."

"Who's their carpenter?"

"A guy who went back to his village. There's food and grain in piles now. It can get contaminated by bugs, get wet. We're not good at this." The woman turned off the stove for Thomas.

"Okay. Let's go take a look." They left together and took a cab to the camp in the south part of the city. It was a compound consisting of rustic buildings, all painted the same sweet yellow on the outside. On some, a stenciled border outlined the windows.

The couple led him to a small building in the back near an open-air kitchen area and a dark independent building that was the actual kitchen. Kids of various ages passed them and turned to stare at the tall, bearded white man. He met a short dark man who was the cook. The Australian woman went to find a contact who could translate.

"You're right," Thomas said, looking at the pile in the pantry. "Rotted wood. Can they get me some basic tools?"

It took an hour and a cup of tea before some kids came running in with a borrowed hammer, saw, and nails. He could see that the shelves had been patched and held together for what the Australian man said was more than ten years. The couple told Thomas clay bricks were easier and cheaper to get than wood, so he designed a combination that would use brick supports with short segments of reused wood between them.

It took days to gather the bricks and locate a craftsman who could build the brick supports. Therefore, Thomas had to return to the camp several days in a row to check on supplies. He was dismayed at the slow pace. Each day, the cook gave him a cup of tea, and kids gathered around, testing their broken English.

It was hard not to bond with the kids. He thought of Dorje. The kids' schooling was minimal, and they would likely graduate to jobs as porters for tourist trekkers. They would carry sixty-pounds on their backs up thousands of feet of elevation for about six dollars a day. They would patch together warm clothes for the high-altitude hikes, where they would sleep and eat in one room. One injury could derail their livelihood. With few exceptions, the trekking companies provided no medical insurance or care. The porters would need English to interact with hikers. With the help of Donald and Jeri, Dorje had found sponsors and attended good schools.

Thomas thought about his family's time as refugees. They'd been lucky it lasted only a few years. Stateless, they could not get jobs in the host country. They'd scavenged everything, all the time, to provide minimal creature comforts. They scraped together enough clothes to wear one outfit while another was washed. They felt desperate because they had no foreseeable future and were at the mercy of strangers who told them to do things they didn't quite understand. They had no control over fundamentals like food, clean water, warm shelter and health care. Thomas decided not to tell Livia about the Tibetan refugee camp. It might throw her back to a dark time and remind her of the huge losses that preceded her time in the camps.

Another Calling

"Eike, eike, wake up." Her Nepali companion shook her shoulder. She said, "A baby's very sick. They need you to come." The village where the sick baby lived was an hour from Eike's house.

She sat up on her cot and shook herself awake. It was dark outside. Night house calls were rare, but part of the job. Her companion went to bring her tea and rice with yoghurt and lentils to get her going. Eike placed a square, heavy-cotton scarf on the bed and started packing: headdress, ritual scarves, mirrors, butter lamps, a bell, juniper, a collection of herbs individually wrapped in papers, some allopathic pills, such as aspirin and acetaminophen. Her sweater and skirt were nearby, and she put them over the cotton smock she had worn to bed. A wool jacket was near the door. Although it was spring, mountain nights were cool. After eating, she set out with the man who had come to get her, the sick baby's uncle. She didn't know him well, but he was someone who passed through her village periodically, probably on his way to a market down the valley.

The sky was ablaze with stars that looked like sequins on a black cloak draping the surrounding mountains. If Eike had not felt urgency about her trip, she would have found the view spectacular. The chill of the night and fear for the child blended and made Eike and the man walk with fast, steady steps. Eike held the bundle under one arm and her other hand was free in case she tripped or needed to grab something to pull herself up steep steps in the path. Unlike older shamans, she was youthfully quick, which was reassuring to people waiting for help. Eike and the man navigated over rocks and between bushes, using memory and the sparkle and glow from above to find their way. In a region with rare electricity, their eyes were accustomed to taking in any available light and differentiating obstacles underfoot. She soon opened her jacket, letting in crisp air.

They arrived at a house that was not as primitive as most. It had proper floors and rooms and furniture, including tables, chairs, cots, and rugs. Unlike most Nepalis, the family was not living on the floor and in smoke. The kitchen was separated from the rest of the rooms by a wall, and rather than ventilating through the roof, the stove ventilated through a vent. An anxious middle-aged woman met Eike and the man, bowing to her with palms over her heart. Eike put her hands out to take the woman's. As they walked to the other room, the woman explained that the baby was listless, would not eat, and was breathing with difficulty. He had been irritable and hot the day before and now was exhausted and limp.

In the other room, the baby was wrapped in several blankets on a bed. A worried young woman, apparently the mother, sat near with her hand on the baby. The room was lit by a small lamp in the corner. A low table was pulled over to the bed for Eike's things. She took off her jacket and sat next to the baby to get a closer look. He was dark, about three years old, with a round puffy face and damp skin. His nose had a smudge of ash to protect him from evil spirits. She tried to see his tongue and felt his pulse in each little wrist. She asked about diarrhea and vomiting, coughing and water intake. The women showed Eike a diaper containing urine so she could see the color.

Eike asked the women to uncover the baby and swab him with a damp cloth to cool him. Eike put the spout of a small pot, like a tiny teapot, to try to get him to drink water. He was still asleep.

Eike set up her ritual materials on the low table: the mirrors, the butter lamps, which she lit, the bell, several card-sized pictures of her favorite deities, some bowls. The family added some rice offerings. Someone lit the juniper branches and held them to the side. Eike wrapped several scarves around her neck like a cape and put on a small headdress. She sat in a chair facing the child and started to chant, ringing the bell, swaying forward and back. Suddenly, she grimaced and shouted, as her deity took control of her body. She stood up, waving her arms over the baby. The family sat back, giving her room. She swooped down to the baby and appeared to bite into his side. They knew she was trying to suck out the evil energy that possessed the child. Eike pulled back and spat into one of the bowls. It was a black fluid. She repeated an extraction several times. The baby moved as if waking up. Finally, she rang the bell and chanted, then sat back calmly. She pulled off the headdress and scarves.

"Give him water as much as you can," she said in Nepali. "And give him one of these now, at mid-day, and in the evening." She handed the women a version of children's Tylenol from her kit. "Also, I will put together herbs." From the collection of herbs wrapped in folded paper, she poured amounts into one of the bowls. These were to be blended into yoghurt and fed to the baby in small increments. Finally, she advised a massage using sesame oil and nutmeg to bring back energy.

By now, day was breaking, and sunlight started coming in the room. Eike's chair was moved to a wall while the middle-aged woman tended to the baby. Someone brought Eike tea and a rice cake.

Suddenly, the door to the room burst open with a loud bang as it hit the wall. A young woman with disheveled hair and clothes rushed into the room, bringing with her a burst of cold piney air, and headed for the bed with the child, shouting in Nepali "You witch! He's mine!" She grabbed the middle-aged woman's hair and pulled.

A man following behind her tried to hold her back. He grabbed her hand on the hair. "Stop! Stop! We're here now."

The woman sitting on the bed covered the baby and tried to get away from the attacker. "Leave us! He's going to die if you take him!"

The man who had fetched Eike dashed into the room and joined the fray. He ran to protect the woman on the bed. "Calm down! Get away from her!"

Finally, they forced the attacker to sit in a chair, where she burst into tears. "What's wrong with you? You can't take him! He's my baby!" She sobbed into her cuff.

"You made him sick," said the other young woman. "You're going to kill him. You go drinking in the market. You stole my beads to pay for it. He's safe with us!"

"No, no. You gave me the beads. I'm not drinking. Ask Jahnu." Her hands were clasped as if begging. Her husband looked at the floor.

"Where have you been for two days? Huh? Explain yourself!" the other young woman said.

"I needed to visit my aunt. I had to go take care of her."

"It's a lie!"

The woman who had burst into the room tried to get up and go to the baby. He was rousing, moving his head, opening his mouth. Eike was glad to see it. The two women scrapped in the middle of the room again. Their men pulled them apart.

"You might as well settle down. He needs to rest here a while anyway. Settle down," said Eike's guide, apparently the uncle.

"Let me hold my baby! I want my baby!" cried the mother.

"All right, all right." The men let go of her and she jumped to the bedside. She gently wrapped the blanket around the baby and put him in her lap. She was crying again, rocking him, stroking his head. The others watched, embarrassed now, remembering that Eike was witnessing the squabble.

Eike's guide, the uncle, spoke first. "Pawo Eike, I'm sorry. The mother's neglecting the baby. Her sister has no children. She tries to care for him. The baby is going back and forth."

"It looks like he's better. I should go." Eike tried to calm their embarrassment.

"You can see we have two disturbed women here," the uncle said.

"Yes."

"Can you tell us how this will resolve?" he said.

Eike was known for her divination skills, too.

"I have to consult my gods," she said. She got up and left to sit in the other room, which was a small room off the kitchen. She sat on a bench and started chanting quietly. Everyone else waited in the first room.

After about half an hour, Eike came back to the chair she'd had before. She looked at the mother, wrapped around the baby. He was drinking water from the little pot now. His eyes were flickering awake. The mother brushed her cheek against the baby's head, as he sucked from the spout, and hummed words quietly into his ear. The aunt sat a few feet away, looking stricken with grief and longing for the child. The two men were drinking tea. They seemed resigned to their difficulties, one with a possibly barren wife and the other with a wayward wife. They were part of an extended family and lived like brothers.

Eike felt her own body giving way to fatigue. In the first hour of her trip, she and the uncle had gained over 1,000 feet of elevation in their hike. She had spent hours in anxious concentration, giving her body up to a trance and eating and drinking very little.

"What can you tell us?"

"The baby will die unless it stays with the aunt," she said.

The mother let out a loud wail as if the child had just died in her arms. The rest of the family were stunned. "Die?"

"Yes." Eike knew she couldn't elaborate on a vision that had come to her. There were never many details. But the message had been clear.

"You're known for being right," said her guide. "It's a serious prediction."

"It's up to you now. I'm sorry. I hope he's better now." Eike got up and packed her things back into a bundle. The journey home would be easier, downhill and in daylight. Another family member came from the kitchen and gave her a bundle of grains and dried apricots as payment. The gift was heavy. The family was not poor.

"Safe journey," he said, hands over heart, bowing.

Eike bowed in return and entered the fresh outside air. She could hear the mother moaning in grief. The image of the mother's tender and visceral attachment to the child stayed with her during the whole journey back.

***

The hills around Eike's village were an undulating sea of green. The valley itself was bounded by steep mountains, which looked like harsh, but beautiful, distant islands rising out of a green sea. Like volcanic Polynesian islands, they were too steep to be accessible. The view most people had was the view they saw going around the mountains. Only a few mountain climbers tried scale the peaks. The peaks, which were mostly above the tree line, were gray and fog-bound, harsh and cold. By contrast, the foothills were a delightful paradise, with alpine flowers, grass and leafy trees. In this garden Eike walked to gather medicinal and ritual herbs. For her, that was a frequent solitary pastime, another form of meditation. Her search was both purposeful and random, as she looked in likely spots for certain herbs and discovered others by accident. On these hikes, she wore her usual long wool skirt and jacket, with her matted blond hair down her back in a loose braid. Except for her clothes, she could have been a hiker in the Swiss Alps. Her shoes were native: wool felt boots on a leather platform, with straps up the shins.

The path Eike took was not a usual route for hikers so she was surprised to see someone coming up a herder's path toward her. She knew most of the people who lived in the valley as she had served many families. From a distance she saw a slick loden-green jacket like outsiders or lucky natives wore, probably wind- and waterproof with a perfect array of hidden pockets. His hair was a brown mop, not unusual for campers. He was tall and lean, and his skin was darker than that of most Americans and Europeans she had seen. He was walking with strong, long deliberate steps, a pace that seemed accustomed to steep treks. He looked up at her occasionally, and she could tell he was aiming to catch up with her. She faced downhill and waited, putting the basket on her hip to relieve the weight of the strap on her shoulder. She was facing the sun, her cheeks red from the exertion of her own trek, but now cooling because she was standing still.

"Hello," he called in English. "We have to stop meeting like this." He was still fifty feet away, too far for conversation, but intent on keeping her waiting.

"Excuse me?"

He moved more quickly to close the shouting distance between them. "Your people said you were up here. It's farther than I thought."

"You're looking for me?"

"Of course." He came near. He had striking good looks, like a Bollywood star, but leaner than most (because the Indian stars tended to live indulgent lives and it showed). He had an Aryan nose, the cheeks and light skin of Northern India, not the round, dark features of the South. "I'm Sam."

"Eike."

"I saw you perform a ritual yesterday. For a relative of mine who passed."

"I see. You're Nepali?"

"No. Anglo-Indian. Bengali mother, English father. Name's really Sahan."

"And the relative?"

"On the Bengali side. Migrated up here to grow tea."

"That's hard."

"They're doing well. Organic. Exports. This valley is god's gift."

"I think so." She smiled thinking about it.

"And what're you doing?"

"Herbs." She pointed to her basket. "It's a big part of my work."

"How do you know what to get?"

"Folklore. My lama taught me everything I know. There's no book."

"Not even a classical text?"

"Some. What do you do?" They were still standing a few feet apart. Eike surprised herself, feeling so friendly. Normally, she was absorbed in her thoughts and discouraged curiosity on the part of strangers. It must be the sunshine, she thought.

"Trekking logistics. I work with the high-end providers. People paying $60,000 to climb Mount Everest. That pays for a lot of tender loving care for climbers."

"They don't all make it, it seems."

"True. Some die chasing a dream. Not everybody can say that."

"Have you gone yourself?"

"No. I'm too caught up in the business. Working with sherpas. That $60,000 helps locals, too. We watch out for locals."

"Are you a local?"

"Kathmandu."

"So what're you doing here, Sam?"

"Chasing you. I've asked around. You've got a reputation." He smiled.

"You came a long way."

"Let's see. Bus. Three-hour walk. Hike up here. Yeah. Let's sit down."

She remembered that the ritual he must have seen was nearby. He was kidding. They looked around and found a few rocks.

"Would you like some chocolate?" he said.

"Sure."

He put his daypack down and pulled out a bandana, a knife, several oranges, chocolate, and dried apricots. "I realize your parents are in Kathmandu. I haven't met them. They're well-known."

"Yes. I grew up there."

"How often do you come down?"

"Every few months. Sometimes I have a ceremony in Kathmandu. My Lama's there."

"Do you specialize?"

"Mostly healing. Some help with departures."

"Ah. And what do you do for fun?"

"This." She took the orange slices he offered and savored them. "How about you?"

"This, too." He looked at her frankly, with affection. They ate pieces of food on his bandana, looking away and taking in the sun. She added some pieces of cheese and nuts from her own bundle. Eike was feeling a little awkward. He broke the silence, bringing her even more discomfort: "Do shamans like you marry?"

"Some. My Lama's married."

"And you?"

"Never came up."

"And if it did?"

"Karma. It's not something you engineer. I've being doing this work since I was fourteen."

"Fourteen! You've been up here since then?"

"No. I started in Kathmandu. There's a long training."

"I've been in Kathmandu for just three years. I must have missed you there."

"Yes. I've been up here over four years. Settled here." She started to pull her basket near, preparing to get up.

"How do I reach you? Can I visit again?"

The thought was alien. It wasn't that she didn't have people visit or contact her, but they were always seeking the services of a shaman. "There's a phone in the shop in the village. They take messages. You can get the number there. Next to the place where the bus stops." They both stood up.

"Can you let me know when you come to Kathmandu?"

"Sure." She wasn't sure. "What's your number?" she asked.

He pulled out a pencil and paper and wrote "Sam Multoone" and his phone number. "Eike." He looked at her intently as he handed it to her. "Are you allowed to hug?"

"Hug?" She was suddenly fourteen. She let her arms open, and he slowly stepped to her and put his arms around her waist. He pulled her tightly against him. It sent a shock through her body, like a heater accidentally tripped to high. She could smell his neck against her face. He was a half-foot taller, very strong, and wrapped around her like a hungry python. He sensed her surprise and let go, again slowly, which only intensified the flush of heat inside her. She was gripping his upper arms and felt reluctant to let go. Finally, they stepped apart.

"Okay," he said, grinning. "Okay. See you soon."

"See you." She was too embarrassed to look him in the eye.

"We'll talk soon."

"Yes."

He picked up his daypack, put it over his shoulder, and started down the slope. After about twenty feet, still shouting distance, he turned and waved. "Bye now!"

"Bye." She was dazed.

Busted

LOUD POUNDING ON THE FRONT DOOR woke Thomas, the girls and the Israeli who slept on the first floor, and they ran into the entry room. It was 3 a.m. The Israeli reached the door first and shouted, "Who's there?" The answer was "Police!"

He unbolted the door and opened it to a group of men in light-blue uniforms with dark lapels and berets, holding thick batons and flashlights. The police pushed past him until five of them were in the entry room, with more standing in the doorway. Two had holsters with formidable *ghurka* swords that appeared to be eighteen-inches long, long enough to cut off a head.

One of the police pushed the Israeli onto a chair and grabbed hold of Thomas and the two girls. He pushed the girls into the space next to Thomas and made them sit on the floor.

"What? What's going on?" the Israeli protested, putting his arms in front of him in case the police started to use more force.

The four residents were in sleeping clothes: shorts and T-shirts, their hair scrambled from sleep, their eyes squinting into flashlights directed on them. Someone switched on the electric light.

Two of the police scouted the rooms on the first floor, and four ran up the stairs and banged on doors. In just minutes, Borys, Jack, the Australians and the other Israeli came stumbling down the stairs and were pushed into the group already smashed into one corner of the entry room. There was lots of shouting in Nepali and some in English: "Out! Out! Now!"

Thomas was in an awkward spot on the floor against the wall. Other residents were between him and the police who were standing over them with batons ready. He felt foolish and confused. It was clearly a raid, but for what? A bunch of volunteers and tourists were living in a plain old house. The Finnish girl next to him was trembling, and he put his arm around her. The Dutch girl had squeezed beside the chair with the Israeli in it. The Israeli was the most convenient target for a beating and had his hands out to protect himself. Swords were a different matter. All the residents were looking at each other for an answer: Was this normal? Were they in some kind of trouble? What happened with police in Kathmandu? Who was going to help them? What were their rights? From their behavior, the residents all seemed to implicitly agree that resistance was not a good idea. They couldn't be sure how many more police were outside. Besides, this raid had to be a mistake.

The Australian man looked at Borys and Jack. "What's going on? Do you know?"

"Shut up!" a policeman shouted in English. "No talking!" This was frightening because it would have been easier to cooperate if the residents knew what the police wanted.

There was a shot upstairs. The housemates quickly looked at the floor around them and assessed whether anyone was missing. They were all there.

An officer came downstairs and huddled with several others, looking at the now-fearful group. He pointed at two of the officers and then pointed at the residents. The English-speaking officer, the chief, faced them.

"Passports. One by one. Go and get passports and wallets and clothes." The English-speaking officer pointed at the Dutch girl and the Australian guy. Another officer pulled her up from the floor and followed her to her room. The Australian guy, followed by an officer, went to his room upstairs. Each resident, in turn, was escorted out of the entry room and came back and handed the chief a passport. He was busy checking nationalities. There were two Americans, a Pole, a Finn, a Dutchwoman, two Australians, and two Israelis. Six men and three women. After they returned with clothes and valuables in hand, they pulled pants and shirts on over their sleepwear.

They were asked to stand up and go outside. Thomas asked the English-speaking chief, "Our things. Are they safe?" The chief nodded. The housemates went outside into the dark. There was a van outside, and they piled into it, sitting down on benches along each side. By now, bystanders were in the street, watching the commotion. The officers tried to shoo them away.

At the police station, the residents were herded into a receiving room. Each was interviewed and escorted to a holding cell. Men and women were isolated from each other. The young women were particularly distressed about being separated from the men because they thought the men might be able to tell them how to get help.

It was a rough night. The holding cells had wooden cots with no bedding. The toilet was a large stinking can in the corner. In the morning, the prisoners were given a bowl of rice with lentils poured over it, and milky tea. Sanitation was a concern. Thomas knew they could get diarrhea in the next hour. Fortunately, he was one of the first to be called out of his cell. He was the oldest, and he hoped the raid was a mistake.

"What's the purpose of your visit to Kathmandu?" the officer asked.

"Tourist."

"How long?"

"Three months."

"How long in the house on Kulabhulu Galli?"

"Two weeks."

"How long did you know the other occupants?"

"Just met them when I moved in, really."

"Anybody in Kathmandu who can vouch for you? Any business contacts?"

"No business. But Jeri and Donald Simons can vouch for me."

The officer raised his eyebrows in recognition. Jeri and Donald were fixtures in the expat community. "We will contact the embassy. You might be released to them."

"That's a relief. Thank you. What's up?"

"Illegal export."

"Of what? Drugs?"

"No." The officer dismissed Thomas to an escort who took him back to the holding cell.

When Thomas got back to the cell, Borys was gone, and the remaining men were curious. "The officer said illegal exports. Not drugs. What can that be?" He looked at the other men. They shrugged their shoulders.

Borys did not come back. The other men were interviewed individually. Around lunchtime, Jack went out and didn't come back, either. After another round of rice and lentils with milky tea, Thomas was summoned again.

In the office was a well-dressed American. "I'm from the embassy. Brad." He held out a hand.

"Gosh, glad to see you. It's been very confusing." Thomas stood taller as a feeling of safety and trust washed over him. "I didn't know who or what was going to help us out of here. Or what we needed to do."

"Have a seat." Brad pointed to a chair. It was the same room in which Thomas had been questioned. The Nepali official had left. Brad and Thomas were alone in the room and sat in chairs in front of the desk. "The police will turn you over to us if we can assure them that you're okay. I need to ask you a few questions."

"Sure." Thomas was now apprehensive again.

"You have a record for growing pot in Oregon State. Cost you a federal job."

"That's true. Regrettable."

"But no record of your actually dealing. I assume you were growing for your own consumption then?"

"Yes. I was deep in a national forest. Money was not in the picture."

"Still, you broke the law."

"Yes."

"No records of subsequent drug activity. No other charges."

"No. There shouldn't be." Thomas tried to remember what expressions to control if you were lying, but he couldn't remember what they were—blinking, tight lips?

"Have you done any drugs while you were here?"

"Smoked a bit. No selling. I thought it was fairly common here."

"Still illegal. But not prosecuted. They found a few joints in your room."

"They searched?"

"Yes."

"What else is going on?"

"Let's finish talking about you. How long have you known the others in this group?"

"Two weeks. I was saving money by living in the house. Just staying a few more weeks."

"Did you know they were involved in relics? Anybody talk about that?"

"No way. My God. Who?"

"At least two of your friends had a wardrobe full of antique statues and scrolls, which are banned for export."

"Who?"

"Borys and Jack. An informant reported them. The police have the collection now."

"We heard a gunshot."

"Probably to break the lock. It was in an upstairs room."

"Wow. I had no idea."

"We can ask the police to let you go. I strongly recommend that you go to a hotel. And watch whom you hang with. The police will not forget your name."

"All right. All right. Is there anything I can do for the others?"

"Their consulates are coming for them. You can't do anything for them, and you shouldn't. After you get your things, stay away from them. As I noted, the police are watching. They're going to be wary that they missed something."

"Okay. Wow. Thank you."

Brad stood up. "I'll talk to the police. They'll probably let you go after that."

"Thank you. I'm really sorry. It's been a shock."

"Happens. Stay safe. Kathmandu has a lot of transients desperate to make money so that they can stay."

"I get it."

Brad left. Thomas stayed seated in the office. About fifteen minutes later, a Nepali officer came in, gave him his passport, and told him he was free to leave. Thomas asked where he was in the city and how to get back to the house on Kulabhuli Galli. It wasn't far, so he walked to clear his mind. It was late afternoon. He had less than two weeks left in Kathmandu.

Reckoning

THOMAS SET OUT FOR THE HOUSE on Kulabhulu Galli at twilight. On his way, he stopped at a restaurant and ate a quick chicken curry and lentils. He could have bought from a hole-in-the-wall shop—a lone cook squatting in a small stall, offering food during most of the day—but cleanliness was an issue. Because he'd been awake most of the night and anxious all day, he was exhausted. When he arrived at the house, it was dark and the front door was locked. He was the first to return.

Overwhelming loneliness washed over him as he unlocked the door and stepped into the dark, silent, empty interior that used to be filled with the mundane movements and small talk of nine people. He locked the front door behind him and thought about his housemates and their miserable internment at the police station. There was nothing he could do for them. Brad had told him to stay out of their affairs, to avoid the appearance of being in cahoots with them.

Thomas went to the bathroom, switching the light on and pausing to give the roaches a few minutes to find hiding places. He wondered if they were glad for some human contact again. They must have thought their giants had gone to another planet. Thankfully, a pot of water that had been boiled for drinking was in the kitchen.

He went to bed. At early light, his fitful sleep was broken by the sound of the front door unlocking. He jumped up in his shorts and ran to the hall to see who it was. The Australians, with the Finnish girl, came in, looking worn and skinnier. Their clothes were dirty from sitting on floors and lying on filthy benches. Dirty hair made them look like beat versions of themselves.

"Hey! You made it back," Thomas said. "Oh my god! Are you all right?"

Wearily the Australian said, "Not happy, but safe again. You got here first?"

"Last night. What about the others?"

"Their embassies are working on their cases," said the Australian. "They'll be all right. Except Jack and Borys. They'll probably spend some time in jail and get deported."

"Did you guys eat?" Thomas said. "Want me to find some yoghurt and rice? Pizza? *Chapattis*, peanut butter?"

"No, no. We'll just get some rest and then go out. We have snacks here. We're sticking together today." The Australian looked at the Finnish girl. The three of them seemed to be holding hands psychologically.

***

The Australian showed him a copy of that day's *Himalayan Times*. There was an article with photos of Borys and Jack and an array of religious items collected in the raid. Thomas's name, along with the names of all the other occupants of the house was listed. The article was scathing, highlighting the black-market purchase of idols, antique ritual items, and scrolls bought from Tibetan refugees, particularly in the Pokhara region. It was not clear how long the business had existed or whether much had been exported. The dark-mahogany wardrobe with a padlock had been completely filled with ornate butter lamps, bells, small prayer wheels, prayer beads, incense burners, ritual weapons, *tonkas*, small snuff bottles with inlaid jade and turquoise, scrolls, and statues of the Buddha. The statues were clearly illegal for export, the other items illegal if they had historical or religious significance.

You could buy antiques like these in the markets. However, the items refugees carried out wrapped in their coats when they fled with great difficulty over snow-covered passes and through dangerous rivers, tended to be very old and very precious. When refugees sold these items, they were trading their heirlooms for money, usually to save the life of someone in the family.

Thomas was reminded of his experience with the forest service when it discovered he was growing marijuana. But the police episode in Kathmandu was not his fault. He was guilty only by association, and for something he truly considered immoral. Few residents of Kathmandu could recognize or judge him, but enough could to make him feel like a criminal. He'd underestimated the innocence of expatriates and transients, people grooving in Kathmandu. What was especially shocking to him was the crime. Young slackers who had enough wealth to travel across the world and were too lazy to make an honest living were exploiting the desperation of displaced persons. Jack and Borys were the kind of criminals who would have exchanged potatoes for Nicholas and Livia's last family jewels.

***

Thomas fell back into bed. At mid-day, he woke again, feeling hungry and dirty. He looked around the room to see if his things were there. The camera was still hidden in a deep pocket of his canvas bag, under dirty clothes, books, extra shoes, and jeans. His battery-run shaver was still tucked in his shaving kit with shaving cream and toiletries. It would have been a prize steal. He dug out clean clothes. Wrapped in a towel, he went down the hall to the bathroom for a shave and shower. The house was quiet now, and he guessed that his other housemates had gone out for a meal. Now grateful that his ordeal at the police station had been short, he returned to the room. He wasn't hurt. He wasn't starving. His stuff was okay. The embassy knew where he was and was on his side. As he sat down on the cot to pull on his pants, he noticed that Paul's urn was gone.

***

Almost immediately, Jeri and Donald asked Thomas to come by for dinner. He was wrung out emotionally, too anxious to sleep, embarrassed to go out and especially embarrassed to see anyone who knew or recognized him. But he felt he had to repay

Jeri and Donald's kindness, because he would be flying back to Seattle in two weeks. The whole time he'd been in Kathmandu, they'd been an anchor for him. If he could redeem himself in their eyes, it would be enough. It was one decent thing he could do: pay his respects and feel their unwavering support one more time.

He opened Jeri and Donald's gate slowly and thoughtfully, savoring the sight of it to keep it in his memory. He was already anticipating missing the feeling of refuge he had when he entered the gate. Jeri and Donald had become familiar allies, and he hoped they still were. He could barely control how distraught he was. He was not used to looking for comfort from others. He didn't know whether he could pretend he was his old self. He knew Dorje must have told Jeri and Donald what had happened to him in Kathmandu.

"Oh, Thomas, come on in," Jeri said cheerfully and genuinely.

Thomas had expected forced cordiality. He wondered at her ability to pretend nothing had happened.

"Hi." He was letting Jeri and Donald take the initiative.

Jeri gave him a friendly, but short, hug. Donald shook his hand, also briefly.

"Let's sit over some tea," Jeri said. "It's breezy today. Maybe inside is best." They sat surrounded by the artifacts that covered the living room, making it seem like a museum of Northern India. This time Thomas could look at each item and know where it fit in the Tibetan or Indian mix. He recognized the collection of small bowls as those used for rituals.

"Dorje said you had a bit of trouble?" Jeri said.

"Yes. I hope you'll let me explain." He found it easier to look Jeri, rather than Donald, in the eye.

"Where are you staying now?"

"Back at the Tibet Hotel."

"Are you clear with the police?"

Thomas spoke, looking down into a cup of tea. "Finally. The girls vouched for me. I hadn't been in the house long."

"What's this about you and pot in the States?" Donald said. He also looked away so as not to appear threatening.

"It complicated things. I lost a job because of growing. National forest."

"You mean the embassy found out about that?" The official in Donald was coming out.

"The embassy helped the police case me out." He kept his tone even.

"But this wasn't about pot," said Jeri softly.

"No. Actually the embassy helped clear me."

"That's lucky." Donald said. Now he looked Thomas in the eye, with less wariness.

They heard the front gate click shut. Jeri and Donald looked at each other in surprise. Was it Helen? Unexpected? They hadn't spoken to her since the news of the raid. She didn't get news from Kathmandu on a regular basis.

Helen came in and put down her cloth bundle. "You!" She frowned at Thomas. She seemed very unlike a nun to him. Uncontrolled. Critical. Maybe he'd finally brought out the woman in her, the woman who wasn't all about harmony.

"Hello, Helen," Thomas said, gripping the arms of his chair. His streak of bad luck wasn't over.

"Had enough of our culture by now?" Her face flushed with anger. She folded her arms and remained standing at the far end of the room. Decades of meditative composure appeared erased, at least at the moment.

"Now Helen," Donald stood up. "He's been cleared. He was not guilty."

"Stealing treasures," Helen said. "Buying from vulnerable refugees. Making some money."

"It wasn't him. He didn't do that."

"I suppose it's fun, like growing marijuana. A hobby." She didn't seem to hear her father.

"Helen," Jeri interjected. "It wasn't him. And pot is not in this picture."

"Did he tell you about the Tantric sex?" Helen asked.

"What?" Donald and Jeri turned to Thomas now, who turned a shade redder than Helen.

"Dabbling in the dark arts," Helen said. "A perversion of centuries of Buddhism. And for what? For sex?" She remained standing, too riled to relax into a chair.

"Thomas, what's that about?" Donald tried to use a calm tone.

"Can we slow down?" Thomas pleaded. "Helen, sit down. Everybody."

"So you can blow it off, like everything else in your life?" Helen steamed. "Join the dharma bums on Freak Street in Kathmandu?"

"Helen. What's gotten into you?" Jeri took over, also in lower tones. She got up, crossed the room and put her arm around Helen. "Sit down, please ... Thomas, what's all this?"

"First, I didn't deal in pot here. At all. I smoked some. People here believe, as I do, that it's not a bad thing."

"But exploiting refugees?" Helen added. She was resisting Jeri's pull toward a chair.

"No. The guys where I rented a room were doing that. Not me. I had no idea."

"It's true, Helen. The embassy cleared him. He's not accused of that." Donald shifted his loyalties to defending Thomas.

"And the Tantric sex?" Helen said.

Jeri and Donald winced.

"As you know, Helen, that's private, and secret," Thomas said. He looked at her. He tried to imitate her usual composure. "People enter Buddhism in different ways. You're not going to tell me my path, are you? Even your hero Alexandra David-Neel dabbled in whatever she could find."

Finally, Helen sat down, her sleeve brushing teacups and causing a clatter. "But you went for the sex."

"No. You can't possibly know. So don't say that. I went for meditation. Reading. And experience. I trust you did the same, in your own way." He resisted taunting her. The color in her face heated up again. They both stopped talking, as if they realized they were verging on regrettable words—poison that would take a long time to wear off. Their respite was a subtle sign, however, that they both cared enough to stop.

"We didn't know you were meditating," said Jeri, tightening her grip around Helen's shoulders as if helping her hold back.

"Four weeks now," Thomas said, in a slow, lower tone. "Helen, I think you said something to me about the need to have faith and how experiences give you faith."

"I did." She pulled her vest tight.

"Are you saying you have faith now, Thomas?" Donald smiled.

"I have much greater interest. I feel like I'm on a respectful path. The stolen relics were like a shower of fire. I'm having nightmares."

"Ah. Demons," said Jeri. "You've joined the culture."

"Let's just say a sober respect. I haven't talked to Jack and Borys, but I hope they get a little hell for the scam they were running."

"What's happening to the relics?" Jeri asked.

"They're going to a monastery in Pokhara," Thomas said. "So people can reclaim them if they want."

Jeri turned to Donald. "Some of our Tibetans might be victims. We can help the monastery do a little catalog, something that shows what's there so it can be reclaimed."

Donald immediately looked interested. "Yes. I'll contact the monastery to see if they want help."

Thomas looked at Helen. He didn't expect her forgiveness. Jeri and Donald didn't know that he'd insulted her barely a week before. "Helen. I'm sorry. I'm really sorry. It's been a confusing time. A lot of new things." He felt Paul's ghost stepping in. The ghost was not angry, just dismayed that the two of them had gotten into a big mess.

"I know."

She was calmer, Thomas thought. Not exactly warm, but maybe not as likely to frost him out of her life.

Like a couple who had reconciled, Helen and Thomas both had cooler skin now.

"You're going to have to cleanse some bad karma." Helen smiled. "If you believe in that sort of thing."

Jeri and Donald got up to lead Helen and Thomas to dinner. They all moved slowly. They all looked at their chairs as if they were noteworthy, pulling them out, and sitting in them. Thomas felt as if he'd fought with his family. They were not going to quit him. Everyone was a little bruised.

Instead of talking, they would eat and change their inner barometers. Retreat into the meal and the pleasure of eating. The cook brought out food in serving dishes. Donald asked Helen about her hostel. She had colorful stories about trekkers who'd passed through. Thomas' issues had been taken off the front burner and put on a windowsill to cool.

"Thomas, you're not eating," Jeri said after they'd had their therapeutic pauses and diversions. "And I must say you look like hell. Did you get sick in jail?"

"No, no. I'm afraid something else went really wrong." Now, he definitely stopped trying to eat. Donald and Helen looked at him. Helen frowned as if she expected another stupid blunder. He felt beyond her approval now. The tension in his face was not going away.

"Well, come on, old chap," Donald said. "You're still alive. You're not sick. You're not guilty. There's hope."

"I lost Paul's ashes." Thomas put his fork down and teared up. The tears took him by surprise. He put his elbows on the table and rubbed his eyes to hide.

"What?" Helen and Jeri said in unison.

"What happened?" Donald said protectively. "Take your time."

Thomas clasped his hands in front of his face. "The ashes were in my room at the house, and they were gone when I got back."

Helen looked as if she were about to cry. Jeri reached to take her hand, which was on the table.

"Do you think somebody took them?" Donald asked. He looked at Jeri, seeking a unified front as parents who needed to be strong as an example for young ones, even if the young ones were in their fifties. He was used to crises, personal and political, and turned on his problem-solving voice. "Where exactly were they? What do you think happened?"

"I bought an urn. A brass thing. Like a little *stupa*. The seller said it was designed for the remains of lamas. I bought it and put the ashes in it." Thomas sounded as if he couldn't tell whether this was a stupid thing to do. Maybe smoking pot had finally warped his judgment. Putting the ashes in the urn had seemed like a gracious idea. Now, it seemed pretentious and silly.

"It was in your room?" Donald said.

"Yes. On a stool by my bed. When I got back from the police station it was gone."

"Did you ask the police about it?"

"No. I didn't think they wanted to see me or the house again. I'm afraid to go to the police."

"But if it was a theft, they should know."

"They said our things that we left in the house were safe. Of course, we're all foreigners with stuff that's pretty interesting."

"Were any of those interesting things missing?"

"No. Nobody said they were missing anything. The house was empty for nearly twenty-four hours."

Donald turned to Jeri. "I think Dorje should go to the police. He can ask them for advice, if nothing else. Thomas, can you draw the thing?"

"Yes."

Jeri got up and brought Thomas paper and a pencil. He made a quick sketch of the urn.

"Does Dorje know the address of your house?" Donald asked Thomas.

"516 Kulabhulu Galli." Thomas sat up and pushed the drawing to where the others could see it. After Jeri and Donald leaned back, Helen picked it up. She put it near her on the table and put her hand flat on it.

***

That night was turbulent for Thomas. Meditation was impossible. He smoked pot to calm himself.

He thought about times when he and Paul, then preteens, had chased butterflies. It was a glorious period of harmony between them. They had a reference book and took pride in identifying butterflies on sight. With homemade nets and a jar of formaldehyde, they spent weeks capturing the insects. They taught themselves to mount them in cigar boxes and make labels and notes about them. They knew the fine points of pinning and preservation. They knew the names of famous butterfly collectors and the rarity of various species.

Nicholas encouraged the boys because collecting butterflies reminded him of his own childhood in Lithuania, where it was a popular pastime. Paul took their collection mounted in several cigar boxes to school as show-and-tell. He left them overnight, and they were stolen.

The theft ended a time of innocence and harmony between the brothers. Thomas thought Paul must have done something stupid and blamed him for risking their work. Paul was supposed to be the smart big brother. He'd failed. Both brothers felt the sting of the theft, though. Thomas never forgot the feeling of violation—that a stranger simply stole part of their life for his own pleasure and would take credit for something they'd created.

Now, Thomas could not stop picturing the lost urn in the hands of a thief—a thief oblivious to what he possessed, happy about the crime.

Thomas returned to Jeri and Donald's house the following day to find out what Dorje had learned.

"The police took the urn," Dorje reported. "They thought it was part of the loot. It's been sent to the Tashiling camp in Pokhara to be inventoried."

"Oh wow." Thomas sat back and folded his arms. "That's sure easier than it being taken into the dark side of Kathmandu."

"You bet," Donald said. "You, Dorje and I need to go to Pokhara tomorrow morning. The monastery in Tashiling is probably going to be the authority on the authenticity of things that were recovered. We'll start with them. I'll get a driver for tomorrow."

After another sleepless night, Thomas, along with Dorje and Donald, drove headed toward Pokhara at sunrise. The car they were riding in could go faster than buses, but it still shared the road with all the other traffic to Pokhara. The hours riding over rough roads were long. It was drizzling, which made the treacherous gravel slippery. To be safe, the driver went slower than usual. They stopped in Pokhara for a quick meal and then went to the Tashiling monastery.

Dorje went into the main building and found an administrator. The monks were not full-time officials, and there wasn't an office. Dorje disappeared for nearly half an hour, looking for someone who might know about the artifacts. He came back with another monk. The monk said the artifacts were in a room, and he would look for a key. After another half hour, he returned and invited Dorje, Thomas and Donald to follow.

Thomas had never been inside a monastery compound. It was like institutions everywhere: a few rooms with tables and chairs, long hallways, people passing on their way through the building. Thomas and his companions crossed an open courtyard, surrounded by pale-yellow buildings with thatched roofs. Young monks in dark-maroon cotton robes that bared one shoulder were sweeping the courtyard. They giggled when they saw the strangers. Donald greeted them in Tibetan.

Finally, they reached the padlocked door of a far room. The monk unlocked it. The room was dark, crowded with dusty shelves. The monk entered ahead of them and pulled aside a small curtain covering a small window. In dim light, they could see rows of artifacts, stacked as if they had been unloaded quickly, and a large amount of dust in the air. The artifacts did not seem organized in any way. Donald showed the monk Thomas' drawing. All four of them moved close to the shelves to look. After about twenty minutes of searching, peering in the near-dark, Dorje reached behind a cluster of small statues and pulled out a larger object behind them. It was the brass *stupa*/urn. He held it up.

"Ah!" exclaimed Thomas. "That's it! That's it!" He reached for it. The monk stopped him and said something in Tibetan.

Dorje translated. "These are treasures. We must handle them with utmost respect." He placed the urn on a nearby table.

"Dorje, explain to the monk how we got here," Donald said. "That Thomas bought the urn and put his brother's ashes in it."

Dorje spoke to the monk at length in Tibetan.

"The monk says they can't part with the urn," Dorje said. "They haven't verified the contents yet."

Thomas stepped back in horror. It was not going to be easy. He didn't understand what sacred or administrative barriers there were to taking possession of the urn, but he hadn't imagined any. He hadn't known how police think in Kathmandu, and he knew nothing about Tibetan monks, either.

"Dorje, ask him if we can verify them together," Donald offered.

Again, Dorje spoke to the monk.

"He has to consult with the head Lama," Dorje said. "If you want to wait, he'll try to do that now."

"Tell him okay. We'll wait," Donald said.

The monk motioned Donald, Thomas and Dorje out of the room and secured the padlock again. He took them to a near room with chairs and left.

Nearly an hour passed. A boy brought them water to drink, but Donald and Thomas were reluctant to take the risk of drinking it. They were getting tired. Finally, the monk came back. He walked them to another room and told Dorje that another monk would be coming. Finally, he returned carrying the object, and the other monk appeared.

"The container is 2,000 years old," the other monk said slowly to Dorje in Tibetan, which Dorje translated. "It was rightfully returned to us. It would not be eligible for export."

"But I don't want to export it," Thomas protested to Dorje. "Tell him I want the ashes that I put inside."

"The monk says the contents may be a relic of a lama," Dorje said. "They haven't opened the urn."

"But I put them there!"

"They have to research it. They have to find out where the ashes came from in Tibet. They could be the remains of a high lama."

"But how will they tell whose ashes they are?" Thomas pleaded with Dorje and looked to Donald for help.

After a long exchange between Dorje and the monks, Dorje said, "They will do the research and get back to Donald."

Obviously, Thomas thought, he was the evil outsider here, the violator of Tibetan sacred culture. He was lucky to be aligned with Donald the Benevolent.

Thomas looked very impatient.

Donald tried to calm him. "You have to realize that the urn is a sacred object," he said. "They're not going to do what you want. They're going to do what they have to do. I'm sorry. We need to leave it and give it time. Dorje, ask them to let me know as soon as possible. Ask them if I can help in any way."

After consultation, Dorje said, "Donald, they appreciate your offer. They know how to contact you or me. We can't do any more right now."

For Thomas, the ride back to Kathmandu was a journey of desolation. He sat in a back seat, watching the gray, hard rocky terrain on the side of the gravel road, trying to wish away the feeling that he had failed Paul and his mother. He couldn't think of what it was he'd done that was irresponsible. Buying the urn? Putting the ashes in the urn? Moving into the group house? It all seemed circumstantial and bizarre. Now Paul—in the form of his ashes—was trapped in a religious vortex, as if a strange force of nature had taken over and captured Paul's material self. Instead of the force of water carrying his body down the Colorado River to a near-certain death, he was captured in a holy vessel inside a monastery, under the misperception that he was a lama who was too precious to be let go. He might as well have been taken hostage, consciously, by believers in a holy cause who were desperate to preserve their entire heritage. Except this was an accident. A case of mistaken identity. A tourist folly. Paul's ashes were in the wrong place at the wrong time.

Thomas tried to deny the significance of the ashes. Paul the living man was gone. Ashes were not the real person. They were a gray shadow in granular form. *Even DNA is destroyed in ashes,* Thomas thought. *Just pretend they are scattered now, except that they fill a crucible in the shape of a stupa, a form that is arbitrary and meaningless to the world outside of Buddhism.* But the ashes weren't scattered. They were imprisoned by ancient brass walls with god-knows-what memories. It was as if Paul's soul who'd had an earthly presence was intact as long as the ashes existed in one mass. You could say: "That's Paul." Or more accurately, "That's all we have left of Paul." He hadn't yet been given up to memory, to history, and to a material form so blended with earth, air or water that it was unrecognizable. Right now, he was in somebody else's house—the urn or the monastery—for eternity. Maybe.

Now, Thomas really believed the ashes had to be scattered. While trying to deny their significance, he'd come around to focusing on this quest instead of abandoning it. He wondered if he could meditate himself out of his misery. Smoke enough pot. What was making him care so much? Was it Paul's taking him by the hand the first day of school? Punching him in the arm in the back seat when they were on vacation car rides? Giving him his BB gun when he left for college? Just being his family, every day, for most of his childhood?

"It's not over," Donald said, leaning back in the car. "You have to trust things will turn out."

"I know," Thomas mumbled, drifting back into a vacant stare as the now-green terrain whipped by in a blur. He wished he could fall asleep.

He declined Jeri and Donald's offer to eat at their house. After a long, mute hug from Jeri, he walked back to his hotel. In his room, his first resort was to smoke a joint. There was a small bottle of Indian rum, but he decided to keep his chemistry pure and let the pot soothe him. He didn't dare call Livia and Clara. He couldn't imagine facing them after this mess.

***

After two more dismal nights of being stuck in a sludge of guilt and the intervening day spent mostly pacing the busy streets as if walking would redeem him, Thomas heard a knock on his door in the early morning. His beard was a crop of brambles with weeds around the edges.

"Thomas! Open up!"

He recognized Dorje's voice and opened the door.

"Wow," Dorje said, seeing the rough hairy face. "You should clean up and then come with me."

"Why?"

"You'll see. Okay?"

"Okay. Give me ten minutes." Thomas motioned Dorje to the armchair at a table and headed for the shower or, more accurately, the room that blasted water all over.

Thomas and Dorje walked out into the streets together. Being with someone, even without talking, was soothing. Thomas was still withdrawn and possibly spacey from smoking pot, and he had trouble keeping up with Dorje's fast pace.

Donald greeted them at the door. "Come in, come in. We've got real coffee for you." He pushed them in front of him. Because of his fatigue, Thomas almost didn't see Helen sitting on a couch. She stood up quickly.

"How are you?" she asked, with civility. She was cordial, back to her serious composure, back to being a nun.

He shrugged his shoulders and looked at her without anger. Since the recent testy encounter, he wasn't sure where she stood and couldn't endure any more of her disdain. He'd doused himself in gasoline and lit the fuse, mentally, many times already. He couldn't bring back the glow he'd felt whenever he saw her before his troubles started. Dorje found himself a chair on the side of the room. Jeri sat a bit farther away, coordinating the delivery of coffee and omelets.

"Sit down," Donald pushed Thomas toward a chair. "We've got good news."

Thomas sat down as if he'd just run a marathon. Four sleepless nights were not easy for a man in his fifties. "That would be welcome."

"Helen got Paul's ashes back," Donald said. He went to the sideboard that was covered with artifacts, lifted a round tin canister the size of a squat coffee can, and placed it on the low table in front of Thomas.

Thomas' arms went up to his head. He ran his hands through his clean, thick brown hair, trying to fully focus his senses. "Wow. Tell me what happened."

"After I called Helen, she went to Tashiling monastery," Donald said. "She persuaded them to open the urn. They decided the ashes are not authentic in their tradition. Helen, you explain it."

"I told them you were not staying here much longer, and they agreed to open the urn yesterday. There are, of course, mantras and sutras that go with such a potent act. They have to purify the environment. But they did it."

"I appreciate that, for sure." Thomas leaned back and clasped his hands in front of him as if in supplication.

"Normally, after the cremation of a lama, the cremation oven is opened, and they take out and separate the dust-like matter and bones," Helen said. "There are bones, joints, pieces of skull and such. With the highest lamas, they find relics. They're pearl-like remnants. They can be crystal-like beads. I don't know how you explain them scientifically, but there you are."

"So what did you find?" Thomas pictured sifting through his brother's body, looking for tiny marbles. It was beyond anything he could imagine.

"There were no relics by their definition," Helen said. "Not even bones. The ashes were finer than any you get here. The consistency. You know what I'm saying?" Helen stopped, seeing Thomas wince.

"Fine ashes." He repeated.

"So fine they agreed they were not authentic to the age of the urn and very likely not the product of Tibetan cremation."

"What a lucky twist." Thomas resisted an urge to open the tin and look. "Saved by technology."

"It is indeed Buddhist practice to scatter ashes, for the most part," Helen said, looking at Donald. "I don't know if Paul was aware of that."

"Thomas will follow through on that with Eike," said Donald.

Thomas stood up and moved to the sideboard to stretch and relieve the tension of four days. "I don't think I'll tell Mom about this. It felt liked we'd just lost him again. I'm so tired."

"You should let it go, Thomas," Helen said. She came up beside him and put a hand on his back. It was the first time she'd touched him. "The guilt. Grief. Feelings like that express attachment to Paul. Attachment interferes with his journey to another life."

"That might apply to you, too." Thomas leaned back and faced her directly. "Letting go of guilt, I mean. Guilt over not telling him about Eike."

She looked at Donald and Jeri. "I do regret it. I was too young to handle it in a good way. I'm sorry, Thomas."

"I appreciate that." Thomas rubbed his face as if wiping away a mask. He and Helen had both been through wringers—Paul's burdens on them. "I haven't been perfect myself."

Fatigue took over, and they fell silent. Jeri waved them to the dining table.

Helen walked over to the dining table and sat next to him. "You know," she said as she settled into a chair and looked at him, "a lama will tell a grieving family to take a pilgrimage and do spiritual things." She put her hand on Thomas' arm. It was the second time she'd touched him. "Especially do something for the deceased. That's what you do to help them move through the *bardo*. And that's exactly what you've done."

Attachment

Eike GOT A MESSAGE at Jeri and Donald's that she should call Sam when she was in Kathmandu. They said the message had been there for days, in case she returned. She and Sam arranged to meet for a walk up to the Swayambhunath Temple, on top of a hill overlooking the city and the valley.

When she arrived, he was standing at the entrance, below the hundreds of steps up to the temple at the top. She noticed his straight posture, used to carrying backpacks. His hair was longer than typical European's, but not long enough to be statement of some kind. In fact, longer hair was common among Bengali intellectuals.

The entry courtyard was lined on all sides by vendors sitting on the sidewalk, their wares spread on cloth in front of them. They left Eike and Sam alone because they looked like locals. She was wearing a long cotton tunic over cotton pants. Both were the same muted turquoise color. Her clothing was more subdued than the hippy style of a Kathmandu tourist.

"This can't be steeper than the hills you climb every day," he said greeting her.

"My steps are usually not so lavishly decorated." They looked up at the ornate concrete statues lining the giant stairway above them. "I am really happy to come back here," she said, taking in the festive display. They started up.

"Sometimes we bring trekkers here right away to test their legs. Of course, it's too late to send them back home if they don't look fit."

Eike and Sam walked slow and steady to keep from getting out of breath.

They stopped at the ten-foot tall Buddhas seated on each side. The Buddhas were painted gold, their striking eyes aimed down at people below them. Sam put his arm on her shoulders. Few people who knew Eike was a shaman would be so bold.

Nearer the top they passed the famous monkeys that had free reign of the temple. The monkeys were considered holy residents. They shamelessly groomed, slept and defecated where they wanted to.

"It took me a long time to get used to the monkeys and pigeons all over," said Sam.

"But they're just like cows. Just like Bengal, right?"

At the top, they went around the large white dome of the *stupa*, running their hands against the rows of hanging brass prayer wheels. Many locals visited just in order to perform this rite. Revolutions of the wheel are meritorious even if the person spinning them is distracted. Performing the ritual together created an intimacy between Eike and Sam. Their merits were spinning simultaneously, intertwined as the two brushed a hand across dozens of the wheels, one behind the other. Spinning prayer wheels was also thought to be a purifying process, erasing negative karma.

The Buddha's eyes painted at the top of the bulging white *stupa* looked down on them. Those eyes were featured in many postcards and photo books, along with the prayer flags and wild monkeys of the temple. Eike knew that the postcards did not show all the dimensions of the place. For example, they did not show that every day before dawn swarms of Nepalis and Tibetans woke the gods with drums and singing. Monks blew giant horns, filling the sky with an eerie moan, as if there were a convention of foghorns.

Eike and Sam sat on a wall within the courtyards surrounding the *stupa*. They watched a man on the top of the giant white dome swing down a bucket of saffron-colored water, painting the dome in streaks of yellow-gold. It was a clear day, and the white mound with gold streaks, a gold spire on top, and tricolor streamers was like a vision.

"Tell me about your family," Sam asked. "Your parents are well-known."

"Except they're my grandparents," Eike said. "My mother is a nun on the other side of Pokhara. I just learned who my father was."

"Wow."

"My father is in the form of ashes right now. I'll be performing a *Chöd* rite for him." Sam put a hand on her arm.

"Were you close?"

She put her hand over his to dispute the assumption of grief. "I never knew him. And my mother left me with her parents."

"Why?"

"She rejected the job, I think. It's all right. I had a loving family and still do."

"But you're not angry."

"I've chosen the same life of religious service. How can I be angry?"

"Are you going to give up your children, too?" he joked.

"I think I can be more like my grandparents." She was conscious of his suitor's interest in her thoughts about the mundane part of life. "You can be close to your family and be close to a cause, however impersonal it is." She smiled and got up to move on.

They walked around the back of the temple. In the openings of many square structures, people were performing rituals: lighting oil lamps, throwing marigold petals on statues, praying. The crowds were a strange mix of curious tourists, fond locals, and serious seekers of godly help and blessing, all stepping over each other. They wore Western jeans, cotton saris, hiking clothes—not matched with any particular other characteristic. In the jockeying for position, mutual respect was lacking. A tourist might be trying to take a great photo while the devout might be trying to get close to a divine figure. The scents of oil lamps and their smoke poured out of recessed stone cavities.

"You've seen the false *sadhus* near the cremation grounds?" Sam asked.

"Yes."

"Performance art. I hear many of the performers are not even holy people. They just paint their faces and dress up like a *National Geographic* photo and pose for money."

"We religious people are all mixed up in real life too, Sam. Authenticity is personal." She leaned over a wall to look into a pond full of coins, her dreadlocks swinging to cover her face. "I'm a tourist attraction too, sometimes. People are curious. It's innocent."

She walked past a stand selling cotton candy in large clear bags with a monkey lurking over the stand to steal a bag. "My father's brother came to town as a tourist. I can't imagine what he thought when he saw me for the first time." She pushed her hair across her face like a veil.

Sam pushed her hair away from her face and leaned in. "Do you live 'on behalf of all sentient beings' too? I was hoping for more a more personal relationship."

She flushed. "Sentient is good." She stood away from the wall, with bright pink bougainvillea draped beside her, complimenting her turquoise. "You must be meeting a lot of exciting foreign women in your job."

"You're one of a kind," he said. "My kind." He looked her in the eyes, then walked ahead for a bit and turned around. "There are professional ethics about that, you know. Although trekkers tend to be young and human. They're on vacation. Climbers tend to act like they're going into battle. The Sherpas think it's sacrilegious to mess around on the mountains. You're in the lap of a goddess."

They reached the end of a long gravel road on the other side of Swayambunath hill and were about to enter the cacophony on the road.

Standing there, she let him hug her, even though upperclass Indians do not do that in public. They were both outside enough norms to do what they wanted. Kathmandu was such a blend of cultures that you could choose your way. With Jeri and Donald, Helen, Jampa, her Lama, Thomas and now Sam as examples, inventing her own way seemed to be the rule.

Trance

THOMAS AND DORJE TRAVELLED up to Eike's village again, this time to be present for her *Chöd* ritual for Paul. They saw the small cluster of stone houses with flat roofs and entered the one where she lived. She'd made preparations that were the same as they'd witnessed before. Copper bowls held water and oil lamps flickered. One of her housemates, an older woman, invited them to sit on a bench along a wall. She offered them tea. Thomas and Dorje had eaten on the way, since they had hiked a long distance. Thomas stepped outside to wash his face with water from a pump and use the latrine in back.

Thomas gave the metal canister containing Paul's ashes to the attendant, which she took to Eike in the other room. Thomas was finally parting with the ashes, leaving them to Paul's daughter, the shaman.

When Eike entered the room she was fully outfitted as a shaman: She wore the tall headdress of pheasant feathers shooting up from a broad band of red cloth, a maroon woolen dress wrapped in front, and heavy long necklaces. She'd laid out the mirrors, bell, drum and a bone horn. She placed the canister, arrowhead, and cap next to the implements. Thomas saw her differently now. She was no longer a stranger, yet he still knew little about her.

Someone started to burn juniper and smoke filled the room, making it hard to see. Several other people were in the room, apparently to witness the ritual and, in that way, gain personal merit.

Eike started chanting, beating the drum slowly and occasionally ringing the bell. Her eyes were directed downward and gradually took on a glazed look—open but not focused externally.

***

In her mind, Eike entered a charnel ground at dusk, after vultures had picked and plundered any flesh they could find there. At night, jackals, circling and howling, took over. She summoned her protective gods and spirits. One of her regulars was a large white owl perched on the only tree beside the charnel ground. It held a dead animal in its beak. It looked very content. Another was a doe. Then, Eike summoned all the people to whom she owed a karmic debt. She pictured her head severed, then her arms, her legs, all cut up into pieces as if she were a corpse offered to vultures. At this point, she had no fear because she had performed this ritual many times and knew the territory, which always included the unexpected.

Wolves came onto the grounds and began eating her flesh. They ripped at skin, tearing strands of flesh away from bones, salivating and chewing with relish. Once they were sated, they moved aside to reveal the entrance to a cave.

Eike reconstituted her spirit and entered the cave, then passed through a stone door and went down to a subterranean level. Bats as large as kites exploded from the ceiling. Ghosts started grabbing at her legs, begging for flesh. She knew the demonic local deities would appear in various physical forms and that she had to maintain equanimity to overcome them. She acknowledged them as ghosts and offered compliments. Then, she began a powerful incantation to pacify them and stepped over them.

She met a well-known holy man who was alive but had no flesh on his body. He instructed a monkey at his feet to draw a mandala in his blood. Suddenly, from behind, the dreaded deity Palden Dorjee Lhama charged at Eike, riding his wild horse on a saddle made of bloody human skin, and then departed. Behind him were *Tsen,* demons with red skin, wearing helmets, riding on red horses.

Eike went through a tunnel down to the third level. It had a black pool of water and was damp and smelly. Bizarrely, through a hole she could see a pastoral scene outside, where a marmot was standing and watching, and she knew that it was Paul. She spoke to him as the shaman who was to guide the travel of his spirit through the *bardo*. "You are dead. Don't come back. You don't belong here. Go forward. Don't look back. You will see radiant, beautiful beings and hideous forms, strange visions, colored paths, frightful apparitions. Go toward creatures who will give you rebirth. Pass through the *bardo*."

Water usually held snakes, she knew. The third level was guarded by a huge tiger that, on seeing her, turned and roared. Then, it vomited snakes that poured to the ground and slithered toward her. When they came close, she could see they were like leeches, with a mouth, instead of a face, and little teeth inside. Horribly, they attached to her legs and climbed over each other up her body. Before long she was covered. After they attached to her flesh, they sucked her blood and became engorged, giant, slimy purple slugs. She used her strength to withstand revulsion and terror. She tried to pull them off, kick them off and brush them off. When they refused to disappear, she realized that all beings and phenomena were products of her own mind. She ceased to resist. They disappeared, and she fainted.

***

The visible Eike was dancing vigorously in circles, beating the drum rapidly and chanting loudly. At this point, her eyes were nearly closed. Even through thick smoke, Thomas and Dorje could see that she was distressed. Suddenly, she fell into a slump.

They were afraid to move her, respecting how her trance protected her. But she was not reviving. She lay, breathing heavily from exertion. Her attendant put a pillow under her head and took the drum and bell from her hands. After another fifteen minutes, they moved her to a comfortable, stretched-out position.

Thomas wanted to go see what happened but Dorje held him back.

Another hour went by. Eike's attendant wiped her face with a cool cloth and took the headdress off. Finally, they moved her to a cot in the other room.

"What happens now?" Thomas asked Dorje. "Is there anything we can do?"

"Not now. She may regain her strength and wake up. If she doesn't, we get help."

"What kind of help?"

"Another shaman. Or help in Kathmandu." It was already nightfall.

"We'll sleep here in this room until morning and see how she is," Dorje said. They'd brought their own food and a blanket as part of their hiking gear.

"I don't know how I can sleep."

"You have to. Nothing to do now."

They lay down and waited for morning.

***

Thomas heard Dorje in the next room talking with the attendant and others in Nepali. When he came out, he told Thomas they'd decided to transport Eike to Kathmandu. They were fashioning a stretcher with poles and blankets. Four people would carry it to make the journey faster. The hike would take at least three hours. The river crossings, with swaying bridges, were the most problematic. Thomas thought ahead and wondered what they would do on the bridges He examined the stretcher and saw that the Nepalis' long experience in the mountains had yielded techniques that made it very secure. The attendant and Dorje lifted Eike onto it, covered her, and then wrapped scarves to hold her onto it. Thomas and Dorje took the front of the stretcher on their shoulders, and Dorje and the attendant took the back. The four men set out.

It was a difficult journey as they maneuvered steep and rocky sections of the path. They managed to cross the rope-and-board bridges that were barely the width of one person by staggering themselves to fit inside the ropes. The bridges did not seem designed for the weight of five people, but they had borne the weight of yaks and horses carrying loads, so they were probably strong enough. Following the lead of the Nepalis made Thomas fearful, but he tried to hide his feelings.

As soon as they reached a road, they looked for a bus to flag down. The first one that appeared was decorated like a flop house or Buddhist temple. Colorful pictures were on every panel, each depicting a different event in the life of Buddha. Each panel was framed in a different ornate border. The bumper was lined with a motif, including the eyes of Buddha repeated about twenty times. Beaded flaps were along every lower edge. The doors were painted in bold stripes. Elaborate hubcaps, like golden crowns, extended five inches from the bus. The bus was a carnival on wheels, celebrating the exhilaration of being able to ride fast, in a place where most people walked the long, steep mountains. The bus stopped. It was only half-full.

The four men quickly assessed the challenge of lifting an unconscious girl up the steps into the bus, carrying her down a narrow aisle, and fitting her into seats that were closely spaced to maximize capacity. Toward the back was an area with sparse seats, leaving room for bundles, large baskets, goats and chickens. Thomas and Dorje picked Eike up from the ground in a fireman's hold, their arms linked to form a seat. Then, they slowly mounted the steps and made their way down the aisle of the bus. Beside some goats was a seat with more legroom and bundles on the floor. In sync they decided Thomas should sit against the window, with Eike draped against his chest, her legs lying across the rest of the seat and extending onto large cloth bundles set against the edge of the seat. Thomas could hold her tight and buffer her from rough turns and bumps. Dorje sat in the seat behind him next to the goats. The other two men found seats toward the front of the bus. They put the stretcher poles and cloth under their seats. With a large cloud of black smoke billowing from its exhaust, the celestial chariot tore down the mountain road.

As a forest ranger, Thomas had never rescued anyone and never had to carry anyone. Long ago, he'd been taught rescue techniques but had not used them. The tools at hand here were, of course, limited. There was no gurney to hold a spine and neck in place. There were no heart monitors, oxygen, or IVs for fluid. There wasn't even water to wash the ashes of juniper incense from Eike's face. He hadn't embraced a woman in a long time, he thought, as he held her tight so her head leaned in against him.

"I feel like her father right now," he said to Dorje. "Will she be all right, do you think?"

"She's still breathing. We'll be in the city in three hours."

"She could be dehydrated by now."

"The spirits will keep her alive."

"You think? Will the bad ones take me over?"

Dorje laughed. "You have to be Nepali. They probably think you're trying to take over."

"If only I could."

Eike was slight and thin against Thomas, smaller than most of the women he'd held in his arms. Her hair and skin smelled of juniper. He thought of Paul. He wondered if she smelled anything like Paul. This was Paul's flesh and blood, in his arms. He looked at the skin on her arms and her hands. He felt her body, her breast, and her head against him. He was like a new father inspecting his baby, marveling at the very existence of a body that shared his DNA. Thomas was worried but not panicked. He didn't know what a distressed shaman looked like, but Eike was breathing regularly, her temperature was fine, she was not gasping and thrashing or acting uncomfortable. No convulsions. She was like Sleeping Beauty, waiting for the kiss. He felt fiercely protective. Caring was a new emotion for him. He wanted her to come back to consciousness, and he wanted to be her uncle and her surrogate father. He felt he would carry her to safety. It was a matter of time.

***

Jeri and Donald were shocked at their arrival.

"What happened?" Donald looked to Dorje.

"She fainted. We don't know why. Maybe you should call a doctor."

Jeri immediately sent a servant to summon her Western doctor whose office was about twenty minutes away. They put Eike on the bed in the room she used during visits. The hikers were given water and food. Everyone waited for the doctor. When he came and examined Eike, he found nothing to treat. She was unconscious with a slight fever and a low pulse, but otherwise she was not ill in a way that required emergency care with allopathic medicine.

Dorje explained that Tibetans believed that shamans could be possessed by a spirit or enslaved by a demon. In either case, another shaman was needed to liberate them. He suggested that Eike's Lama Yeshi, who still lived in Kathmandu, could help. Donald and Jeri agreed. Dorje left to find the Lama.

Thomas telephoned his mother in Seattle. It was very early morning there. He told her what had happened.

"Thomas, do you think we can help?"

"If you want to. Dorje left to fetch the shaman."

"When do you think the shaman will perform the ritual?"

"Soon. An hour. Or a few hours. When he gets here. I'll call you."

"All right. Please call. We'll be ready."

About an hour later, still before nightfall, the shaman arrived in a pedicab with Dorje. He was shown to the room in which Eike lay. Thomas called Livia to tell her the ritual was imminent.

The wrinkled old man moved slowly across the room and, with measured movements, seated himself on the floor. He was brought water to drink. Thomas thought: Winthrop residents would say someone that emaciated "looks like he could use a hamburger." The shaman pulled out his kit and took out implements—a headdress made with white owl feathers, a worn drum, and a small bell. He put a necklace of bones over his head. Dorje put a red-silk cloth on the floor, placed copper bowls on it, and lit some oil lamps. The shaman started to chant slowly in a broken, aged voice. Thomas could see his eyes blank out just as Eike's had. They did not roll back, but they were no longer seeing the room.

Dorje whispered to Thomas: "The advanced shamans do not need to dance about. They can accomplish everything with their minds. He needs to communicate with a demon or spirit and negotiate the liberation of Eike's spirit. It might require a sacrifice. The shaman might offer his 'double' as a replacement for the possessed spirit. It could mean a fight with a demon. It could mean repeated fights. If the shaman's strong, he'll win. This one is as strong as they come."

Thomas reached into his pocket and put his hand on the obsidian arrowhead. *I don't believe in this, but, Paul, you got her into this and you better get her out.*

***

In Seattle, Livia woke Clara. Next, Livia called Nancy, Victor, Alice and Phil and asked them to come to the house. The four friends rushed over in the dark of early morning. Before leaving his place, Victor grabbed some mandarin oranges, Alice brought fresh strawberries she had in stock, and Nancy brought an exotic cheese she'd bought the day before. Clara made them breakfast and coffee while they awaited the call from Thomas. Livia set up the round dining table again. In the center, she placed an enlarged photo of Eike facing the ceiling and arranged several candles around it. She placed Paul's keepsake urn there, too. She also included the little snuff bottle with a painted samurai wielding a giant sword. That seemed like a perfect surrogate for Paul. For good measure, she placed a photograph of him next to Eike's.

Right after Thomas called, Livia, Clara and the four friends sat down around the table, held hands and prayed. Each, in turn, called on personal guides, spirits, and family members to help in rescuing Eike.

"I am calling on Ona, my grandmother, the healer, to come to the aid of our child Eike," Livia said. "Ona, come and lend a hand. We know you can do it. Paul, you too. Paul, you need to help your daughter right now. You need to muster anybody you know there. Use all your connections. Seriously, Paul. She was trying to help you, but you must help her now."

The group of friends put their hands on the table, each touching the photo of Eike.

"Bring Eike back," said Clara. "Bring Eike back. We're asking for help. Everyone, please pull this girl back to life for us." They mentally pictured her lying on a bed in Kathmandu.

They continued for an hour. Bill, who was sleeping in Clara's bedroom, woke up, ran to the dining room, and climbed into Clara's lap to continue his snooze. The sky lightened during the hour they prayed and spoke. The twilight before sunrise was turning into a blue-sky day. Suddenly, noise jarred their quiet, serious concentration. They looked at each other, startled out of their contemplative reverie by the loud honking of hundreds of geese flying overhead, energetically flapping white wings to stay in formations, returning north for the summer.

***

Eike's consciousness woke to see her lying on the shore of a wide river. She didn't have the strength to get up. She was bloody, her flesh broken and torn, hanging in pieces. She was in extreme pain and couldn't summon her protectors. A large snow leopard slowly walked toward her. It paused to contemplate her. She couldn't tell if it was about to finish her off or help her. Something, lethargy or confusion, was keeping it from moving toward her. Near her side, she could see dead snakes or leeches spread on the ground, like worms after a heavy rain. There was a raft beside the water, but she couldn't reach it.

Suddenly, her owl-protector, with great fanfare, flew down from the sky and landed beside her. He simply stood guard. Next to the owl, a Native American chief incongruously appeared.

The snow leopard, undisturbed by the owl, moved toward Eike again. Like alert protectors, the owl and chief simply watched. The eyes of the leopard seemed familiar to Eike. Her *Chöd* had transformed Paul from a marmot, who was content on a hillside and stuck in the afterlife, into a formidable snow leopard with a benevolent spirit. The snow leopard was not yet used to this new spirit edition and was still coming into his power.

The snow leopard turned Eike's helpless body over, delicately gripped the back of her dress in his teeth, and dragged her, gradually, inch by inch, to the raft. She was completely limp and could not move herself. Once the leopard had gently put her on the raft, he nudged it into the water with his nose. She drifted slowly downstream and across to the other side of the river. She looked back. The snow leopard vanished into the sky, leaving a flash of lightning.

***

The physical body of Eike stirred as everyone at Jeri and Donald's house watched the old shaman. Eike opened her eyes. She looked disoriented and exhausted. The shaman asked her to turn her head slowly from one side to the other. He massaged her forehead and the crown of her head. He told her to stretch her arms and arch her back.

"Where am I?" Eike looked at Lama Yeshi and Jeri.

"At home in Kathmandu," the Lama said. "You've been in a long trance. A trance gone wrong."

"Ah. Can I have some water?"

Everyone in the room laughed with relief.

A servant came to talk to Jeri. She looked up at Donald and left the room. In the living room stood a young man, his sandals already parked near the door.

"Hello," Jeri said to him. "What can I do for you?"

"I'm a friend of Eike's. How is she?"

"She's good. She's back." Jeri seemed to flounder, not knowing what to do with the young man. None of Eike's friends she'd met looked like him. "Would you like to see her?"

"I sure would. My name's Sam."

"This way. She just woke up. We're all still in her room."

Jeri walked the young man back to the bedroom. Donald and Lama Yeshi were sitting in chairs nearby, while Thomas, Dorje and the two villagers stood. Eike was sitting up and drinking. .

"Sam!" she said with new energy.

"Eike!" He quickly walked over to her, sat down beside her, and leaned in for a long hug.

She seemed surprisingly comfortable with the contact. The others in the room were stunned into cool observation.

Sam pulled away and held her face in his hands. "You're okay, then?"

"Yes. Yes." She was blushing now at the intimacy. She put her hands over his but didn't pull back. "I lost power. My father was there. I think he and Lama Yeshi pulled me out."

"Wow." Sam proceeded to gently kiss her forehead, her cheeks, and then her lips. He was oblivious of the audience. Finally, he sat back and took her hands in his.

Lama Yeshi was grinning. Most of Eike's ritual accoutrements were gone, but she was still fresh from a ceremony, wearing ceremonial robes. It was incongruous. Eike and Sam were both young, and suddenly the intimacy seemed natural.

"Mom, this is Sam. Sam, this is Jeri, Donald. My Lama Yeshi. My uncle Thomas. Dorje. And friends who carried me here."

"I know Dorje. We have some friends in common." Sam smiled at Dorje.

Dorje nodded. "Back street friends." It seemed that somehow he might have alerted Sam about Eike's trouble.

261

Sam stood up as Donald stepped forward to shake hands. Then, Thomas stepped forward. Sam reached out a hand. "Dorje told me about you, Thomas. Sorry about your brother."

"My brother's in good hands," Thomas replied.

"Well, shall we let you two visit?" Jeri started to corral everyone except Sam toward the door. "I'll get you something light to eat, Eike. Sam, you'll eat with her?"

"Sure," he said, turning back to Eike. "Very sure."

She looked tired and limp, as if she'd landed in his arms.

***

Thomas finally felt he could leave. Everyone at the house was exhausted, physically and emotionally. Dorje would take Lama Yeshi back with a pedicab. The two Nepalis from Eike's village would spend the night in the house and then travel back in the morning.

"Dorje." Thomas stopped Dorje on the way out. "Here." Thomas handed him Paul's fancy sunglasses. He couldn't remember feeling so drained. Forest fires were easier than this.

***

After a few days, Eike was up and about, eating bowls of yoghurt with mango and honey, sunning in the garden. Jeri told her about the séance in Seattle and suggested a phone call while she was still in Kathmandu.

"Hello?" Livia picked up the phone. It was evening in Seattle, morning in Kathmandu.

"Hello. This is Eike."

"Oh my, Eike! Clara, come here," Livia shouted from the kitchen. Clara was watching TV in the living room. Livia put the phone on speaker. "What a surprise. We think of you all the time. How are you?"

"Much better. Still at my mother's house in Kathmandu. It's quite comfortable."

"Thomas told us everything. How we nearly lost you. And you were with Paul."

"Yes. Yes, I was. He left as a snow leopard. Do you understand what I'm saying?"

"I think we do. Did Thomas tell you about our séance for you?"

"Yes. I'm sure it helped."

"We have several friends who are powerful. It was quite an exercise. Even Bill, Clara's monkey, was rooting for you."

"She has a monkey?" Eike had forgotten the photo.

"Yes. A small one with beady eyes."

"I've seen it." She laughed.

"Oh! You have?"

"I had a dream of meeting a flock of swans. There was a very wide-eyed little monkey in the bushes. A yellow vest."

"Oh. We did have you come for Easter, you know," Livia said. "Bill acted like he saw you. He was pretty shocked. He jumped to the top of the curtains."

Eike laughed again. "Oh my."

"Thomas told us about your rituals. We were so happy to find you. I wish we could visit."

"How old are you and Clara now?"

"We're in our eighties. Too old to travel. It's such a long flight. We can't suffer the walking and sitting on a plane for nearly a day."

"I've never flown, myself."

"Well, I hope you'll think about it. And soon. I prayed to St. Nicholas. Our family was Russian Orthodox in the old country. Like you, he was very young when he became religious."

"I'll do a meditation on him."

"You'd have liked Paul," Livia said. "He was always far from home, but he had a good spirit."

"I have his ashes now. I'll scatter them."

"Beautiful. We'll send more photos to Jeri's house for you. I'm sure Paul's going to watch out for you now."

"Yes. I need that."

"Well, if you ever get a bug to travel, think of us. We both give you a big hug."

"Thank you. It's nice to talk to you. You and Clara and Bill."
It was Thomas, Eike thought, *who brought us all together. A cigar box brought to Kathmandu.*

"We're here. Stay in touch. Bye now."

"Good-bye."

DEAR CAROLINE,

Thanks again for taking care of Sally for me. It's been great to be free to roam and take in this other world. I never appreciated why Paul liked to travel so much. It's like jumping into another movie and getting to know a new cast. Not that the old one was not good! If anything, travel has given me an awareness of many other people and their choices.

I'm sad for Paul having a shorter life than he should have and the fact that he missed staying and getting close to some remarkable people. I guess we all make up for missed opportunities for each other. You just don't know the directions everyone will take. We gamble at every juncture about how much we should hitch with others—the riches we will gain or lose by it. I'm sobered that we don't know much when we make those gambles, and we're worried that we're limiting ourselves by staying when we might find out later we limited ourselves by going.

I never expected to be so amazed, puzzled and attracted to the strange realities of other people. I guess they could say the same about me, if they landed in my territory and saw me there.

At one extreme is the flood of people in Kathmandu who are barely scraping by, walking down the street in rags while carrying a little can of cooking oil or a bag of lentils. People who fervently worship, dream, and struggle with gods and demons on a daily basis. To me, their extreme poverty seems like the end of the world, and yet they laugh, talk to their friends, sit around with a cup of milky tea, get haircuts in the street, and nap on a nice patch of ground in the middle of the square.

At the other extreme are people like Jeri and Donald Simons and their daughters, who're very idealistic and secure in the world. They could rocket out of here, but they don't because they care about this community. They like being in it and tending to it. To me their life is like a

265

carnival. You feel as though you are enjoying the carnival every day and, at the same time, helping to put on the show.

I've grown to love them, I think. Who would've guessed? During Eike's crisis I found myself caring with ferocity. I would've jumped off one of those rope bridges for her. Suffered a hundred leeches. Well, maybe not a hundred. She's definitely in my heart now.

I just want to say that I feel as if I want to settle down more than I ever did. I like being in my world of Winthrop, too, just as Jeri and Donald like being in Kathmandu. I see now that you can be in your place, and be there differently, depending on your state of mind and attitude. You can embrace it, or you can be cool. I want to embrace it and you.

I know you already made a soft spot for Sally and wonder if you can make another one for me. You were kind enough to feel cured of your progressive DLLDYHS disease—Don't Let Losers Drain Your Heart and Soul—when you met me. I promise I will try to be as attentive and warm as Sally although you know that's impossible. For one thing, I'm not furry, my nose is not cool and wet, and I have no wagging tail. I worry whether she'll take me back. I will use what I do have: my hands, my mouth, my eyes, my skin and etc. to tell you you're the best and we should seek a common path. As Helen says, "Sometimes just living your life well is mission enough."

I should be back in a week and ready for a fabulous summer in Winthrop with you and Sally and your horse friends.

Love, Thomas

***

Thomas boarded a plane out of Kathmandu, this time prepared for the long flight. That old barn he was tearing down was now leveled. Jeri and Donald saw him off. They'd cared for him like they did other refugees: soothing the wounds and listening for new hope.

He thought about his new family. Dorje was a kindred spirit. Helen thought of him as a flawed but acceptable human being. Paul's daughter Eike gave him a warm familial hug. He sensed that part of it belonged to Paul, and he didn't mind that anymore, either. He'd given his mother and Clara a new feeling that they had roots again and a happy future in spite of Paul's passing.

From the plane, Thomas saw the jagged peaks surrounding Kathmandu. They were no longer dangerous but full of settlements of quiet, hard-working people, a few people he loved, and some ghosts, demons, and *dakinis*. Paul was right. The foot of the Himalayas was a paradise of sorts. The air was different, and it was a nice place to be reborn.

Monsoon

Eɪᴋᴇ's ʙᴜs ʀɪᴅᴇ ꜰʀᴏᴍ ᴋᴀᴛʜᴍᴀɴᴅᴜ took several hours. As usual, she hiked up the hills toward her village. When she came over the last ridge, she saw her village and her house, which was on a hill slightly higher than the others. It was late, and she was tired, but elated, to return home.

Nearly every building was strung with hundreds of new white prayer flags, on ropes stretched from rooftops to other roofs or to trees. In their center, the flags were imprinted with the icon of the wind horse, carrying good fortune and harmony to all. It was as if thousands of white birds swarmed the area, flapping their wings in a gentle wind. Like souls on the way to a new incarnation, a new start. *Sam,* she thought.

***

Eike packed a water bottle and nuts into her cloth sack. She folded an extra shawl around the tin urn and placed it inside her large, bronze singing bowl before putting them in the sack. She placed the strap of the sack over a shoulder, and the sack hung under her chest. It was heavy. She knew hiking up to her destination would take over an hour.

The path was so familiar that she hardly needed to look down, but getting around rocks with the heavy sack was more difficult than usual. It threw off her balance, and she slipped, surprised that she nearly fell. The path was steep, and a fall could mean tumbling more than thirty feet down a rocky slope. Treacherous, sharp glacial rocks were hidden under the greenery. A mist caressed the hillsides and clusters of trees, like a white scarf waving in slow motion just a few feet above the ground. She could hear her favorite marmots whistling but could not see them. They were like friends in the neighborhood, and she was sure that they knew her.

After nearly an hour, the path turned on a high ridge, and she saw a cluster of snow-beaten, scraggly cedars. Hunched over from years of snow-pack, they huddled together against the wind. Like bonsai trained into unnatural, forced postures, they'd grown resilient and hearty, ready for the next onslaught of snow and fierce winds. The fog gave them a dark grey-green hue, which contrasted with the white bones of trees that hadn't made it. Those stood within the cluster, helping to shore it up and cut the wind.

Eike's destination was behind the trees. It was a flat outcropping of dry earth and rocks shaped into a shallow cave that looked out on the valley below. When chipmunks saw Eike, they scrambled, interrupted in scouting the ground for seeds that blew into cracks between rocks. Besides the view, the best part of the place was shelter from winds that could blast the ridge. The trees took the blows first, letting through what felt like a mild breeze, while rocks were being worn down on the other side .

Eike felt so comfortable there that she could sleep, before or after meditating for hours. When some of the fog lifted, a spectacular, imposing vista of deep valleys and giant mountains was revealed. The view was so dramatic and forceful that Eike could imagine images of the malevolent Tibetan gods, unattractive with their uncensored, proud, forceful raw power, whose breath was the violent wind. The raw beauty of the scene seemed secondary. In sunshine, the valley glowed like paradise.

The monsoon was due any day, possibly any minute. Moisture hung in the air, on rocks, on trees, on her skin. Through gaps in the fog, she could see heavy dark clouds moving fast toward the valley. The drenching rain would start and go on for months, incredibly seeming to never dry. It was a massive bath, indifferent to plants and tiny creatures threatened with drowning in the runoff. They had to learn to avoid shelters that would soon flood, as soil and rocks were washed into raging rivers, and the valley was cleansed.

To calm herself, Eike chanted the Song of Vajra, which links the internal energy of someone in a confused state with the universal flow of energy. The chanter enters the dimension of sound. Her body is massaged internally by vibrations linking the music to the vibrations of the universe.

Eike took out the large bronze bowl and removed the urn packed inside it. Her Lama had carved the teak mallet she used. It was small to suit her hands and had a pattern of flowers on the handle, unusual in their delicacy and a tribute to her gender. She struck the side of the bowl and moved the mallet against the lip of the bowl to make it sing. Its deep harmonic tones rang out in the silence. She knew it would call up her guardians and focus her mind. She thought about whether travelers in the valley below could hear the tones far above them and think the gods were humming.

For the first time, Eike opened the top of the urn. Inside was gray powder, her father. He had the consistency of a ground spice but had no aromatic scent. The powder was as light as the mist around her and nearly the same color. Powders were familiar to her from cooking to rituals that required spices with different consistencies. She knew how to grind thousands of things into powder, patiently, with muscle, using mortar and pestle. She had witnessed many Hindu cremations and seen the remains washed away. She tried to imagine the human body that was the source of the powder. The only picture that came to mind was one Thomas had given her. It showed a robust, fleshy torso filling out a white cotton shirt with the neck open, revealing blond chest hair. He was smiling, his thick blond hair was curly and his calm eyes showed a hint of humor. He was standing outside with a blue sky behind him. He was good looking. A man she could like.

By now, the rain clouds were nearly above Eike's ridge, and she could see the sheet of rain heading up the valley. She set the open urn to the side and took up the bowl again. She cleared away gravel on the outer edge of the area in front of her. She struck the bowl and moved the mallet around it again, this time building up a loud, complex harmonic, which she sustained for several minutes. She looked at the gnarled trees witnessing this commotion. She thought about chipmunks and marmots hearing strange sounds. She pictured her guardians summoned to her side and sensed their warmth. Her body heated from the movement. Her consciousness went into trance as she saw herself, sitting over the valley, with the rain approaching behind her, as the winds picked up, driving and herding massive dark clouds over what looked like the entire world.

She placed the singing bowl on the gravel and poured the ashes into it. In the next minute, drops of rain hit her face, at first gently and in warning, then insistently, until torrents drenched her hair, her shoulders, her lap, and everything around her. She sat back and watched for a long time as the deluge filled the bowl and turned it into a small, round infinity pool. The water started to pour over the sides. She wept as it carried ashes over the lip of the bowl and down the steep slope beyond, merging with the mineral sediment that filled glacial rivers in early spring.

THE END

About the Author

Ruta Sevo spent years in Calcutta and Madras (now Chennai) as a scholar, doing field work for a Ph.D. However, in the 1970s, a degree in Indian studies did not lead to a job. Three different careers later she was able to take up writing full time.

White Bird came of wishing she'd had time to go to Nepal and into the Peace Corps. Reading about thirty books satisfied a long-latent interest in Nepal and Tibetan Buddhism. A fierce trek up the Annapurna Valley topped it off.

The novel is in the tradition of writers bringing the East to the West, like E.M. Forster, Alexandra David-Neel, and Madam Blavatsky. *White Bird* draws on Tibetan Buddhism which spread out of Tibet by Chinese force after 1959.

In 1973, Sevo received one of four national PEN and NEH/Columbia University Translation Fellowship awards, which she used to translate three Bengali novels. She published scholarly articles in several fields and wrote hundreds of professional reports (see http://www.lulu.com/spotlight/sevo). Her ethical will, a.k.a. letter from the grave, was published by the Association of Personal Historians in *My Words Are Gonna Linger: The Art of Personal History* (Paula Stallings Yost and Pat McNees, editors). She recently wrote and self-published a novella (*Vilnius Diary*) and a translation of her grandfather's memoir from Lithuanian. She has a BA in comparative literature and a PhD in South Asian civilization studies with concentration in literature from the University of Chicago.

Sevo lives in the shadow of Washington, D.C. An author's statement and blog about *White Bird* can be found on http://goodreads.com/sevo.

Made in the USA
Lexington, KY
19 August 2014